FUMBLED LOVE

S. JONES

Editor: Marla Selkow Esposito

Proofreader: Virginia Tesi Carey

Cover Designer: Kate Farlow @ Y'All That Graphic

Illustrated Cover: Sarah Grim Sentz @ Enchanting Romance Designs

Photographer: Lindee Robinson Photography

Models: Denise & Travis Bendall

Formatting: Leanne/Irish Ink

CHAPTER 1
KINLEY

"WHAT DO YOU MEAN, MY FLIGHT IS CANCELED?" I WAS ON THE verge of tears as I stared at the gate agent behind the ticket counter. The day was already off to a bad start before I even left for the airport. Thanks to the near-standstill traffic, I barely made it here on time. I'd taken the entire week off to spend with my family. If only I had booked an earlier flight like I had planned.

"I'm sorry, ma'am, but there are snowstorms up along the East Coast and all flights are grounded." She stared down at her computer monitor and clicked away at her keyboard. Her tone implied she was anything but sorry. "The earliest I can get you out is on Saturday, at 10:05 a.m."

"That's three days away." She couldn't be serious. I frantically scanned the kiosks showing the arrivals and departures. Sure enough, everything was delayed or canceled. "You do realize Thanksgiving is tomorrow, right?" I wanted to cry at the thought. This would have been the first Thanksgiving I spent with my family in four years. "Surely, there has to be a way to get the other passengers and me there before then?"

"I'm afraid not." She didn't look like she was going to relent anytime soon. "There is a staffing shortage as well due to the holiday." She shrugged. "It looks like we will both be stuck here for Thanksgiving."

My eyebrows shot up to my hairline. "That's not my problem. I paid over seven hundred dollars for that ticket."

The news had been reporting nonstop about the Nor'easter shutting down the East Coast. They've had plenty of time to prepare for this. I even checked my app before I left, and it only showed one flight delay. I knew there was a chance my flight would get canceled, but I was hopeful they could get me there by tomorrow. I glanced around to see if there was a place to sit, so I could pull my laptop out and search for other options, but all the seats were filled with pissed-off travelers, complaining everywhere I turned. I thought about renting a car for a quick second, but looking at the blizzard building up outside, it didn't seem like a safe choice.

"Ma'am. We are doing the best we can here. We have no control over the weather."

"But you do have control over making sure you're staffed properly, correct?" My hands went to my hips in frustration. "Like for the busiest travel holiday of the year?"

"Ma'am." She looked over the frame of her glasses like she was exhausted from trying to explain this to me.

I smacked my palms on the counter, causing her head to bolt up from the keyboard. "Will you stop calling me ma'am!"

I was at the end of my rope and on the verge of losing it in the middle of the crowded airport. My mother and grandmother were counting on me being there, and I was looking forward to seeing them.

"I'm sorry, do you mind?" I jolted at the deep voice that came from behind me. I turned my head and was ready to tell the little intruder that, yes, I did mind. But when my eyes locked on his, my only response was a blank stare. It took me a minute to process what was happening.

His hair was dark, and his skin was tanned from all the

hours he spent throwing a football around on the field. I knew that damn face. It looked different and yet exactly the same. I used to write about how handsome he was and drew little hearts next to his name in my high school diary.

Deep brown eyes framed by thick lashes swept over me like they were seeing me for the first time. This could not be happening right now. Either karma was a bitch, or the island of Manhattan wasn't as big as I thought it was.

There was no way in a city of eight million people it could be him. I never believed in fate before, but what were the odds of this happening? My teenage crush, actually every female at Henninger High, had a thing for Maverick Cross. He was the boy every girl wanted to date and the big man on campus all the guys wanted to be friends with.

The corner of his mouth kicked up into a cocky grin. "Hey, doll, could you please stop staring?" He gripped my suitcase and pushed it aside. "And if you kindly move out of my way, I might feel generous enough and let you take a picture with me for all your friends."

I smashed my lips together. There were so many retorts on the tip of my tongue, but my head was spinning so fast that I couldn't form a response.

He leaned in close and whispered in my ear, "I would appreciate your discretion." He looked over his shoulder at the small crowd gathering behind us.

"Discretion?" Momentarily confused, I blinked up at him.

He looked me up and down, and I suddenly grew self-conscious. Seeing him up close and getting a good look at that five o'clock shadow in all its glory made my knees go weak. A ripple of goose bumps broke across my skin because he was a million times hotter than he was in high school. I found myself pulling my coat tighter around my shoulders because I didn't know what to do with myself. "Don't play cute and try to act like you don't know who I am." His smile was smug. "The last thing I need is all the autograph seekers stopping me from making my flight." He placed his hand on my hip and tried to edge his way to the counter.

My palm landed squarely on his ridiculously hard chest. Ugh. Why the hell did he have to fill out like that. "I don't think so, buddy."

He angled his head to the side. "Oh, I get it. You're a fan girl. What will it take to move things along here? I'm trying to get home for the holidays, and you're holding up the line." He stepped closer and lowered his voice. "What do you want? Tickets to a game? Box seats? A signed jersey?"

He flashed me a grin that probably got him what he wanted ninety-nine percent of the time. And then it hit me. *You're obviously a fan girl.* Holy Shit! He didn't recognize me. Talk about being rendered speechless.

"Are you serious right now? Fan girl?" I stared up into his stupidly handsome face that only got better looking with age and waited for a flicker of recognition to cross his features. But it never came. He had no clue that I was his sister's best friend or that I had been secretly in love with him since I was fourteen.

Maverick was three years older than Rylee and me. We didn't travel in the same social circles when we were younger, not just because of the age difference, mainly because he was a jock and I was just the shy, nerdy girl. I carried a bookbag instead of pom-poms.

He hasn't seen me in twelve years, but he should still recognize me. Mortification, like I'd never felt before, hit me square in the chest. What I initially thought was fate was actually kind of depressing. My teenage heart cracked into tiny, itty-bitty pieces.

"Does it look like I'm joking?" His tone implied he was serious, but then he flashed a cute little grin at the woman behind the counter.

I folded my arms across my chest. "Do you honestly think

you can just waltz up and smile your way to the front of the line?"

The corners of his eyes crinkled in humor like he found this whole thing amusing. "You're actually cute when you huff like that. It makes me wonder what other sounds come out of your mouth in the heat of the moment."

My face turned a bright shade of red. "You are unbelievable."

He raised his eyebrows. "I've heard that before too." And then he squeezed his way over to the ticket agent, who had stars shooting from her eyes. They seemed to grow bigger with each blink.

"Mr. Cross. We sincerely apologize for the disruption to your trip. Please be assured that we have put you on the priority list. The next available flight is on Friday, at 1:15 p.m. We will notify you through the online app and ensure your first-class seat is secured. We have booked you a room at the Four Seasons and will cover your expenses free of charge."

My mouth flew open. I didn't even get a voucher for a five-dollar sandwich. Inhaling a deep breath, I scanned the boarding area and felt a tiny bit of tension melt away when a few other passengers started to grumble about his preferential treatment.

He looked at me over his shoulder, winked, and pulled out a signed player's card, which he slid across the counter to the woman kissing his royal ass. "I guess things could be worse. Hopefully, the storm will pass soon."

"Yes, our deepest apologies. We have also arranged a car service to pick you up at the front gate. They will meet you outside Concourse C."

"Hey, wait a minute." I raised my finger and pointed to her computer monitor. "You told me the next flight out was on Saturday."

"I'm sorry, but the flight leaving on Friday afternoon is

oversold, and Mr. Cross is a Diamond Member, so therefore he gets priority."

I've officially heard enough, and arguing with her was getting me nowhere. I gripped the handle of my rolling carry-on and lugged it through the crowded terminal. The look of victory on his face paused me in my tracks. I turned and cupped my hands over my mouth and screamed as loud as I could, "Oh, my God! It's Maverick Cross, the quarterback for the Atlanta Arrows!"

Before he knew it, at least thirty people collapsed in around him with pens, paper, and cameras in hand, begging for an autograph or a selfie.

I quietly smiled to myself as I stormed my way through the airport and ordered my ass an Uber.

CHAPTER 2

KINLEY

"I'M SO SORRY, MOM." I SIGHED INTO THE PHONE AND SETTLED into my seat at the bar.

"Honey, no one could have predicted a blizzard at the end of November." She tried to disguise her disappointment, but I could still hear it through the phone, making me feel even worse.

"I know, but I should be sitting by your nice cozy fireplace sipping on hot chocolate. Not at a bar in Midtown Manhattan."

"What can I get you?" the bartender asked, plucking a napkin out of the holder and setting it down in front of me.

My eyes scanned over the drink menu, considering my options. "I'll have a dirty martini, extra dirty."

"My kinda girl." He winked. "What kind of vodka?"

I covered my hand over the phone. "Surprise me."

"You got it." He knocked his knuckles on the counter and walked away.

I set my purse down and watched him grab a bottle of Tito's from the shelf. His black T-shirt stretched across his broad chest, and I could see his black boxers peeking out from the waist of his tight-fitted jeans. When he turned and caught me staring, I looked away and focused on my phone call.

"Maybe you could take an extended leave and spend a few extra days around Christmas," my mom suggested.

I played with the paper napkin in my hand. "I was actually thinking the same thing."

"Oh, Kinley. That makes me so happy." I could hear the joy in her voice. It wasn't fair that she always had to make the trip to see me, but she never complained. That's why I knew it was the right thing to do.

The bartender came back a few minutes later and placed my drink down. He settled his thick forearms on the bar top directly across from me. "Anything else?"

"I'm good for right now. Thank you," I whispered. The twinkle in his eyes made me blush, so I picked up my martini and took a long sip.

"Kinley, are you still there?"

"Yes," I said once I swallowed my vodka. "I'll let you know the exact dates once I get them approved."

"They better not give you any trouble. You are long overdue for a vacation. I bet Rylee would be overjoyed to have you in town." I hummed in agreement, not bothering to mention that I ran into Rylee's famous brother at LaGuardia Airport. "What will you do for Thanksgiving?"

"Taylor has plans, but I think Chad's parents are in town. I'm sure I can go to dinner with them."

She'd met my friends a few times and had mentioned on more than one occasion that she was glad I had those two to watch over me. She hated that I was a young, single female living in the city alone.

"Oh, good." She sighed in relief.

I checked the time on my phone and noticed it was getting late.

"I'll let you get back to baking. Make sure Spencer doesn't eat all the pie, and try to keep Grandma away from the booze." I laughed, knowing neither one of those two things would be happening.

"Oh, I've already thought of a good hiding spot for both." She laughed, but I still sensed her sadness over my flight cancelation. "I'll call you soon. I love you."

"Sounds good. Love you too."

I hung up and typed out a quick email to my boss, telling him my plans had changed and I needed to talk to him about taking some additional time off at the end of December.

I sipped my martini as my eyes drifted to the flatscreen TVs mounted on the wall. All three of them were reporting about the weather. The storm was lingering over the Tri-state area while the Southeast was getting pounded with freezing rain and strong winds. Unfortunately, there was no break in sight.

I slid my empty glass across the bar, letting the bartender know I was ready for a refill. Maybe a good buzz would put me in a better mood.

"Well, if it isn't the woman responsible for my needing a security escort to help get me out of the airport," a deep voice came from my side, startling me to the point that I almost fell out of my chair. My head whipped to the left, and I opened my mouth to speak but shut it quickly. Maverick had one elbow propped up against the bar top, looking like he found this whole thing entertaining. I blinked my eyes, wondering if this was really happening again. "I hope you don't mind a little company." He gestured to the empty stool next to me. "Considering it took me almost two hours to sign autographs after the little stunt you pulled earlier."

"What?" I said innocently. "I figured you liked being fawned over, so I just assumed I was doing you a favor."

He rolled his eyes. "Sure you were."

My lips turned into a scowl as he pulled his gloves off and unwrapped the scarf from his neck. He unbuttoned his coat and draped it along the back of the chair as if he were about to get comfortable.

"You realize there are plenty of other places to sit." I gestured to the line of empty stools.

Was I being mean? Yep, but I couldn't help myself. It took me over an hour to calm down after I stormed off and left him to his little group of adoring fans. My ego still stung from the fact that he had no clue who I was.

"Is there a reason why I can't sit here, because this seat looks pretty comfortable?"

"You can sit wherever you want, but I haven't had the best night, so don't expect me to make small talk."

"You might want to work on your people skills. If you didn't notice, they didn't get you very far with the airline earlier."

I swirled around to face him, wishing I could toss his arrogant ass off the stool. "Apparently, it didn't get you very far either, seeing that you're sitting next to me."

He moved closer, and the smell of something warm and musky hit my nose. "Are you always this standoffish with people you've just met?"

I wanted to point out that we already knew each other, but I kept my lips closed tight. This was already awkward, and I was starting to feel lightheaded from his nearness.

The bartender passed by, stopped, and did a double-take when he noticed the man next to me. "Holy shit!" He grinned. "You're Maverick Cross."

"I get that a lot." Maverick smiled back, looking uneasy. "But no, we just look alike."

I tilted my head to the side and met his eyes. They pleaded with me to keep my mouth shut this time.

"Damn," he said, throwing a rag over his shoulder. "You could totally be twins. You're even built like him." He shook his head. "It sucks about his injury though. Me and my buddies have a bet going on whether or not he'll be back next season. That hit he took to the leg didn't look too good."

"I wouldn't count him out just yet." Maverick pulled his wallet out and grabbed a few twenties. "I'll take a Jack and Coke and this should cover the cost of her drink too."

"Sure thing." He turned to me. "Same as before, beautiful?"

"Yes, thank you. Wait." I grabbed my purse and searched for my credit card. "I still owe you for the first drink." I tried to hand him an American Express card, but he waved me off.

"That was on the house."

Maverick's curious gaze bounced between us. "Thank you." I smiled and slid a ten-dollar bill in his direction. "Please let me at least cover the tip."

"Nah, I'm good. I'll let your boyfriend tip me when you're done."

"Oh, he's not my boyfriend."

"Good to know." He smiled, causing a dimple to pop out of his left cheek. I was a sucker for dimples—another reason why I should have avoided the man sitting next to me because he had two.

I sighed and twisted around in my stool. "I guess I should thank you as well," I said, softening my voice. I didn't want him to think I was ungrateful, but I couldn't pretend to be enamored with him either. If I were still that same teenage girl who was infatuated with every smile and word that came out of his mouth, then I would be completely on board with this encounter. But I wasn't that young girl anymore. I was older, smarter, and well aware of how cautious I needed to be with him.

He slanted his head to the side and studied me. "Think of it as a peace offering." He winked, and we both turned our attention to the end of the bar. A few guys were staring in our direction. Maverick adjusted the beanie on his head and kept his face turned away. His shoulders were hunched forward in tension, and I almost felt sorry for him. He had to know that he would stand out. He was too big, too broad, and too recognizable.

I raised an eyebrow. "Not in the mood to take a selfie or sign anymore autographs?"

He blew out a breath. "While I'm thankful for my fans, I don't want to spend the next hour talking football or my torn ACL." He turned and stretched out his injured leg.

Now I felt guilty for calling attention to him earlier. But seriously, how did a hotshot like him think he could blend in with a crowd? Even if you didn't watch football, you knew who Maverick Cross was.

I cleared my throat and tried to think of ways I could ruffle his feathers because he seemed to enjoy my sarcasm. "Was the lounge at the Four Seasons out of alcohol tonight?"

He turned so his knee brushed against mine. Just that little touch made my body tingle in places it shouldn't. "So you were paying attention, huh?"

I moved back because he smelled too damn good, and I needed a little space between us so I could think clearly.

"Don't flatter yourself, buttercup." I patted his leg, and he lifted his eyebrow. "I know you think you're someone special just because you know how to throw a spiral, but it takes more than that to impress me."

His grin deepened. "Is that the extent of your knowledge when it comes to football?"

"You mean that and the fact that you guys can wear tight pants better than most females and probably more padding than those cheerleaders stuff in their push-up bras?"

"Wow!" He scratched his chin while holding in a laugh. "I think we got off on the wrong foot." I made the mistake of looking into his eyes; they were twinkling with humor. I tried hard not to notice every little thing, but it was becoming impossible. "Maybe we should introduce ourselves?" He held out his hand and turned that flirty smile on me. That swarm of butterflies that released in my stomach needed to calm down. "I'm Maverick, but my friends call me Mav."

There wasn't a chance in hell I was reaching for that hand. The second our fingers touched, he'd be able to tell how clammy mine were.

Instead, I held my drink up and gave him the first name that popped into my head. "Ivy. Nice to meet you."

"Ivy?" he repeated as if he were testing out the name. He reached over and grabbed a handful of nuts from the glass bowl. "So, Ivy, do you live in Georgia, or were you just visiting family?"

"Are we making small talk now?"

"Would you rather we talk about the weather?"

"I think I'll pass." I rolled my eyes and tried to ignore that little voice in my head telling me that lying about who I was would come back to bite me in the ass. But I was already two drinks in to care if he recognized me or not.

"So, which one is it?"

"Which one is what?" I asked, confused because, clearly, I was losing focus and couldn't keep up.

"Visiting family or going home?"

"I guess you could say both?" I knew I should quit while I was ahead, call it a day, and put this encounter behind me, but this opportunity was too good to pass up.

God, I needed a therapist. I watched the bartender fill a row of shot glasses for a group in the back. I was tempted to order one for myself to take the edge off.

"What part of Georgia are you from?"

"Aren't you just full of questions?"

"I'm just trying to get to know the beautiful woman sitting across from me."

Was this real or some crazy dream? It had to be a dream, right? Maverick Cross called me beautiful. What the hell was happening? I shook my head and gave my teenage heart a minute to calm down. Focus, I reminded myself.

He doesn't know who you are. He thinks you're someone else. Play it cool, and don't let him get under your skin.

"I'm afraid there is nothing special about me," I said, trying to steady my nerves.

"I highly doubt that." His gaze raked over me. "What do you do for a living?"

"I'm a celebrity stalker for TMZ."

He took a sip of his drink. "I figured that out earlier."

I narrowed my eyes at the smart-ass. "You're lucky I only caused a small scene as opposed to what I really wanted to do."

"Yeah, I'm felling pretty lucky." He sat back in his chair as a slow smile slid onto his lips. "So, what do you do when you're not stalking celebrities?"

"My life isn't nearly as exciting as yours. I work for a start-up company."

"What kind of company?"

"Do you really want to talk about work?"

"When you put it like that, I guess not."

"Good, because it would be hard to compare myself to a football legend." I rolled my eyes playfully.

He chuckled. "You're really not a fan of the sport I play, are you?"

"Not really." I shrugged. "I mean, if there's a game on, I'll cheer for whoever my friends are rooting for. I don't pay much attention, to be honest. I know you throw the ball to someone who runs it into the end zone, and you have a guy who kicks for an extra point. And from what I can tell, it looks like it can get a little rough on the field sometimes, but personally, I think you guys are just trying to show off," I said, trying to play dumb even though I knew much more than that. "Honestly, I prefer baseball over football."

"Ouch." His hand went to his chest. "Then I guess the fact that I'm a star quarterback in the NFL doesn't impress you then, huh?"

"Afraid not." That was the truth. I loved the man before he became famous. I used to doodle little hearts in my diary and sign my name in cursive, *Mrs. Kinley Cross*. I even named our future children and clipped wedding dresses from bridal magazines on the pages of my scrapbooks. I had it bad for my best friend's older brother. And it crushed my spirit beyond repair that he had no idea who I was.

"Has anyone ever told you that you have a terrible poker face?"

My martini glass paused on its way to my lips. "Pardon?"

"Admit it." He picked up his whiskey and swirled the amber liquid around his tumbler. "You know a lot more about football than you're letting on. Don't forget, my job is to study my opponents, so I can read people pretty well. I think you're a lot more knowledgeable than you claim to be."

My shoulders sagged in disappointment. For a slight second, I thought he knew it was me. "I hate to burst your bubble, but I told you, it's the uniform. I really have a thing for those tight pants they force you guys to wear."

His eyes flickered with amusement. "Damn. Now I'm pissed that I didn't wear my uniform tonight."

And I was glad I didn't play poker because I'd be broke. He was right, my face would give my hand away. I wouldn't be able to keep up with this charade for much longer. He would eventually find out the truth and realize who I was.

A group of guys walked through the door, and Maverick cleared his throat. "So, listen, I'm going to head out. People are starting to recognize me, and I don't want to push my luck. I'd rather spend my time talking to you instead of fielding questions about my injury." He paused and wiped his thumb across the corner of his lip. "I have a hotel room nearby."

At first, I thought he was joking until I realized he was serious.

"That's convenient." I stared straight ahead. "Any reason why you're telling me that?"

I could see him grinning out of the corner of my eye. "I like to keep my options open."

"And I plan on keeping my legs closed, so you might want to look into other options."

He could tease and flirt with me all he wanted, but it wouldn't get him anywhere. I had already drawn the line at this little encounter, and there was nothing he could say that would make me cross it.

He barked out a laugh. "It was an invitation."

I was seriously starting to get a headache. "And I just declined."

"What?" He looked like that was the first time a woman had ever told him no, and it probably was.

"I'm not interested," I repeated, just in case he was having trouble understanding English today.

He jerked his head back quickly. "Impossible. Every woman is interested."

I snorted because, honestly, I had no idea how to respond. "I'm sure one-night stands are completely normal for you, but I don't sleep around, especially with someone I don't know."

Ha! Take that. I patted myself on the back at how unaffected I appeared.

His brows dipped down. "Who said anything about sleeping? And we don't need a whole night, just an hour or two." He started laughing, but his hands went up in mock surrender when I didn't. "Sorry, bad joke. That's why I play football instead of performing stand-up comedy."

"You actually get women to go home with you with lines like that?"

He shook his head, and I saw a hint of embarrassment jump in his features. "Honestly, I can't remember ever having to work so hard in my life just to get a woman to talk to me, let alone like me."

Of course, he didn't. Everyone loved him. He assured I was just playing hard to get. He had no idea that I was only protecting my heart.

"Listen, Maverick. I'm sure a famous good-looking guy like yourself has plenty of young, beautiful women to pick from." I pointed across the bar and toward the window. "You won't have trouble finding someone."

When he leaned in close to my face, I had to suck in a breath. His scent, his stare, and the close proximity were too much and not enough at the same time. It took all the willpower I could muster to pull away. He was offering me more than I'd ever thought I'd have.

"I don't know why you are hell-bent on fighting this, but you're like a goddamned mystery that I want to solve." He swirled his whiskey around in his glass before bringing it to his lips. They were full and pink and way too tempting, just like the rest of him, from his short-trimmed beard to his warm chocolate eyes. Everything about him was alluring. "Don't take this the wrong way, because I swear, it's not some cheesy pickup line, but I feel like we've met before, which is crazy because I would have definitely remembered you."

I blinked up at him and allowed his words to hang in the air. My body went completely still. My mouth would not move. My mind was firing blanks. My chest was so tight it was about to explode. The way he looked at me. The suggestion in his eyes. The implication of his words, was too much for me to process.

"I'm going to need a yes or a no, sweetheart." His eyes held mine, and I wasn't sure how much longer I'd be able to play this little game, because it felt like I was already in over my head.

I picked up my drink and drained the rest of it. A little liquid courage would help. It certainly wouldn't hurt, I thought to myself as I set the empty glass down on the coaster.

"Why are you being so persistent?" I asked, finally finding my voice. I wasn't being very nice to him. Sure, it was all an act, and I only did it to protect myself, but he didn't know that. He's had plenty of reasons to excuse himself and sit far enough away from me. The bar was big enough. But he stayed and engaged with me, and without even trying, made my night better. I'd smile when he wasn't looking, and even though I'd never admit it, I liked that he hadn't moved from his seat.

Was I softening up to this idea? It had disaster written all over it. Saying no would be the right thing to do because saying yes would be a horrible idea.

"Honestly, maybe, because your little attitude has made this night a lot more interesting. Although, I do find it a little odd that you're rejecting me because that never happens," he teased, then his tone turned serious. "It's a refreshing change to have a conversation with someone who isn't kissing my ass because they have an agenda."

Could I have a one-night stand with Maverick and keep my feelings detached? The answer was no. Not a chance in hell, but if this were my only shot, I'd be a fool not to consider it.

"That's sad that you're in a world where you always have to question people's intentions."

He shrugged his shoulders. "Story of my life."

There was a devil on my shoulder telling me I would be crazy to walk away and the other telling me he would be pissed when he found out the truth. Despite the mixed emotions in my head, his offer was too good to refuse.

"The ball is in your court."

When he scraped his stool back, getting ready to leave, my mind was made up. This might be the only way to know for sure if I had built him up in my head all those years. I'd be crazy to let this opportunity slip through my fingertips. I just needed to remind myself that there would be no tender smiles, or sweet words. This was strictly physical. There would be no emotions involved. The hurt feelings and broken heart could be dealt with tomorrow. Tonight, I would find out once and for all if those teenage fantasies I conjured up in my mind were as good as the real thing.

I didn't trust my voice, so I stood and held my hand out for him to lead the way.

He smiled in victory, snagged his jacket from behind the stool, and shrugged it on. He placed a hand on my back and led me out the door.

CHAPTER 3
MAVERICK

With shaky hands, I slipped the key card into the lock. The second we stepped inside the suite, I spun her around and pressed her against the wall.

The room was dark, with only a sliver of light coming from the window. Yet, the flush in her cheeks that spread down to her neck was as clear as day. Fuck, I never wanted to worship a throat so badly in my life.

"Tell me you want this."

Her gaze held mine, and all I could think was she was so damned beautiful. "I wouldn't be here if I didn't."

"I'm just making sure we understand each other." My gaze raked over her body. "I'm also going to need you to confirm that whatever happens in this room will stay private," I explained as gently as possible. I wasn't trying to be an asshole, but I couldn't take any unnecessary risks.

"Trust me, the last thing I want is to end up in the tabloids as one of your cleat chasers."

Her snark turned me on. Normally, women whimpered and bowed down at my feet. Not this little spitfire.

Bringing my mouth to her ear, I whispered, "You act like being associated with me would be a bad thing."

"I'm pretty sure any decision concerning you would be bad for me."

I ran my nose along her neck, inhaling her scent. It was light and peachy, and I wanted to devour her on the spot. "Stop acting like there is anyone else you'd rather be bad with."

She seemed to get a kick out of pushing my buttons. I didn't understand why and it annoyed me that I wanted to figure out why.

"Did it ever occur to you that you might be my second choice? Maybe it was the hot bartender who I had my eye set on."

I wasn't the jealous type, but I didn't like how he looked at her. Every time he would call her beautiful, she would smile and blush, and I wanted to take the martini glass he kept refilling and shove it down his throat.

I moved my hand up her thigh, keeping a firm grip. "You know what I think?" I slid my hand up a little farther until it reached her panties. "I think you want me just as bad as I want you."

Her lips were plump and perfect, practically begging for mine. So, I took that as an opening and brought my mouth to hers. Everything about this woman was hard and soft. From the way her hands gently tangled in my hair to how she gripped my shoulders to pull me closer.

Our tongues stroked and moved in perfect rhythm as if we'd kissed a thousand times before. I roamed her body with my hands, splaying my hand along the width of her hips. I wanted her naked and writhing underneath me. I wanted to taste every inch of her and savor every damn second.

I pushed her jacket off her shoulders. Her eyes met mine, and I worked a deep swallow down my throat. I studied her and contemplated why I worked so hard to get her here tonight. There was this inexplicable pull that kept me from walking away. Because she sure as hell gave me plenty of reasons to.

She was immune to my fame, something I rarely encountered. Perhaps that was why I was all twisted up inside. There had to be a reason, I thought as my eyes flickered across hers as if I was expecting her to know the answer.

She was, without a doubt, attractive with her blond hair, blue eyes, and a body that looked like it was made to sin, but that wasn't enough.

"I don't know what it is about you, or what you're doing to me." I pulled her hair back gently with one hand and cradled her jaw with the other. "But you're driving me crazy. You have me tied up in knots. I don't usually want for anything, but I want you so bad it physically hurts."

"I bet you say that to all the girls," she said, kicking her jacket that landed on the floor to the side.

She'd been taunting me all night, and I would pay her back by ruining her for anyone who came after me. She would remember this night. I would make sure of it. I squeezed her ass, roaming my hands along her curves and stopping at her opening.

"You're not a girl." I inched my hand into her panties and slipped my fingers underneath the fabric. "You are all woman." I kissed the column of her neck and pressed my arousal against her heat. She clawed at my shoulders when I slammed my mouth down on hers. The little sounds she made every time my stubbled chin scraped against her cheek only spurred me on. She could kiss. That was for damn sure. It had me questioning if she was as innocent as she claimed to be because she either had a lot of fucking practice or she was a natural.

"On your knees, sweetheart." Was I testing her? Damn, right I was, and I wanted to see if my instincts about her were right.

She smirked, accepting my challenge. There was no

missing the mischief in her eyes as we breathed each other in. My eyes flickered down to her mouth, and a whole list of confusing emotions raged within me.

Need. Want. Lust. And something indescribable swirled inside me.

My blood heated as she lowered herself to the plush carpet and brought her fingers to my zipper. I hissed out a breath as she slowly undid my fly. She licked her lips and studied the outline of my dick like she couldn't wait to see it.

"You keep looking at me like that, and this will be over before we even start." I shoved my pants down, stripped my boxers off, and let my cock spring free. The hitch in her breath went straight to my swollen head. I brushed her hair to the side so I could see her face. "You're beautiful."

"So are you," she said, glancing up quickly and staring into my eyes.

"I can't say I've ever been called that before."

She grinned. "There's a first time for everything."

My nostrils flared as her red-painted lips wrapped around my cock. She teased my tip with her tongue before it disappeared into her mouth. It felt better than I imagined. I was mesmerized by watching her take me in, inch by inch. The harder she sucked, the harder it was for me to hold back. She teased me with her tongue, moving it up and down and squeezing my head with enough pressure to make the room spin.

I was on the brink of losing control, but I wanted to take my time with this woman. Yet every smooth glide of her tongue made my dick grow more impatient. I tried to pull away, but she held me in place, slanting her head to take me deeper. I fisted her hair, wrapping it around my hand in a firm grip. Watching this was enough to send me over the edge. I focused on holding on for as long as possible, but my self-restraint had limits. She sucked me off while raking her nails along my thighs, and I knew I was close to losing it.

When I hit the back of her throat and saw her eyes water, I'd had enough.

I jerked away from her, trying to get my breathing under control. "We're moving this over to the bed."

"You're awfully demanding." She looked amused as I helped her to her feet.

"I'm impatient." I pulled her dress over her head and inhaled deeply.

I backed her up to the mattress, and laid her down gently. Her skin was smooth and flawless. She was toned and fit, curvy in all the right places. I wanted to map out her body with my hands and mouth and memorize every inch of her. When she peered up at me through her lashes, something I couldn't explain moved through me. My heart pounded in my chest, and I had to take a deep swallow to calm down.

I kneeled on the bed and took a minute to admire her. Why did this feel different? The chemistry and the connection didn't feel forced or foreign. It felt oddly familiar. I knocked that thought out of my head because, clearly, I was losing it.

I unzipped her boots and slid them off her feet. She laughed when I threw them over my shoulder, and they landed on the chair.

"You've got quite the throw."

I flashed her a grin while sliding her panties down her legs. "Some people would say my arm was worth about thirty-million dollars."

She rolled her eyes. "It's a good thing I only need you to use your hands and mouth then."

"Don't forget these." I parted her open and gently moved my fingers in and out.

"Oh, yes." She arched her back. "You definitely need to get those insured too."

I laughed and brought my head between her legs. "And don't forget this." I swiped my tongue against her clit. She squirmed beneath me as I searched for that bundle of nerves that would set her off.

"That," she said in between breaths, "is worth a hefty ahhh…" she cried out as I drove my tongue in deeper. Her fingers landed in my hair as she pushed my face closer. She was trying to position me where she wanted me, but I had other plans for her.

I grabbed her wrist and lifted my head. "I want you to turn the other way and put your hands on the headboard." She looked like she wanted to argue, so I dragged my tongue along her opening. "Please."

She turned over, got on her knees, and I moved up the bed and positioned myself exactly where I needed to be. I looked up at the beautiful sight above me and dug my fingers into her ass cheeks. "Now ride my face, beautiful."

She gripped the headboard and started rocking against my mouth. Her head fell back in a moan as she got into a steady rhythm. I grabbed her ass, pulling her tighter against my mouth. Her soft sighs grew heavier, matching the rise and fall of her chest. I added a finger for extra pressure, letting her know who was still in control. Maybe I needed the reminder for myself because the woman had me feeling powerless and unsettled.

She squeezed her eyes shut, so I buried my face deeper, pushing her to the point of no return. I was already teetering on the edge, but I wasn't stopping until she was finished. I wrapped my arms around her legs, holding on tight as her thighs began to tremble. Watching her fall apart and lose control was a sight I never wanted to forget.

Knowing I had the power to bring such a strong, independent woman to the brink felt almost as good as scoring a touchdown. Actually, it felt better. So much better. I needed to be inside her, and I had a feeling once I had her, it wouldn't be enough.

She collapsed on my side, landing on her back, seeming

utterly satisfied. I stood up and swallowed tightly at the sight in front of me. Her breasts were full and heaving, her lips were parted open, and her messy hair hung lazily along her shoulders. She was beautiful. She was perfect, and at that moment, she was all mine.

My body vibrated with need as I tore off the rest of my clothes. The shirt I wore sailed across the room, landing in a haphazard mess with the rest of our clothing.

Planting my knee on the bed, I licked my lips, still tasting her on my tongue. I grabbed her hands and pinned them above her head. My mouth closed around her nipple while my free hand found the other one.

Trailing my fingers up her thigh, I kept my touch featherlight. Her body tensed with anticipation when I pushed her legs apart. Placing a hard kiss on her lips, I rubbed my thumb over her clit and moved my fingers in and out. Her arousal gave me the power to keep going, all the while hoping like hell my release wouldn't come before I was ready.

I lined myself up at her entrance and pushed inside. Everything felt tight and warm as I inched my way in slowly. My head fell back in pleasure, my eyes slid closed, and my cock jerked in happiness. Every nerve ending in my body burned hotter as her nails dug into my back. My eyes pinched tight, and I gave her a minute to adjust. I started to move until my hips found the perfect rhythm. I couldn't remember anything ever feeling this good in my life. So hot. So warm. So...My body stilled.

Fuck! My eyes flew open. "I forgot the condom."

I jumped off the bed so fast you would have thought my ass was on fire. I fished the condom out of my wallet, tore the wrapper off, and slid it over the body part where it should have been all along.

How could I be so reckless? What was it about this woman that made me lose all common sense?

"Sorry about that," I murmured as I kneeled back on the bed. "I didn't mean to react like that. I just…"

"It's okay. I'm glad one of us was thinking." She sounded calm, unlike me, who was flustered. And I never got flustered. To be fair, she was different, and for the first time in my life, I wished this could be more than one night.

I kissed my way down the curve of her neck to her shoulder, trying to salvage the moment I almost ruined. I stroked her clit with my thumb and then slid the base of my cock inside. I made sure my strokes were slow and measured, trying to keep myself from exploding too soon. I needed to pace myself and draw this night out as long as possible. She tried to meet each movement as I kept hitting that same spot over and over again. We were all hands, tongues, and teeth. I don't know what I did to deserve this, but I sure as hell wouldn't regret a single second.

My breaths came out in pants, and beads of sweat trickled down my forehead as I pounded into her like a madman. I was possessed.

Typically, sex was just a physical act for me. Yet, something about how our bodies connected made me want to break every vow I ever made to myself.

When her eyes flew open, I wanted to promise her things I had no business promising. But instead, I brought my lips to hers, willing myself to get a grip. This was sex, nothing more. So why did it feel so different with her? It felt like I'd known this woman for years instead of hours.

My body started to shudder, and that ball of pleasure I fought to hold back came tumbling forward. I came with a roar, and I came harder than ever before.

I collapsed on the mattress next to her, needing a minute to get my breathing under control. She turned sideways and rested her head on my shoulder. I pulled on the back of her neck and captured her mouth again. Cuddling wasn't something I usually did, but I was too sated to overthink it.

"I think we'll need to do that again," I said, leaning on my elbow and staring down at her. I would need a few minutes to recover, but I knew it wouldn't take long to regain my strength.

She let out a low chuckle. "What makes you think you were good enough to earn another round?"

I couldn't help it. I fell back against the mattress and laughed. "Don't act like you didn't enjoy every damn second of it."

She shrugged her shoulders. "You were all right, I guess."

I arched an eyebrow. "All right?" I tickled her, and she started squirming beneath me. "Take that back right now and admit I'm the best sex you ever had."

I couldn't deny that this woman brought out a playful side in me. Hell, she brought out many different sides of me. Some I didn't want to examine too closely.

"Okay, Okay." She was out of breath. "It was the best." She tapped her lips. "You get the top spot, like A number one, top of the list, king of the hill." She smirked. "How's that?"

"What the fuck?" My eyebrows pulled together. "Did you just compare my lovemaking skills to a Frank Sinatra song?" Her response was to laugh harder. "Oh, it's like that, huh?" I said, climbing over her and pinning her hands to the bed.

"What?" she asked innocently. "You don't like Old Blue Eyes?"

I glanced down at her. Everything inside me went soft. "I like your blue eyes."

An uncomfortable silence took over the room. I watched her work a deep swallow. I got this strange sense that she was trying to hide something and didn't want me to look too closely, which was odd because most women went out of their way to get noticed by me.

She went to stand up, but I grabbed her wrist. "Where are you going?"

"I assumed you wanted me to leave."

Was her radar that off? Not once did I hint that I wanted her gone. "You assumed wrong. Besides," I said, trying to rationalize this, "it's still storming outside. Why don't you get some sleep and wait till it clears up tomorrow?"

She arched an eyebrow and leaned forward. "Are you sure?"

"Positive." I smiled, tucking a piece of hair behind her ear.

She nodded and moved to the end of the bed, pulling the covers up to her chin. I pulled her across the sheets until she was nestled into my side. Thank God she didn't fight me because I was exhausted and just wanted to close my eyes and sleep. Instead, we stayed awake until the wee hours of the morning, telling jokes and teasing each other until the only noise in the room was her light snoring.

And for the first time in my life, I fell asleep with a smile on my lips.

When I woke up the next morning and reached for her, the bed was empty. Typically, I was the one sneaking out at dawn. I should be thankful that she spared me the morning after speech. The one that made things awkward. Where I gave a list of excuses for why we couldn't see each other again; instead, I felt disappointed.

Grabbing my phone from the charger, I pulled up the weather app. The storm was letting up a little bit, but another one was right behind it. I needed to get back to Georgia because we had a game on Sunday that I couldn't miss. Even though I wasn't an active player, as the team captain, I was still expected to show up and support my team.

I pushed the covers aside, the ones that still smelled like her, and shuffled into the bathroom to take a shower. Once I was finished, I wrapped a towel around my waist and grabbed my shaving cream off the counter. There was a hickey on my neck and scratch marks running down my shoulders.

The guys in the locker room would never let me live this

down if they saw these marks, but all the ribbing and jokes would be worth it.

I didn't have an ounce of regret. Did she? Is that why she left without a trace?

She would have at least left a note or phone number, right? Maybe she left something behind, and I missed it. A tube of lipstick or an earring? I searched the room, looking under the bed, near the door, and under the loveseat. There was nothing. And then my eyes landed on a scrap of fabric rolled up inside the messy sheets. Bingo!

A smile graced my lips at the black lace thong. At least I had something, and it was better than any souvenir I'd find in a New York City gift shop.

I made myself a cup of coffee and walked over to the window. The sidewalks, usually filled with people, were empty, except for the guy shoveling across the street. Everything was covered in snow. Even the few cars parked along the street were buried.

How did she get home? Did she walk? Take a cab?

My phone pinged with an email from my agent letting me know that I had secured another endorsement deal. I fired off a reply, letting him know that I was still in New York if they wanted to meet one more time before I flew home. My focus needed to be on football—not wishing for something that would never happen again. Because I needed to get my old ass back on the field, and a distraction was the last thing I needed.

CHAPTER 4

KINLEY

"Knock, knock."

"Hey, Taylor." I looked up from the mess scattered over the length of my desk. "I thought you were out of the office today?"

My friend strolled in, all decked out in a red sweater dress, a Santa hat, and snowflake earrings dangling from her ears. It was comical how much she loved Christmas.

She collapsed into the leather chair at the corner of my desk and moved a few files aside to make space to set her coffee down.

"My meeting got canceled, so I thought I'd check in on you and see if you were feeling any better."

"Just a little more tired than usual," I said, saving the file I was proofreading before closing out the document. I didn't have time for small talk, but I didn't have the energy to turn her away either. She was our operations manager, and I needed her help with a past-due project.

"That's what happens when you work fourteen-hour days."

I shook my head, not even bothering trying to deny it. "I

need to get this marketing proposal done so I can have every-thing wrapped up before the holidays."

"Are you excited about your trip back home? It's long overdue."

Wasn't that the truth? It had been a rough two weeks for me. Our CEO was determined to push our product launch through weeks ahead of schedule to help secure some Christmas sales revenue before the end of the year. The problem was that there were too many issues on the service end, and I was convinced our finance department was over-projecting the potential sales figures. As a result, everyone in the office was stressed and being pulled into multiple projects.

"I am." I leaned back in my chair and crossed my legs. "How was your date last night?" I asked, knowing she would have an exciting story to tell me.

"Get this." Her eyes lit up. "He teaches at Julliard, so he took me on a tour of the school and played a piece just for me in one of the practice rooms."

That made me smile. "Sounds romantic."

"Oh, it was, especially when I thanked him by having sex on the piano when he was done playing."

I laughed. "That date will be hard to top. Are you going to see him again?"

"Not sure." She shrugged. "Speaking of dates, are you ready for tonight?" She pulled a mirror out of her bag so she could adjust her bangs. I tilted my head to the side in confu-sion. When I didn't answer, she looked up and shook her head. "You forgot, didn't you? It's Chad's holiday party tonight."

"Shit, it completely slipped my mind." I picked up my phone to check the time. "Why did I even commit to this?"

She chuckled. "You agreed to go because it's for a good cause."

That was true. Chad worked for a nonprofit that supplied

food and resources to help get homeless people off the street, and tonight was their big fundraiser.

I set my phone down and sighed. "I don't know why I allowed him to talk me into this."

"Probably because you can't say no to your lovesick friend."

I refrained from rolling my eyes. She was constantly digging to see if I'd somehow slip up and admit that there was more to our friendship than I let on.

"I've told you a thousand times. It's not like that." This was an ongoing argument, one I lost every time. "You need to get that crazy idea out of your head."

"Why else would he ask you to be his date every year?" she asked, swiping a cookie off my desk and shoving it in her mouth.

"Maybe he doesn't want to go alone." I pushed the tray of cookies out of her reach before she could steal another one. "Now, did you swing by my office to check to see how I'm doing or are you just here to annoy me, because I have work to do?"

"Actually…" She inched forward, but I dropped my arm over my tray, preventing her from stealing another one.

"Stop eating my cookies. You have your own."

She crossed her arms. "You're mean."

"You'll live." I rolled my eyes.

"Fine." She rolled her eyes right back at me. "Want to take a guess who I saw last night?"

"Considering you were on a date last night at Julliard, I don't have a clue."

She grinned. "I saw your one-night stand. The football player."

"Where?" I sat up in my chair and placed my hand over my pounding heart.

Her grin deepened into a full-blown smile. "On one of the

flat screens at O'Grady's. We stopped on the way home for a drink."

"Are you trying to give me a heart attack?" I kept my hand pressed against my chest as if that could somehow get it to stop beating so fast. For a split second, I got excited, thinking he was back in town again. God, I was such a head case.

"Speaking of heart attack, he got mine going pretty damn good. Have you seen that new bodywash commercial that just came out? Jesus." She fanned herself. "It only showed him stepping out of the shower from the waist up, but damn."

Instead of answering her, I looked off to the side. I had firsthand knowledge of how beautiful his body was. It had been two weeks, and my heart was a flipping mess of emotions. He was the reason I was falling further behind with my work. He was the reason why I couldn't sleep at night. I was too busy being distracted by remembering every little detail and wishing we could do it again.

That night was a mistake, even though it didn't feel like one, because clearly, it did more harm than good to my already fragile heart.

Taylor snapped her fingers. "Earth to Kinley."

"Sorry." I leaned back in my chair. "I spaced out for a second."

"Where did you go?" She smirked. "You looked like you were seeing stars, or maybe..." she paused for dramatic effect. "Football helmets."

"Knock it off," I scolded, and rearranged a stack of papers on my desk that didn't need rearranging.

"Have you thought about reaching out to him?"

I looked at my office door to ensure no one was listening to this conversation. "And say what?"

"I don't know." She shrugged her shoulders. "Maybe ask him if he's interested in hooking up again." I gave her a blank stare. "Or maybe tell him who you really are. I mean, you are still friends with his sister, right?"

"I'll always be friends with Rylee, we just don't keep in touch as much as we used to." I shifted in my seat. "And there is no way he will ever find out it was me he slept with, because I don't ever plan on seeing him again."

That night kept replaying over and over in my head, leaving me unsettled for many different reasons. I was ashamed and embarrassed and never expected to feel so much guilt. Not for spending the night with him but for pretending to be someone I wasn't.

"Do you think it would have mattered to him if he knew who you were?"

Her comment gave me pause. "Oh, I'm pretty sure that night never would have happened if he knew it was me."

I'll never forget when he came home from college to attend a high school football game. The team was headed toward a state championship, and he decided to make a surprise appearance. I was one of the few people who knew he would be attending the game. So, I went to Hollister, bought a cute pair of tight jeans and a white, revealing tank top and drowned myself in a bottle of perfume from Victoria's Secret. I even splurged on an expensive makeup palette from Sephora.

When he walked up the bleachers to greet everyone, I stood up and expected a hug and kiss on the cheek like everyone else. Instead, he ruffled my hair and said, "how are you doing, kiddo?"

No hug. No kiss. Nothing but a pet on the head that lasted all of five seconds. All my well-earned babysitting money went down the drain, along with the tears I shed from the humiliation.

"Well then, you better hope you don't run into him while you're home visiting your family." She chuckled and took a sip of her coffee.

I shot her a look. "Atlanta is a big city, so unless I seek him out, which I won't, I don't see that happening."

"Gotcha." She seemed to ponder my response for a second and changed topics. "Let's talk about tonight. What are you wearing?"

I craned my neck from side to side. "Probably the same dress I wore last year." This will be the third year in a row that Chad has guilted me into going. "I don't understand why he doesn't take a real date. He'll never meet anyone if people think we're together."

"Because he wants *you* guys to be together." She stuck her tongue at me, and I rolled my eyes.

"You've been watching too many Hallmark movies."

"I don't have time to watch cheesy Hallmark movies. I'm too busy living my real life." She checked her watch and stood up. "Not to mention, all those movies end with a kiss. My nights end with a bang."

I chuckled and shook my head. "Wait." I held my hand when she headed to the door. "Do you really think Chad has a thing for me?"

A smile grew on her face. "Fifty bucks says he tries to kiss you tonight."

I sank back in my chair; my lips twisted in annoyance. "A hundred bucks says he doesn't."

Her laughter followed her out of the room, and it was so loud it drowned out the sound of her clicking heels along the tiled floor.

———

"Have you started your Christmas shopping yet, Kinley?"

I tore my eyes away from the beautifully decorated Christmas tree and the string lights flickering across the courtyard. Tavern on the Green was an iconic restaurant nestled in the heart of Central Park. I'd walked past this building many times, but this was my first time inside.

"Um…that would be a solid no," Chad answered for me and swung his arm along the back of my chair.

"I'm a last-minute shopper," I informed his coworker Brenna. We were the last three left at the table. A band was set up on a makeshift stage in the front of the room, playing a mix of holiday music and soft ballads, drawing the people onto the dance floor.

"I can relate," she said as a server came and picked up her empty plate. "Every year, I swear off shopping. It's so much easier to buy gift cards and shop online."

I pushed the mason jars filled with cranberry and flickering light tea candles aside to make room for the dessert trays. "I'm the same way. I hate the crowds and long lines," I said, taking a bite of my crème brûlée. Unlike the atmosphere, the food was a little underwhelming.

Chad bumped my leg with his. "Your gift is already wrapped and under my tree."

"Why do you have to go and make me feel bad?" I teased, swatting his arm.

"You can make it up to me by switching desserts," Chad suggested, motioning his fork between our plates.

"No way, this is my favorite, so I'm not sharing."

He snickered and polished off the rest of his cheesecake. Once he was finished, he squeezed my shoulder. "Don't forget you owe me a dance."

"No, I don't."

He leaned in, and the sleeves of his dress shirt tickled my bare arms. "Please."

"I'm a terrible dancer, remember?" I said, noticing the band had started playing a slow song.

His eyes twinkled. "That's what makes it fun."

"I don't want to hear any complaints when I step on your feet."

Brenna raised her glass to her lips in an attempt to hide her disappointment. I sighed because my friend was clueless.

Chad's hand splayed along my lower back, bringing me to his chest. We've danced many times, so why did this feel different? It felt weird, and I couldn't understand why.

"I never understood these functions," I said, glancing over at the boisterous laughter coming from the bar area. I was trying to keep the conversation light and shake the weird vibe I was getting from him.

Chad followed my gaze as we swayed back and forth. "What do you mean?"

"None of these people know what it's like to be homeless or hungry, yet they hold these fancy functions to flaunt their money around." I grimaced once I realized how judgmental I sounded. "Sorry, that wasn't very polite. I'm sure they're nice people. It just seems like it would be easier to write a check instead of doing all this."

He laughed. "I've always loved your honesty." He twirled me around in a circle and pulled me back into his arms. A strand of hair came loose from my bobby pin and he tucked it back behind my ear. Maybe I was just being sensitive, but I could feel his thumb skimming along my neck. It was so brief I thought I imagined it.

"I'm glad someone does," I said, trying to relax and push aside that uneasy feeling that kept creeping in. Either Taylor was right, or I was losing my mind because her comment from earlier popped up in my head for the hundredth time tonight.

"By the way, you look beautiful. Red is definitely your color." He held me tight and moved us across the crowded dance floor. The tiny hairs on the back of my neck rose. It was an innocent compliment, but it didn't feel that way.

I laughed nervously and took a step back. "You have to say that, because I'm your friend."

"Friend." He cleared his throat and looked away. "Right."

My stomach somersaulted, hoping and praying that I was misreading things. I looked over at Brenna, who was watching us closely. Why couldn't Chad show an interest in her? Maybe he just needed a little nudge in the right direction.

"I'm going to make a phone call." I patted his chest and started backing away. "Why don't you mingle a bit? Maybe ask Brenna to dance."

His smile fell, and he nodded his head. "Okay, sure."

I left him on the dance floor and walked out of the room, trying to ignore the look of disappointment on his face.

Maybe Taylor was right after all. There was a slight chance my friend had feelings for me.

CHAPTER 5

MAVERICK

I WAS GOING THROUGH MY LAUNDRY WHEN MY EYEBROWS SHOT up to my hairline. I'd been on the road, traveling with the team for the last two weeks, so this was the first chance I'd had to get settled. My mouth kicked up in a smile while staring at the scrap of lace at my fingertips. I forgot about stuffing these in my suitcase, but I sure as hell didn't forget about the woman who left them behind in my hotel room.

I looked for her in every crowd and searched for her name on social media, which was pointless because I didn't even know her last name. I gave every woman with blond hair a second glance that passed me by. It was official, I had completely lost my mind.

"Dude, what the fuck is that?" My buddy JP shot me a look like I was crazy. JP was my closest friend on the team and the best wide receiver in the NFL.

"None of your business." I stuffed the panties in the bottom of the laundry basket, hoping he would just let it go. I looked down and willed my hard-on to disappear.

"Did you hook up with someone in Dallas or Chicago and I didn't know about it?"

The two of us roomed together while we traveled with the

team for the past two weeks. I might not have been on the active player roster, but I still needed to attend practices, meetings, and cheer my guys on from the sidelines.

"I didn't hook up with anyone on the road," I said, wincing as my knee stiffened. The weather was affecting my joints. Ever since they put my knee back together with pins and needles, my leg would flare up whenever it rained. Sitting on a plane for five hours with limited mobility didn't help either.

Playing in the NFL, I learned how to push past the pain, but sometimes I wondered if I'd reached my limit.

"Mav," he gave me a skeptical eyebrow, "we've been friends for a long time. Either you have a fetish with women's underwear that I don't know about, or you're into drag and ashamed to admit it."

"Fuck off." I laughed. "They belong to the woman I met in New York."

As one of my best friends, I shared a few details with him about that night. He knew me better than anybody and noticed I'd been acting a little strange. I've had my share of one-night stands back in the day, but this encounter with Ivy felt different.

He arched a brow. "The blonde you brought back to your hotel?"

I didn't bother denying it. "That's the one."

"I know you said she wasn't your usual type, but you wouldn't be carrying around her underwear if you didn't really like her."

"Never said I didn't like her."

"You know what I mean."

He was right. I did know what he meant, and she was the exact opposite of my usual type, but she still fascinated me for some reason. Her mixed signals and hot and cold attitude definitely held my attention.

She was witty and wild, and one night with her had me

wanting more. The fact that she was a bit mysterious just added to the attraction.

She didn't share anything about her past with me, which was unfair because my life was an open book. All she had to do was type my name in the search bar, and she would know everything from where I grew up to what fruit I put in my morning smoothie. Yet, I knew nothing about her. All I knew was her name was Ivy. She was great in the sack, and she intrigued the hell out of me. I couldn't remember the last time I pursued a woman. It was usually the other way around because, for me, finding a warm body to pass the time with was as easy as shooting fish in a barrel.

My phone buzzed in my hand, and I glanced at the screen and hit accept. "What's up, Morris?"

"Yo!" Morris was an offensive lineman on the team and a big party boy. It was hard to hear him over the vibrating music in the background. "We got a table down at Deluce. You ready to come out and enjoy a little action with the boys?"

I glanced over at JP, who nodded his head. "Yeah, let me shower and grab a bite to eat. JP and I will be there in an hour."

I hung up and raked a hand through my hair. The last thing I wanted to do was go clubbing, but it beat the hell out of staying home and doing nothing.

———

"You don't look very excited to be here tonight," my friend Della said, bringing her glass of wine to her mouth.

"I didn't have anything else to do," I said, tapping my fingers against my empty tumbler. "I figured it was better than staring at the walls of my condo."

She rolled her eyes at my response. "Careful there, your

charming personality might attract the wrong kind of people."

"Considering you've been sitting next to me for the past hour, what does that say about you?"

"That I'm immune to your charm." She beamed, and I chuckled.

Della and I went way back. We met toward the end of our freshman year at the University of Georgia. We dated briefly, but somewhere along the way, we realized we were better off as friends.

A camera flashed from a few tables down. It annoyed me that I couldn't go anywhere without someone trying to take my picture. Sometimes, I just wanted to have a drink with my friends and relax. The sound of laughter broke out around me. Another flash came from my left, and my body tensed.

"Relax." Della squeezed my leg. "Forget about them. Security won't allow them to approach you."

I looked past her and swallowed. "I'm just not in the mood to deal with anyone tonight."

Part of my shitty mood was because I was tired and running on little sleep due to the heavy travel I had to endure these past few weeks. The other part I didn't want to admit out loud was I was in a funk from sitting along the sidelines and watching my backup complete pass after pass and execute plays that had him looking more like a starter than a backup.

"You've been distracted and irritable lately." She took a sip of her drink. "Has your leg been bothering you? Are you icing and stretching?"

"I've been doing everything you told me to do."

Della wasn't just my friend. She was one of the physical therapists on the team and damn good at her job.

"I can fit you in for an extra session this week if you think you need it."

"I'll let you know."

Della knew how hard I'd been working on my recovery. She knew I wasn't letting up until I was feeling back to one hundred percent better.

"You know you can talk to me about anything, right?"

"There is nothing to talk about. Just jet-lagged, that's all."

"Are you forgetting I've known you longer than anyone in this room? I can tell when you're avoiding something."

"Speaking of avoiding." I gestured to the next table over. "What happened between you and the lawyer over there?"

I recognized him the second she took the seat next to mine. The dude looked like he wanted to rip my face off. He's stopped by the training facility to pick Della up from lunch a few times, but I haven't seen him around lately. The poor guy's been staring at her all night, trying to get her attention.

"He's not my type."

I knew from personal experience that Della was hard to please. So, her comment didn't surprise me.

"Let me guess, he wanted more."

Della was beautiful and confident and attracted a lot of attention. She'd dated her fair share over the years but was known for not keeping anyone around for too long.

"Ending it was better for both of us. You know firsthand how high maintenance I can be." She chuckled, trying to play it off.

"I hate to admit it, but you're right." She smacked my arm playfully. "But don't worry, when the right guy comes along, you won't be able to stay away from him."

"Since when are you an expert on relationships?" Her tone grew defensive like it always did when I brought up her lack of commitment issues. "It's not like you're out there trying to hunt down a wife. I'm the closest you'll ever get and the only relationship you ever had."

"Della, I never said I didn't want to settle down at some point. I just haven't had the time or met the right one yet."

I had a feeling that once I did find that woman, my friend would have a hard time accepting it. She didn't like sharing the spotlight.

She narrowed her eyes over the rim of her glass. "Your focus has always been on football, Maverick." She took a sip of her drink and made a sour face. "Besides, you're too picky, that's why I've been the only woman in your life for the past decade. I don't see that changing anytime soon."

She had a point. Over the years, I've grown very selective about whom I spent time with and who shared my bed. Being the team captain came with a lot of responsibilities, and everything I did was a reflection on my team and the franchise. One picture with a catchy headline could be devastating. I've seen how bad decisions can damage and destroy careers. So I did my best to stay out of the tabloids.

"Mav, you came, dude." Morris came up and patted me on the shoulder.

"Where the fuck have you been?"

His smile was wide. "On the dance floor where all the action is." He jerked his hips playfully. "JP is still down there busting a few moves. My old ass can't keep up with him. I need a drink." He wiped his hand across his sweaty forehead.

"I'll join you." I stood up and glanced at Della. "You need anything at the bar?"

She looked disappointed that I was leaving her alone. "I'm good." She hurried out of the booth. "I'll go find someone to hang out with now that you're leaving me behind."

Morris shook his head, and I cleared my throat uncomfortably. Della rubbed people the wrong way and wasn't loved by everyone. Usually, I'd make an excuse for her behavior, but I didn't feel like defending her tonight.

"Let's go get you a drink." I pointed to the bar. Morris looked like he wanted to say something but gave me a hard pat on the back instead and followed me across the room.

The club was packed tonight. There was a private party in

the back room, so the servers were stretched to their limits. I placed an order at the bar and turned to face Morris, who was typing on his phone. "Sorry, bro." He slipped his phone into his pants pocket. "That was Dwayne." Dwayne Poteete was our offensive coordinator and one of the few people I regularly butted heads with on the team. While standing on the sidelines, I've watched how well he worked with my backup, Brent Wilson. Brent allowed him to run plays where I liked to call them on my own.

"I'm surprised he isn't out celebrating tonight."

Morris's eyes filled with sympathy. "Wilson is good, but he still has a lot to prove."

"Well, he sure fucking proved that he can get the job done." I knew my mood was shitty and acting irrational, but I was worried about keeping my job.

"Don't be so hard on yourself, bro. You are the one who is going to be in the Hall of Fame. Wilson is starting to think he's God's gift to football; he still has a long way to go. You have been in the league long enough to know what happens with the rookies with a God complex."

"I know." I looked over my shoulder to make sure no one was listening. I needed to snap out of this funk before the wrong people started to pick up on it. "I'm just a little bitter. I want to hang in there as long as I can without worrying about boy wonder stealing my job. I'll feel better once I'm back on the field."

"Mav, we all know this is just temporary and we can't play forever. Yeah, his performance is good right now, but he hasn't learned everything from the school of hard knocks like you and me. You're still our QB1. You've got to focus on getting better, dude, and stop driving yourself crazy. Your time ain't up until you say it's up." He leaned forward, placing his hand on my shoulder. "Wilson might have a bright future ahead of him, but he's not ready to lead the team like you can."

"You'd think after all these years I'd be a little less paranoid, huh?" I muttered.

"Nah." He patted my chest. "It's that fire in you that makes you a warrior on the field. It's what earned you those three Super Bowl rings. Besides," he took a sip of his drink, "Coach has a hard-on for you. Pretty sure you could fuck his wife and he'd still thank you for doing his job."

We both laughed. I was lucky to have a coach who not only believed in me but built an entire team around me.

A head of long blond hair caught my attention. My eyes bugged out of my head. Could it be her? When the woman turned, giving me a clear view of her face, I quickly realized it was most definitely not her.

Morris snapped his fingers in front of my eyes. "Mav. Did you hear me?"

"Sorry," I apologized, giving my head a quick shake. "I thought I recognized someone."

"Are you doing okay?" His concerned gaze did a quick sweep across my face. "I know this is a lot to handle."

No one has asked me that. Sure, they asked if I missed playing or if I knew when I'd be back, but he was the first person to ask how I was feeling. Morris and I played at the same level. He understood the pressure I was under.

"I'm good." I patted his shoulder. "Thanks for the talk, Mo. I appreciate it."

We made our way back to the table. The windows gave us a clear view of the dance floor below. There were women in every shape, size, and color, but not one of them piqued my interest. I found myself staring off into space, wishing I was somewhere else. My thoughts kept drifting back to Ivy.

I couldn't lie. It felt great being with a woman who wasn't the slightest bit impressed that I was one of the best quarterbacks in the NFL. I laughed because I was pretty sure she didn't even like me very much. She was a bundle of blond hair and blue eyes wrapped up in a mystery. Too bad the only woman that had grabbed my attention was someone I'd never see again.

CHAPTER 6
KINLEY

THE TWO PINK LINES ON THE WHITE STICK TAUNTED ME AS I paced the length of my living room. It's been thirty minutes since those lines appeared, and I've spent the entire time hoping they would fade away. I walked over to the window, pulled up the sash, and stuck my head outside. I let the cool air hit my face for a long minute before shoving the window shut.

This felt like a bad dream. Maverick was the last man I would ever want to knock me up. Okay, that wasn't entirely true, but I had a baby to think about, and I didn't have the first clue how to handle this. My mind began to play out every possible scenario. And no matter how I tried to spin it, the result was the same. My life was changed forever.

My laptop pinged from the coffee table, alerting me of a new email. What was I going to do about my job? One of the reasons why I accepted a position with Vitalmed was because I was young and single. I've been telling myself that if I was going to make a name for myself in the marketing industry, now was the time to do it. I had the rest of my life to settle down and start a family. Getting pregnant was definitely not part of my five-year plan.

I started pacing my apartment, taking in a few calming breaths, but it wasn't helping me relax. What did this mean? I worked ten-to-twelve-hour days to get ahead. Would I have to hire a nanny? What if the baby got sick? Who the hell would I call when there was a problem? My eyes stung with tears; never in my life had I ever felt so alone.

I sighed and picked up my phone to call Taylor. I needed to tell someone before I went crazy.

———

I was curled up in my favorite chair when a knock sounded on my door. I wiped my eyes and threw my soft blanket on the couch. "Come in," I hollered, not bothering to get up.

Taylor came strolling in, took her boots off on the mat, and unzipped her coat. "What was so important that I needed to come over right away?" she asked, dropping her purse in the chair.

"You might want to sit down for this one."

She perched herself down on the edge of the table in front of me. I probably looked like a mess. "Is everything okay?"

I swung my legs off the couch and walked over to the window. I wanted to believe I could get through this, but honestly, I wasn't sure I could. A voice in my head told me I needed to accept this, but the change this would bring to my life terrified me.

I closed my eyes, knowing there was only one choice for me, and while I might not have planned for this to happen, it was my reality. Admitting it out loud would be the first step toward accepting the truth.

"I'm pregnant." I sighed, and tugged on my hair, something I did when I was upset.

"Who's the baby daddy?"

I snapped my head in her direction. "Who do you think?"

"Oh no!" Her eyes widened in recognition. "The quarter-back you sacked at Thanksgiving?"

"His name is Maverick, Taylor."

She scratched the back of her neck. "Are you sure you're pregnant? It's only been a few weeks since you slept together. Isn't it a little early to tell?"

"Not for me. I've never missed a period in my life."

My cycle came every month like clockwork. I started to panic when I realized I was a couple of days late. By day five, I was about ready to crack. I finally bought a test and prayed that only one line would appear—no such luck.

"Damn. What are you going to do?" She leaned forward and waited for me to fill in the blank. Wasn't that the million-dollar question?

"I don't know." I looked down at my stomach in disbelief. This news was a lot to process.

She gave me a look of sympathy. "Do you think you'll keep it?"

I was terrified of doing this alone, but I would have to push those fears aside. I knew I had options, but I didn't even consider them.

"Yes, I'm keeping it."

She blew out a breath and shook her head. "I can't believe you didn't use protection."

"We did use protection, but we got a little carried away at first," I told her without going into too much detail.

"Are you going to tell him?"

"Of course, I'm going to tell him." I sighed, dropped down on the couch, and threw my head back.

She leaned forward. "Other than being knocked-up, what has you so worried? Are you scared about his reaction?"

"What am I supposed to say? Surprise! I've got a bun in the oven and you're the one who baked it." I shook my head. "Oh, and I have another surprise for you too. I know this sounds crazy, but we already know each other. I'm Kinley, the girl who was best friends with your sister growing up."

I wasn't ready to have that conversation. I wasn't sure I'd ever be ready.

"I think you should say whatever feels right." Her voice was gentle, but it did nothing to calm my nerves. "I know this isn't ideal, but you're not alone."

"I feel alone," I said, feeling my throat close up. "How am I going to do my job and raise a baby? How am I going to explain this to our families?"

"Listen to me." She reached for my hand. "Having a baby isn't the end of a world. And you have nothing to explain. You don't owe anybody anything. And anyone who judges you can fuck right off. This is the twenty-first century. Women raise children on their own all the time."

I was ashamed about my lack of excitement. Of course, it wasn't the end of the world, but it sure felt like it at the moment. I felt guilty that my first reaction was about the instability it would cause. The news was unexpected, but it didn't give me a free pass to act so selfishly.

"I feel like I'm already screwing things up. I know nothing about being a mother. Shouldn't a small part of me feel happy and excited?"

"There are no rules about how you're supposed to feel. So you're not doing cartwheels across the living room or shouting from the rooftops. That doesn't make you a bad person."

"Thank you." I brought my hand down to my stomach. I couldn't believe there was a life growing inside me. "And thanks for being a good friend."

"So, what's next?"

"Now," I reached for the laptop and placed it on my lap, "I look to see if I can change my flight and leave for Atlanta a little earlier than I planned."

CHAPTER 7
KINLEY

I stepped out of my rental car and walked up the familiar driveway. Multi-colored lights blanketed the white columns, and a holiday wreath with a red bow hung from the door of the two-story brick house.

Now that I was here, I wished I had called first. What was I supposed to say when Beth and Vinny asked why I wanted their son's address? They would no doubt know something was up and wonder why I didn't just reach out to Rylee instead.

I wanted to puke at the thought because my friend was not going to be happy with me.

With shaky hands, I rang the doorbell. If I was this nervous asking for his address, I didn't want to think about what a mess I would be when I finally faced him.

"Kinley." Mrs. Cross blinked her eyes in disbelief. "This is a surprise." She stepped forward and wrapped her arms around me. "It's been forever since we've seen you. Oh, my gosh. Look at you." She held me at arm's length. "I barely recognize you."

Join the club. Your son didn't either.

"Vinny," she called out. "You're never going to believe who's here."

Mr. Cross came rushing down the hall but stopped short when he saw me standing there. His eyes widened, and then a smile appeared on his lips. He was wearing his signature short-sleeved plaid button-down and Levi jeans. I forgot how strongly Maverick resembled his dad. "Kinley Roberts, how the heck are you, kiddo?" He let out a throaty laugh. Vinny was always a smoker, and it didn't sound like he was close to quitting anytime soon.

"I'm well, thanks." My nose got a whiff of the familiar smell of Marlboro Lights. It wasn't strong, just enough to know that I would find an unopened pack on the top shelf of his tool bench in the garage because he was forbidden from smoking inside the house.

"What a lovely surprise." Beth studied me, probably wondering why I was showing up at her house out of the blue. I smiled at the short, beautiful woman who was always kind to me growing up. Her dark hair was still in her signature bob, with a bit of gray peeking out around her temples.

"Come inside." She squeezed my arm gently and closed the door behind her. "Let me take your coat."

After handing her my coat and taking my shoes off, I followed her into the family room. It felt like I was traveling back in time. Everywhere I looked, there were memories from my youth.

"It looks like you've done some updates," I said, noticing that they had extended the family room and updated the kitchen.

"Yes." Beth chuckled as she settled into the seat across from me. "Maverick tried to buy us a house, but there were too many memories, and we couldn't bring ourselves to sell it."

Vinny leaned forward in his chair. "What brings you by,

Kinley? Rylee didn't mention anything about you being in town."

I eyed the giant tree with twinkling lights in the corner. "Yeah." My voice cracked with nerves. "I'm actually looking for Maverick. I was hoping you could give me his address."

I tried looking online, but surprise, surprise. My search came up empty, and while I could have just called my friend, I figured this was easier.

Vinny's eyebrows pulled together in confusion. "Oh."

I rubbed my twitchy hands down my thighs. "I'm in town visiting my mom." That was partly true. "And my stepfather is a huge Atlanta fan. I was hoping to get him a couple tickets for the next home game for Christmas."

Lying to them and keeping this secret was killing me, but what else was I supposed to say? *Oh, by the way, I'm pregnant with your grandchild, and your son has no idea.* The sooner I got this news off my chest, the better I would feel.

"I'm sure he would be happy to get you those tickets. Would you like me to call him and save you the trip?"

I ran my sweaty hands together and placed them on my lap. "That's very kind of you, but I'd rather approach him in person if that's okay?"

"Of course." Vinny stood and paused for a beat. At first, I worried he didn't believe me, until he reached into his pocket and pulled out his cell. "Do you want me to write his address down or do you want to add it to the contacts in your phone?"

I pulled my phone out and unlocked the screen. "I'm ready when you are."

Once I was done programming his information, we sat and caught each other up to speed on each other's life over a shared plate of chocolate chip cookies. I was getting ready to leave when Vinny handed me a keycard.

"You're going to need this to access the building and the elevator. It will save you time from dealing with the people at the front desk. They aren't always the most pleasant people to deal with, but they keep the building safe, so I guess that's all that matters. This should save you some time and trouble. You can either leave it with Maverick when you're done, or swing by after. Whatever is easiest."

There wouldn't be anything easy about this visit, but I was thankful for one less barrier to go through.

———

I stared up at the large building in front of me and closed my eyes briefly. Of course, the show-off had to live in an exclusive high-rise in Buckhead.

The reality of what I was about to do hit me when I passed the doorman and walked through the massive front lobby. My fingers shook as I pressed the button for the elevator. Unfortunately, the two blocks I walked after parking my car did nothing to calm my nerves. Every possible scenario played through my mind on the ride up. The most likely, he would be pissed. The best case, he would just be in shock. Either way, things were going to be awkward. The closer I got to his floor, the more my stomach churned.

As soon as I stepped off the elevator, I spotted Maverick in the doorway. Whatever courage I had disappeared. He was dressed casually in a pair of gray sweatpants and a black hoodie. He was talking on the phone, and the sound of his voice alone sent shivers down my spine.

He was about to lock his door but looked up. His eyes met mine in surprise.

"JP, I'll call you back." He hung up and slid his phone into the front pocket of his sweatpants.

He crossed his arms and hiked an eyebrow up. "Ivy?" He stepped forward in shock. A small smile played on his lips as he got closer. "What are you doing here?"

I shuffled on my feet as his eyes raked me over. My blond

hair was in a messy ponytail, and my red sweater had a small stain on the front from the smoothie I had grabbed at the drive-thru this morning. I looked nothing like I did the night we spent together. There wasn't a stitch of makeup on my face, and I regretted not putting any extra effort into my appearance this morning. "Can I come in?"

A crease formed between his eyebrows. "How did you know where I lived?"

"Your parents told me?"

"Are you fucking kidding me? How the fuck did you find my parents?" His eyes flashed down the hall as if he were expecting a camera crew to pop out of the woodwork. He looked seconds away from tossing me back in the elevator.

"I promise, I can explain."

My heart beat like a drum in my chest as he stalked forward and towered over me. He looked every bit the tall and intimidating football player he was.

"You bet your ass you will, Ivy." He slammed his hands on his hips and clenched his jaw.

"First, my name isn't Ivy?" He flicked his hands in the air like he couldn't care less and signaled for me to make my point. Instead, I stood there for a moment, unable to speak because it was hard to think with him standing so close to me. Finally, I swallowed and forced myself to get this part over with. "My name is Kinley."

He stared at me and tilted his head to the side. Then, slowly, very slowly, I saw the recognition sink in.

His mouth opened and closed, and his eyes seemed to double in size. "Kinley Roberts?"

"Yes." I stuffed my hands into my coat pockets. "Can I come in? We need to talk."

"Uh, yeah. I guess." He staggered back a little. "Kinley fucking Roberts. I'll be goddamned," he mumbled, holding his hand out for me to make my way through the doorway.

I walked into the living room that stretched to a wall of

windows leading to an outdoor terrace. Taking a quick glance around, everything appeared sleek and modern. It was a hell of a lot more impressive than what I lived in—just another subtle reminder of how dissimilar our lives had become.

He ran a hand over his stubbled jaw and drew a long breath. "Why didn't you say anything to me when we first met?"

"You didn't recognize me and I was too embarrassed to bring it up."

"Yeah, well. You look different. You know, a lot more grown up." He ran his hand through his hair and down the back of his neck.

"I'm going to look even more different in about eight months."

He stilled.

"I'm pregnant."

CHAPTER 8

MAVERICK

My memories of her were nothing like reality. From the moment I laid eyes on her, I knew there was something familiar, but I couldn't put my finger on it. Now I knew why she felt different.

Holy Fuck! I slept with Kinley Roberts! And now she's... my gaze dropped down to her stomach. It was still flat.

"You're pregnant?" My brain felt like it was short-circuiting as the implications of her words spun in my head like an out-of-control rocket that was about ready to crash. Her eyes closed, and I said the stupidest thing a man could possibly say. "And you think I'm the father?"

My mind went back to that night, trying to remember every detail. This couldn't be right. There was no way. It just wasn't possible.

She crossed her arms over her chest. "Are you serious? Or are you just trying to piss me off right now?"

It was a dick thing to say, and I deserved her attitude. Probably deserved worse. But I didn't have a clue about how to handle this situation. I was in utter shock with a million damn questions that needed answers.

"Well, excuse me. It was one night. Do know how many

women have made this kind of accusation to men like me? It happens more than you think, so you'll have to forgive me for thinking you're any different."

I wasn't trying to be a jackass, but it seemed like everyone today had an ulterior motive. Women were all about cash and drama. They either wanted my dick or my money. I closed my eyes and shook my head. I had to remind myself that she wasn't some cleat chaser I met at a club. She was Kinley. My little sister's best friend. Someone I've known most of my life.

When I opened my eyes, hers were narrowed on me, and holy hell, was she scary when she was pissed.

"Do you have any idea how insulting you are? Clearly, all the fame has gone to your big, fat, inflated head. So, let's get something straight, Mr. I'm a Fucking Big Shot, who thinks he has the right to act like a shithead." She stabbed a finger in my direction. "If I was here trying to shake you down for a few bucks, then I'd give you a price here and now. Instead, I came here because it was the right thing to do and you deserved to know." Her voice started to shake with emotion. "That's my ulterior motive, so you can take all that other bull-shit you were spewing and shove it."

"Damn it," I shouted out. "How could I be so damn stupid to sleep with you?" As soon as I said it, I realized my mistake and felt like the world's biggest asshole because that was not how I meant it.

Her mouth hung open as she tried to blink the tears away. "I don't know what I was thinking." The devastation on her face dimmed something inside me. "But I shouldn't have come here."

Her boot-clad feet smacked against the cold tile of my penthouse. Christ, I couldn't seem to say anything right. I stepped in front of her. She seemed so small at that moment. Nothing like the spitfire I had the pleasure of spending the night with and certainly nothing like the girl I remembered from my youth.

"I didn't mean it like that, I swear. I'm just shocked, that's all." I tried to explain, but hurt, angry eyes stared up at me. "I owe you an apology. I'm sorry."

"You don't owe me anything." She turned up her cute little button nose in attitude. It turned me on in ways it shouldn't have. "I don't expect anything from you. If you want to forget that night ever happened, that's your choice. If you want nothing to do with me or this baby then I'll accept that too. But I plan on raising this child, with or without you."

"Is that so?" I said, trying to move on from her little speech. Forget the night ever happened? Yeah, right.

"Yes." The word fell from her mouth so easily. "I never want my child to feel like a mistake or unwanted."

"*Your* child?" My chocolate eyes met her blues. I pointed to her flat stomach. "I believe I had something to do with that. Wait…" I don't know what made me think of it, maybe because I was still trying to wrap my head around everything. "How the hell did this even happen? I wore a condom."

Her eyes flashed to mine in anger. "Not at first you didn't."

My mouth opened and closed. "I was wrapped up when I needed to be." How dare she imply that I didn't know how to roll that shit on. I've had plenty of practice. Never, ever, have I forgotten before that night. It was a tiny slip-up on my part, which I immediately corrected.

"You obviously didn't do a very good job." She sighed. "Look, we all know that condoms aren't one hundred percent effective. I didn't plan this, and I'm not trying to trap you." She swallowed, looking pissed. I couldn't blame her, but then again, I was caught off guard. What did she expect?

She flattened her mouth, causing my eyes to narrow on that beauty mark above her top lip. That should have given it away. Kinley looked different but still somehow the same. I should have known it was her.

I lifted my gaze to her blue eyes; they were so bright they practically glowed. They held a look of sincerity as opposed to the dollar signs I was used to seeing. Gone was the nerdy little bookworm who wore sweatshirts and turtlenecks. Little Kinley Roberts turned into a real looker. She wasn't the kind of stunner that stopped traffic and preyed on celebrities looking for their next meal ticket. She was cute in a girl-next-door sort of way. The kind that you took home to your parents. The type you settled down with—the exact opposite of what I'd been chasing since high school.

There wasn't a fake thing on her body. Everything was soft and smooth, perfect for my roaming hands. And I remembered vividly how she felt under my palms. Maybe it was crazy, reckless, or a little bit of both, but I didn't want her to just disappear. Now that I knew who she was, it changed everything.

But her life was in New York now. Mine was still in Atlanta. Georgia had always been my home. I couldn't imagine living anywhere else, especially in New York. I liked driving my truck down country back roads, where the only thing I needed to worry about hitting was a possum instead of a person crossing a crowded intersection. I liked the feeling of the hot sun beating down on my back during my morning run, as opposed to jogging on noisy sidewalks. Panic started to take hold and tighten inside my chest.

She rubbed at her arms, completely unaware of the chaos running through my head. "Look, Maverick. I don't know what to expect from you, so I'm giving you an out. I know this is coming out of left field, but you have a choice and I'll accept whatever you decide. Regardless of your decision, I wanted you to know that I'm keeping this baby."

I wasn't sure what pissed me off more. The fact that she assumed I wouldn't want anything to do with my kid or that she was using a baseball metaphor to make her point.

I crossed my arms and tightened my lips in displeasure,

letting her know what I thought about her little theory. "So, you think I want to forget that my baby exists? Walk away from my responsibilities?"

She held up her hands in the air. "I don't know what to think, okay?"

"I'd also like to point out that you're in no position to be upset with me. You haven't exactly been truthful."

"I never lied to you," she said, keeping her eyes straight on me.

"No?" I raised a brow. "*Ivy*?"

Her eyes slid shut. "I'm sorry, okay? You had no idea who I was, and I didn't know how to tell you."

"But you knew who I was though, didn't you?" She hung her head in confirmation.

"Kinley, I haven't seen you since my sister's graduation party. You were practically a kid back then."

She didn't like that answer for some reason. "Of course, you would say that. You always thought of me as a kid. You never saw me for who I was. I grew tits and an ass, all the boys at school noticed but you. I was always your little sister's pesky friend."

"I was three years older than you. You were fucking jailbait back then." Sighing in frustration, I ran my fingers through my hair. I was messing everything up. "Obviously, emotions are running high right now. Give me some time to let this news sink in."

I was there. I participated. I knew this could potentially happen. I've seen it happen. I've heard of it happening. It's never happened to me. So now I needed time to figure a few things out.

"That's fair enough. I can give you my cell number. I'm staying with my mom until after New Year's."

I blew out a relieved breath. "Good." That gave us a little bit of breathing room to figure things out before she flew back home. "Are you free for breakfast tomorrow morning?"

She wrung her hands in front of her. "Sure. Let me know where and when and I'll be there."

I handed her my phone so that she could program her number. "I'm sorry about the way I acted a few minutes ago. I'm just as responsible for this as you are. My parents raised me better than that."

She nodded her head in understanding.

I walked her to the door and held it open. She gave me a quizzical look and paused like she wanted to say something. Instead, she gave me a tight smile and left.

CHAPTER 9

MAVERICK

"Mav, I'm in the middle of something. Can I call you back?"

"It's important." I inhaled sharply, dreading this conversation.

"How important? I don't have time for chitchat. I have a meeting with a Nike executive in ten minutes, and I still have to run a few numbers before the call."

"I need to talk, and it's urgent." My stomach tightened because he was going to be pissed and give me shit.

Julian Steinberg recruited me right out of college. There was a reason why he was one of the highest-paid and most sought-after sports agents in the industry. He not only negotiated the best contracts, but he made sure his athletes toed the line. He wasn't a fan of scandals because they cost him time and money to clean up. And money is what he lived for.

"This doesn't sound good. Please don't tell me you went and knocked some random girl up."

I choked on my damn Gatorade. "Um…" I pulled the phone away from my ear and looked around, expecting him to be standing there.

"Who is it?" His tone was all business mode now, and I

could hear the keys clicking on his laptop and the chair scraping across the floor.

"Someone I hooked up with last month." He didn't need to know Kinley's name or our history. Or my lack of fucking memory.

He sighed. "How do you want to spin this? I can make it go away, just tell me how much you want to spend?"

"Whoa, slow down there, Julian." His offer wasn't uncommon, considering what he did for a living. His job was to fix my mistakes and look out for my best interests. But Kinley didn't feel like a mistake, just unexpected. "I'm not looking to pay her off," I stated firmly. "I'm just giving you a heads-up."

"Fine. Give me a name. We need to run a background check on her."

"Not necessary," I said, stalking across the room. I wasn't sure why I was so upset about this conversation. All I knew was it felt wrong.

"Do you still have a concussion along with your injury? Of course, it's necessary. The last thing you need is some gold digger looking to link herself to a baller."

My jaw clenched, and my hand balled into fists. "She's not a fucking jock juggler. She is the mother of my child, so show her some respect."

The line went silent. "Am I missing something here? Was it not a random hookup?"

"Yes, and no." I ran a frustrated hand through my hair. "We kind of grew up together. She was best friends with my sister when we were younger."

"Why didn't you lead with that?"

My eyes slid shut. "Because I didn't know it was her until she showed up at my door and told me she was pregnant."

"Wait." He laughed. "You fucked your sister's best friend and didn't know it was her? Man, I need to get you re-enrolled in concussion protocols."

"Watch it. Not fucking funny," I warned. This intense

feeling of protectiveness for her surprised even me. I didn't understand it myself, but the feeling was there.

"So, what now? How do you want me to proceed? Do you want me to have legal documents drawn up? Which reminds me, you're going to need to get a paternity test."

I could hear him typing away on his computer. I understood where he was coming from. It was standard procedure in this business. But Kinley wasn't a part of our world. She was different, and I was going to treat her differently. My family would kick my ass if I didn't give her the respect she deserved.

"That's not necessary."

"Mav, this will eventually get out in the media. You're a big fucking deal in the eyes of a lot of people. You have a reputation to uphold. You've done a good job steering clear of scandals. Don't go getting sloppy now. Trust me, the last thing you want to do is piss off our sponsors."

I opened my mouth to speak, but nothing came out. I needed a damn drink. "Right now, the only person pissing someone off is you."

"Look, I'm doing my fucking job," he barked into the phone like he was losing patience with me.

I raked a hand through my hair. It felt like my entire world was unraveling right before my eyes. "I appreciate you looking out for my best interest, and if you feel the need to run a background check, I'm not going to stop you." The feeling of guilt edged its way through my stomach. "As for a paternity test, I'll decide if I need to get one."

"Fine. It's a start." I let out a sigh of relief as he pressed on. "You need to think about how you want to address this with the media. I can have Sylvia draft up a statement."

"Give me a little a time and I'll come up with something."

"Don't take too much time. We need to get ahead of this news before it turns into a scandal. This story is tabloid gold and could spin into a public relations nightmare if you don't handle it right. Don't forget, you're in the middle of contract negotiations for next season and you have a very strong morals clause that ownership could use as a bargaining chip in our negotiations. You have the potential of being the highest paid franchise quarterback in the league next year."

He had a solid point. My injury had given my backup quarterback a platform to show off his football talents. I was drafted to the Atlanta Arrows during my senior year of college. It didn't matter how many rings I'd earned or how many trophies I had on my shelf. Everyone in this business was replaceable.

———

"I hope I didn't screw up your breakfast plans?" I asked, taking a sip of my coffee. Kinley and I were seated in the back of the restaurant. It was a little after ten a.m., just between the breakfast and lunch crowd. I was facing the wall, hoping to stay out of view from the customers coming and going.

"Not at all. I was a little tired from traveling, so I enjoyed the extra sleep."

Kinley looked cute with her blond hair pulled back in a ponytail; she was the definition of girl-next-door. It was a look I was becoming fond of and a reminder of who she was. After she left my condo last night, I replayed our conversation a million times in my head. I had no idea she had a crush on me growing up. Back then, the only things on my mind were scoring the ladies and throwing for touchdowns. Being three years younger than me, and being friends with my younger sister, had kept her completely off my radar.

"Have you talked to Rylee lately?" I asked, starting with small talk, something I hated.

I watched her sweep her spoon through her oatmeal. Who the hell ordered fruit and oatmeal at a diner? "Not recently." She looked guilty. "She doesn't know I'm in town yet, although after showing up at your parents' house yesterday, I'm sure she'll find out soon enough. Which reminds me." She pulled something out of her purse and slid it across the table. I looked down and saw the keycard I had given to my parents to access the building. I guess that explained how she was able to show up unannounced. "I need to make sure that gets back to your parents."

I set my fork down on my empty plate and accepted a refill from the girl walking by filling up everyone's cup. "Were you not planning on seeing my sister while you're in town?" I asked, stuffing the card inside my wallet.

Rylee and Kinley were tight growing up, but I had no idea how often they still talked. Or if they kept in touch at all.

"I wanted to talk to you first and go from there."

"I appreciate that." I sat back in the booth and studied my baby mama. She drummed her fingers along her cup and seemed to shift nervously in her seat every thirty seconds. The irony of knowing almost nothing about the woman I've known for nearly half my life was not lost on me.

"This is pretty weird, isn't it?" she said as if she could read my thoughts.

"That's an understatement." I chuckled and took a sip of my water. "Maybe we should get the heavy stuff out of the way first."

Her eyelashes fluttered over the rim of her decaf coffee. "Sure."

"Is there anyone in your life that I need to know about?"

Leading with that question wasn't my intention, but I couldn't deny I was curious about her answer.

"Do you think I would have spent the night with you if there was?"

I held my hands up. "Just making sure there isn't anyone else in the equation."

"No one. How about you?" Her concerned eyes met mine. It was hard to get a read on why she would be worried. Was it because she cared or was she just nervous about how it would affect the baby?

I shook my head, wishing I had any insight into her thoughts. "Nope."

She folded her hands under her chin. "Why not?"

"Football takes up too much of my time. The games, travel, and commitments can be tough on a relationship. Not that I've done a lot of dating." I took a guzzle of my water. "And once you reach a certain level of fame, it gets harder to tell who's genuine. It's one of the downsides to being in the public eye."

"I hate fake people." Her cheeks heated like she was upset on my behalf. "I can only imagine how tough it is to live a normal life when you're so well-known."

She had no idea how much I hated all the fakeness. My status and money were all most people cared about. It wasn't just that, though; I was constantly being scrutinized and talked about by the media and fans. Having a personal life was too much work.

I sat up straighter in my seat and adjusted the baseball cap on my head when a few younger guys walked in. Out of the corner of my eye, I'd seen them snap a few pictures when they thought I wasn't looking. Thankfully, they kept their distance.

"It is tough. That's why I keep my private life out of the headlines. I only allow people to see what I want them to see."

She trailed her fingernail along the edge of the checkered tablecloth. "Speaking of that," doubt and something else flickered across her features, "is it okay if we keep this between us for now? I don't mind our families and close friends knowing I'm just not ready to be thrust into the spotlight yet."

"I understand." I picked up the steaming hot cup of coffee in front of me. It tasted bitter. The life I lived wasn't for everyone, so I wanted her to be as comfortable as possible before she got dragged into the daily media circus.

"Thank you." She swallowed. "There are a lot of moving parts to this and I'd like to work through them in private for as long as possible."

Having the press catch on would add a lot of stress, so I got where she came from. It was another way she was different from the girls who went out of their way to attract attention.

"Take whatever time you need. But I agree, we need to tell our families soon. I don't know how long you are in town for or when you'll be back, but I would like to tell them together. We can't keep this a secret for too long and I'd rather them find out from us."

"Okay, the only person I've told is my friend Taylor." She looked remorseful. "I hope you're not upset. I needed to unload on someone when I first found out."

"Relax, I get it."

"Good." She sighed in relief. "The only other person I plan on telling is Chad."

My brows furrowed. "Who the fuck is Chad?"

"He's one of my closest friends." She blinked at my harsh tone. "He also lives across the hall in my building."

I braced my forearms on the table, noticing she used the word *close* to describe this Chad schmuck. "Does Chad have a girlfriend?" I gritted out, surprised by the sudden level of agitation I felt for a guy I had never met. "Is he married?"

"No, but why would that matter?"

A scowl took over my face. "Because you're pregnant with my baby," I told her as if that was all the explanation needed.

Apparently, I was wrong.

"And?" She folded her arms across her chest. My little spitfire was coming out. I adjusted myself in my jeans.

"And I don't share things that are mine."

"Well, this child is also mine and Chad is someone important to me. He's my friend."

I wanted to tell her I wasn't just talking about the baby being mine. But I had a feeling if I did, I'd end up with a plate of food in my lap. I didn't want her dating anyone while she was carrying my kid. Things were complicated enough. Could I ask that of her? No, I couldn't. Patience, I reminded myself.

"Okay. Friend. Got it," I said, moving my gaze over toward the window. "How have you been feeling?" I asked, deciding to switch gears.

"Not bad, just tired, although it's still early yet."

I found myself playing with the condiments on the table. I knew nothing about babies and wish I had paid better attention when my teammates talked about their pregnant spouses.

"Have you had any weird cravings yet?" Didn't women get those when they were expecting?

She laughed lightly, and the sound pulled a smile from my lips. She had a beautiful laugh. "I've been craving blueberries. Like blueberry everything." She motioned to the blueberries in her oatmeal. "Blueberry pie, blueberry scones, blueberry muffins, blueberry bread, blueberry smoothies, blueberry bagels, blueberry coffee…"

"Stop right there." I held my hand up and wrinkled my nose. "Blueberry coffee? Who the hell would create a blueberry flavored coffee?"

"Probably the same people who created blueberry flavored beer." She laughed at my expression.

That sounded like a lot of blueberries. Hopefully, our kid wouldn't turn out blue.

"That's a weird craving, but I guess it could be worse."

She blew a chunk of hair out of her eye. "Tell me about it. I've been told that the cravings could change, so who knows what it will be next week."

"Excuse me," one of the teenage boys said as he reached our table. "You're Maverick Cross, right?"

I pulled on the brim of my ball cap even though hiding was useless at this point. "I am. What can I do for you, kid?"

"Holy fuck!" He looked back at his friends. "I can't believe it's you."

I plastered on the fake smile I reserved for my fans. "It's me, but as you can see, I'm having breakfast with a friend. Do you have something you'd like me to sign?"

His mouth dropped open. "I don't, but can I get a picture?"

My eyes moved over to Kinley, who was watching this exchange. His friends were standing off to the side, already drawing attention to my table. Great! It was just my luck that this would happen right out of the gate—our very first meeting.

My fists clenched at my sides because I couldn't turn this kid away without looking like an asshole. Disappointment, frustration, and a whole other mix of emotions settled in my gut.

I cleared my throat and stood up. Kinley was already skittish about my life, and this little exchange wouldn't help my case. It would also be the end of our breakfast because once this kid got his picture, it would be fifteen seconds before word hit the street and fans came streaming into the diner.

I needed to find out how I would balance my two worlds. Now that I was going to be a father, my privacy would be my number one priority.

I tossed a hundred-dollar bill and gently reached for Kinley's hand. "Time for us to get out of here."

CHAPTER 10
KINLEY

"Look at you." My mom held her arms out for me to walk into them. "I can't tell you how happy I am to have you home for Christmas." She squeezed me tight, and a wave of emotions hit me in the chest.

I felt guilty for staying at a hotel last night, but I knew I would need some time alone after talking with Maverick. Now, after all the craziness of the past twenty-four hours had passed, the only thing I wanted was the comfort and familiarity of my mother's arms.

"You look good, Mom." I stepped back and noticed her blond hair was a little darker since the last time I saw her.

She patted the side of her head. "I just got it colored last week."

My grandmother came limping around the corner. I could practically hear her grumbling under her breath. "I tried to tell her that her hair is going to fall out by the time she's sixty."

My mom rolled her eyes. "She's been saying that since I was fourteen."

"It's all that Aqua Net you used back in the eighties," my grandmother quipped while leaning against the wall.

I was too tired to deal with these two. I slept like crap last night, and the pregnancy hormones were starting to kick in. The only thing that could perk me up was coffee, and seeing that caffeine was no longer an option, I just wanted a nap.

My mom put her hand on her hip and glared. "Be careful, you old bird, or I'll make sure to reserve you a room at Serenity Shores."

My grandmother always had a retort on the tip of her tongue, and my mom always threatened to put her in a nursing home. I'm not sure how they've survived living together all these years without killing each other. It always felt good to come home for a visit, but something told me I'd be ready to return by the week's end.

"You can always come live with me in Manhattan, Grandma." I pulled her in for a light squeeze. Grandma Deanne wasn't big on affection. She hated hugs and all the mushy stuff, but it'd been so long since I'd seen her that I couldn't resist. She had her hip replaced last year, another sign that she was slowing down. That was another reason why this visit was so important to me. She wasn't getting any younger, and I knew I would regret it if something happened to her and I didn't take the time to see her.

"Hmm…" Her eyebrows folded together as she adjusted her floral housecoat. "You look different."

Most people were born with five senses. My eighty-year-old grandmother, however, was born with a sixth. I shifted uncomfortably and forced a smile. "What do you mean?"

She pushed her glasses to the bridge of her nose and leaned her face forward. "You're glowing."

Oh, God. Please no. The longer I stood there, rocking on my heels, the longer she stared. I squirmed and dropped my eyes to my mom's tiled floor. I folded my hands in front of my stomach, which ended up drawing more attention to it.

She inched closer, and I stepped back, bumping into the wall. Her gaze traveled to my stomach; her thin lips curled in a smirk. "Well, I'll be damned. You got a bun in the oven. Who is the lucky fella that knocked you up?"

All the color drained from my mom's face. "Kinley, do you have something you want to tell me?"

My eyes closed, and my shoulders sagged. There was no point in denying it. The truth would only come out in eight months. "I'm pregnant."

"What?" my mom shrieked. "You're not even dating anyone. How did this happen?"

Despite the miles between us, my mom and I were extremely close. She's been supportive of me and every decision I've ever made. So the thought of disappointing her had an unfamiliar emotion forming in the base of my throat.

"Do you remember Rylee's older brother, Maverick?"

"Of course, I do. You had a huge crush on him," she said, wiping the tears from under her eyes.

"It's a long story, but we ran into each other the night my flight was canceled."

"And?" She held my gaze. Disbelief mixed with confusion and maybe a little excitement was written all over her face.

I wrung my hands in front of me. "And I'm pregnant with his baby."

"Oh, my." She brought me back in for a hug. "I have so many questions," she said, pulling back and squeezing my arm.

I unbuttoned my jacket so I could hang it up on the hook. "I will do my best to answer them."

She pulled on my hand and led me to the family room. My grandmother followed closely behind us. She picked up the pitcher of sweet tea, poured me a glass, and placed it in my hand.

"Thanks," I said, staring at the familiar-looking Christmas tree in the bay window. It was decorated with green and red bulbs, and the angel I made in pre-school sat at the top. If I squinted hard enough, I'd see a few handmade ornaments I made when I was younger. Everything felt nostalgic—even the dozen presents already wrapped under the tree with handmade bows.

So many memories from my childhood came rushing back to me. Would my child have the same traditions I had growing up? Would my mom go overboard every year with gifts? Or would they spend the holidays with the Cross family? I couldn't imagine not waking up with my child and missing out on those magical moments. Especially since you only got to experience them for a few short years.

We still had so much to figure out.

My mom sunk into the spot next to me. "Does he know?" she asked softly.

I leaned my head back and nodded. "He does, and he wants to be involved." My lips quirked up in a smile at how easy it was hanging out with him. Much easier than I ever dreamed it would be. There was also a glance here and there that I noticed, and a few comments I picked up on that hinted at maybe more. But it was too early to determine what more meant for us.

"I think that's great." She patted my leg. "I have no doubt that with or without his help, you'll do just fine. You know I'll support you in any way I can." She paused, and I could hear the wheels spinning in her head. "You could always move back home, you know," she said with a hopeful look in her eyes.

"One thing at a time, Mom." I smiled, trying to get her to hold off on that conversation. I knew it would be brought up and that she would do everything in her power to convince me to quit my job and start looking at houses nearby. I just didn't expect it to be today.

I looked to my grandmother to see if she had anything to add. Frankly, I was surprised she'd stayed quiet for so long. "Well?" I asked, twirling my hand in a circle, giving her the go-ahead to get whatever she had to say off her chest.

She pressed her lips together and scratched the side of her head. "Raisin' kids ain't cheap these days. Make sure he pays his fair share."

I don't even know why I bothered asking. "I'm not worried about that."

My mom cleared her throat and threw my grandmother a death glare. "Let me help you get settled."

I grabbed my suitcase by the door and rolled it down the hall. My mom flipped the light switch, and I glanced across the room. The last time I stepped foot in this house was five years ago, and it was exactly as I remembered it—tan walls with long red curtains and a bedspread to match. Besides the dark cherry furniture, there wasn't much else in the room besides a few boxes in the corner with scrapbooks and photos.

"Do you mind if I lie down for a bit? I'm feeling wiped out." I sat on the edge of the bed and shifted my weight when I heard a little squeak. I forgot how uncomfortable this mattress was.

"Of course not. Take all the time you need. If you need help putting your things away, let me know."

"Thanks, Mom." Just as she was about to shut the door, I called out, "Would you want to do a little shopping later? I need to pick up a few gifts."

"I'd love to." She smiled. "Get some rest, sweetheart."

Once I was all alone, I plugged my phone into the charger and clicked on the last text exchange between Maverick and me. I promised to text him when I was all settled in.

Me: *Thanks for breakfast today. I'm glad we talked.*

I knew he had a physical therapy appointment and a team meeting this afternoon. That's why I was surprised when he texted right back.

Maverick: *Me too. What are your plans later?*

I read his message several times, trying to figure out why he was asking. Did he want to see me again? Today?

Me: *Taking a nap now and shopping with my mom later. What about you?*

Maverick: *My schedule is wide open. Get some rest, and I'll check in with you in a few hours. I want to see you again, but I don't want to monopolize all your time. Have fun shopping with your mom.*

A smile stretched across my face.

Me: *I'd like to see you again too. I'll text you when we're done shopping.*

Maverick: *Thank you. You and the baby should get some rest.*

I snuggled into the blankets and rested my head against the pillow, knowing I would be dreaming about a bearded, super-hot football player with deep brown eyes and full lips. Very full kissable lips that I wanted to kiss again.

CHAPTER 11
KINLEY

Usually, holiday shopping was something I dreaded, especially so close to Christmas, but I found myself laughing and smiling more than I have in years. My mom and I spent the afternoon browsing in all the retail stores while mixing in with the crowd of shoppers looking for last-minute gifts.

We grew tired of the long lines as the day drew on, and seeing that we didn't have anything left to buy, we left the hassle behind and slipped into a little salon for pedicures. She listened patiently as I filled her in on my job, even though she probably thought it was boring, and she brought me up-to-date on all the latest gossip with her bible study group.

One of the things I didn't miss about small-town living was everyone knew your business.

"Mom, you have to promise me that you won't say a word about the baby until I give you the go-ahead?" I reminded her for the tenth time today.

She balanced the shopping bags in her hand while looping her free arm with mine. "I already gave you my word, didn't I."

"You did. Although, you might want to hide all those packages you bought for the baby. I'm not sure how you're going to explain having all those infant clothes and a baby monitor laying around the next time Betsy and the girls come over for paint night."

My mom was a closet artist who only painted as a hobby, even though she had natural-born talent. But every first Wednesday of the month, she hosted a wine and paint night with all her friends.

"God." She got a dreamy look in her eyes. "I can't believe I'm going to be a grandmother." She stopped and paused for a minute. "You do realize this child will be spoiled rotten, right?"

I eyed the multiple shopping bags hanging from her fingers. "I can see that."

She resumed walking toward the parking lot. "I just wish you didn't have to go back next week. I need more time with you."

This trip was already going by too fast, and the thought of leaving caused a heavy sadness to settle in my chest. "The feeling is mutual."

"I hope you don't mind, but I have to pick up Spencer from work. His car is still at the dealership getting repaired." She looked at her watch and started walking ahead of me. "If you want to sit on the bench, I'll go get the car."

The parking lot was packed when we arrived, so we were forced to park far away. As bad as I wanted to sit and rest, I was afraid if I did, I would end up falling asleep. The catnap I took early in the day wasn't nearly enough.

"That's okay, I'll walk with you." After all, New Yorkers were used to walking, but even I had to admit this little bean growing in my stomach was sucking all the energy out of me.

We were each balancing shopping bags in our hands when my cell dinged with a message. I slid it out of my pocket and grinned.

Maverick: *How's the retail therapy going?*

Me: *The long lines and frustrated shoppers are stressing me out. I'm ready to call it a day and buy the rest of my gifts online.*

Maverick: *That's what you get for waiting until the last minute.*

Me: *I'll let you know that most last-minute shoppers are MEN!*

Maverick: *Notice I'm not one of them< inserts sticking tongue out emoji>*

Me: *Pfft…you probably have an assistant who does all your shopping. < inserts middle finger emoji>*

Maverick: *You sound angry.*

Me: *I'm hangry< inserts mad face and a bunch of random food emojis>*

Maverick: *Good. I just finished up with my meetings. Want to grab a bite to eat?*

Me: *You want to share another meal with me? Two meals in a row?*

Maverick: *Well, you are carrying my kid. I want to make sure he's well-nourished.*

I bit down on my bottom lip, smiled, and was about to respond when another text came through.

Maverick: *Seriously, we just finished up, and I'm looking for something to do. If you already have dinner plans tonight, I understand. Enjoy your time with your mom.*

Me: *She has to pick my stepfather up from work. His car is in the shop. If you want to meet me, we can grab something nearby.*

Maverick: *Text me where you are. I'm on my way.*

———

"Hi." I walked over to Maverick's truck as he rolled down the window.

He leaned across the seat, keeping one hand on the steering wheel. "Hop in."

"I'm afraid I'm not much of a hopper these days." I

stuffed my bags in the back and buckled my seat belt. "But thanks for picking me up. I'm starving."

He pulled away from the curb and headed toward downtown Athens. "You were just giving me shit a little while ago about always wanting to feed you."

"I did no such thing. I was simply pointing out that this is two out of three meals in the same day that we will have eaten together. I just don't want you to get too clingy," I teased.

"So, you don't want me to get too attached. Got it." He winked.

I smacked his knee playfully. "Eyes on the road, mister." I shifted in my seat and crossed my legs. He'd been staring at me a little too long, and it was giving me these fuzzy little feelings.

"You're awfully bossy today." He glanced in the rearview mirror.

"I hate shopping."

"Really," he mocked. "I couldn't tell." He clicked his blinker and shifted lanes. "If you don't enjoy it, then why bother? Just buy gift cards."

"My mom enjoys it and I was looking for something we could do together. Oh, look what she bought." I reached behind my seat to grab the bag from the back. I placed it on my lap and pushed the tissue paper aside. I pulled out the milestone mat and held it up.

"What is that?" he asked, glancing out of the corner of his eye.

"It's for the baby's first year. You lay them on the blanket next to whatever month they are so you can see how much they grow throughout the year."

He glanced over briefly and swallowed. "That's cool. What else did you get?"

"Just a few outfits and a couple maternity shirts."

His eyes swept over me, and I was suddenly very self-conscious. "You don't look like you need those yet?"

"I will eventually," I said, crossing my legs. I was hyper-aware of how physically close we were to each other. Every single one of my senses was going into overdrive.

We eased down Clayton Street and found an open parking spot. The sidewalks were filled with young families sipping hot chocolate and admiring the window displays. The road was blocked off and scattered with elves handing out candy canes, and children were lined up for pictures with Santa. Maverick secured the hat on his head and perched his sunglasses on his nose. He was dressed in a pair of dark wash jeans and a gray Nike hoodie. Even dressed down, my baby daddy looked hot.

We spotted a food truck at the end of the block, ordered a few tacos, and snagged a small bistro table underneath a white tent. Maverick took a seat facing the back so that no one would see him, and I took the spot closest to the outdoor heater because, even if the sun was out, the air was still crisp.

"So, what's it like living in Manhattan?" he asked, taking a bite of the taco.

I kept my gaze carefully focused on the plate in front of me. "Not as glamourous as it was in the beginning."

"That's pretty vague," he said between bites of his food.

I lifted my shoulder. "I work a lot and don't get out as much as I should."

His eyes studied my face to see if I was serious. "Sounds boring."

I laughed. "When I first moved there, I saw it all and did it all. After a while, the excitement wore off."

"What do you do on the weekends for fun?"

I shifted my eyes to the display of holiday decorations and thought about that for a minute. "Nothing too exciting. I like to go to the outdoor markets in the city when it's nice out. Chad and I will buy some fresh vegetables and browse the tents. Sometimes I'll pick up a few handmade soaps and scented candles."

"Chad, huh?" His jaw ticked at the mention of my friend's name.

I pointed a finger at him. "Don't start. We're having a nice afternoon and I'd like to keep it that way."

"Fair enough." He held his hands up in mock surrender. "I'm not a farmer's market guy, but I've always wanted to check out the Christmas Village at Bryant Park."

"That can definitely be arranged. Don't get me wrong, it's nice being back here and I am enjoying the warmer weather, but there is no place on the planet that's as magical as New York City during the holidays."

"Maybe you can show me around next time I'm in town. We can play tourist for the day." He flashed me that boyish grin that didn't have a trace of innocence to it. "Maybe catch a show on Broadway."

I tilted my head to the side. "Are you a fan of Broadway?"

"Fuck no." He snorted. "The only show I half enjoyed was *Spiderman*, and even then I ended up falling asleep before intermission. My buddy JP is a huge Marvel fan. We were literally in town for two days, but if you ask me, it was two hours of my life I'll never get back."

I chuckled because I could totally picture it. "Then why did you suggest it?"

"Because I thought it would be something you would enjoy doing," he said without missing a beat. "Spending the day with you sounds a hell of a lot better than watching drills from the sidelines or shooting the shit with the guys in the locker room."

"Wow, you really know how to make a girl feel special."

"You didn't let me finish." He winked. "I suggested it because there is no one else I'd rather spend time with. When I'm with you, I don't give a shit about my career and neither do you. I don't have to put on a mask and be who the fans expect me to be. I don't have to worry about your intentions. Around you, I can let loose and relax."

I was not expecting that.

"You really are a smooth talker," I said, trying not to read too much into that comment. I could handle confident and cocky Maverick, but sweet and charming was pushing it. Especially after the night we shared because it only made my feelings for him grow stronger.

Maverick leaned forward, braced his forearms on the table, and licked his lips. "Funny, because being with you makes me feel off my game."

I rolled my eyes at the ridiculousness of that comment. "Trust me, your game is just fine."

He tilted his head to the side. "Is that your subtle way of saying you're into me?"

"What if I am?" I wasn't usually this bold, but I was slowly testing the waters. I blamed it on the pregnancy hormones. Not to mention, the way he kept looking at me was messing with my head. The man could have any woman he wanted. Why on God's earth would he want me?

"Then I'd say we're off to a great start, because I wouldn't mind one damn bit if you were. In fact, it would make my year."

Both dimples poked out, and I pointed my finger to his cheek. "Don't go flashing those. I'm hormonal, so you can't hold it against me if I start making a fool of myself."

His grin only widened. "You probably shouldn't tell me that."

I was swooning hard. "Back to the topic at hand. We'll skip the theater and the museums next time you're in town."

"Thank you." He blew out a relieved breath.

I was worried that things would be awkward between us, but between breakfast this morning and the impromptu meal tonight, things felt nice.

"How did you end up in New York in the first place?" he asked before plopping a tortilla chip into his mouth.

"I picked New York because I wanted to live in a place where I could be free to be myself and not worry about who I was in the past. In a city of eight million people, no one knows your parents, cousins, or all the stupid stuff you did growing up. It felt like freedom. So, I applied to the Stern School of Business at NYU. I fell in love with the city immediately and decided that's where I wanted to stay."

"That's impressive." There was pride in his voice as he spoke. "Do you see yourself living there forever?"

It was pretty obvious where he was going with this. I couldn't blame him, even if I wanted to. We were going to be co-parents living in two different states. He had every right to ask and be concerned.

"Honestly, I'm not sure. It's a great place to live if you're young, but raising a family there is a whole different ballgame."

He swallowed nervously. "At some point we're going to have to talk logistics."

"I know."

Why did the mention of that feel like I was just smothered with a wet blanket? Logically, I knew I had a life to return to, but after spending a few hours with Maverick, I realized how easy it was to get swept away by him.

"Would you ever consider moving back to Georgia?"

The turn of this conversation had me squirming in my seat. "I would never say never, but it would have to be for the right reasons. How about you? Could you see yourself living in a big city, or do you see yourself happily living here forever?"

He leaned back and rested his hands behind his neck. "I'm not sure I'm cut out for the big city. Atlanta might be as urban as I'll get. I love the campfires and loud football games. Maybe because I'm always in the spotlight, it's nice to come home where my friends and family are. I don't need attention twenty-four seven. I hate being constantly surrounded by crowds and always smiling for the camera. It's nice to relax and chill after constantly being under the scrutiny of the public."

I always assumed he loved the spotlight, but maybe I was wrong. In fact, I got the impression I was wrong about a lot of things.

I found myself fiddling with the napkin on my lap. "I'm surprised no one has recognized you by now."

He pulled on the brim of his hat. "I'm grateful," he said, watching a mom push a stroller with a fussy toddler up to the table next to us. "My life comes with a lot of perks, but I can't do normal things without hiding as much of my face as I can and watching and listening to everything around me. It's one of the drawbacks. It would be nice to walk into a grocery store and pick up dinner or go for a walk in the park without worrying about being recognized. Someone always wants a picture or an autograph, and as much as I hate it, I don't feel like I have a right to complain."

"I'm sorry," I said, glancing over my shoulder. "I wasn't thinking when I asked you to stop here."

"Hey." He reached across the table and placed his hand on top of mine. "I'm having a great time. Even if someone spots me and people start pulling out their cameras, it will be totally worth it."

I ducked my head to hide my blush. I was in deep trouble with this man.

CHAPTER 12
MAVERICK

I pulled into Kinley's parents' driveway and killed the engine. "Don't move until I get you." I hopped out of my truck and jogged along the back to grab the packages out of the trunk.

I opened her door and extended my free hand so I could help her to her feet. "This isn't necessary." She grinned as I settled her onto the pavement.

"Yes, it is." I angled my body toward hers. "If I wasn't holding up the lane earlier, I would have helped you when I first picked you up. I was born and raised in the south. My mom would tan my hide if I didn't treat you right."

"You always were a mama's boy." She patted my shoulder with a look of amusement dancing across her face.

If there was a response on the tip of my tongue, I couldn't find it because, with each lingering second that passed, the urge to pull her closer began to build. This woman has been all I've thought about for the last five weeks. And now that I knew who she was, I didn't see that changing anytime soon. Last night was unexpected, today was nice, and now I wasn't sure how I was supposed to function when she left.

She must have seen something on my face because she angled her head to the side and asked, "Are you okay?"

"Yeah." I coughed into my hand. "I just drifted off there for a second."

"Well, thanks for picking me up and spending the day with me." A slight breeze picked up, and a hint of her perfume hit me. The fact that it was the same scent I recalled her wearing the night we spent together wasn't lost on me.

"I should be the one thanking you. You saved me from a day of boredom. I had such a good time with you that I think we should get together again tomorrow," I suggested, fighting the urge to reach out and touch her like I wanted to.

"I'm officially changing your name on my phone from Maverick to Smooth Talker." Her smile stretched wide across her face, and I found my own doing the same.

I glanced down at her, not realizing that I'd moved closer. "How about Baby Daddy?"

She laughed. "What am I going to do with you?"

I brought my knuckles up to her cheek and studied her face. "Is that a trick question? Because I can think of a whole list of things."

Her eyes were sparkling, and her rosy cheeks were turning a darker shade of pink. "I probably don't want to know what that list entails."

"Oh, I'm not sure about that. You might be surprised."

We both smiled from ear to ear.

Maybe it was the pregnancy glow, or perhaps it was simply attraction. Whatever it was, I couldn't stop staring at her.

"I meant what I said earlier." I rubbed my hand gently along her arm. "I want to spend as much time with you as possible while you're here."

"Can I ask you a question?" She ran her tongue along her bottom lip, and now I was picturing molding her mouth against mine.

What the hell was wrong with me tonight?

I dropped my hand and shoved it into my pocket before I went and did anything stupid. "You can ask me anything, Kinley."

"What are we doing here?"

I knew what she was asking, but I didn't know how to explain it. How did I tell her that she was under my skin and I hadn't been able to stop thinking about her, and she was making me feel things I didn't know were possible?

We might have grown up together, and she might have been my sister's friend, but right now, I was mentally trying to find a place for her in my life. We didn't even live in the same state, but in less than eight months, that wouldn't mean a damn thing. This baby would tie us together forever, and that thought didn't scare me like I expected it to.

"I want to get to know you, really know you," I explained, waiting and watching for her reaction. "Not just as the woman who's having my baby." I stopped, unsure how to finish the sentence. Jesus, she had me all tied up in knots.

She tilted her head to the side. "In what way do you want to get to know me?"

Guess she wasn't going to make this easy on me.

"Whatever way you'll let me. I think we owe it to ourselves and our child to explore these feelings."

Crossing that line with her might come back to bite me in the ass, but things were moving too fast for me to process it all. We didn't have time to play games. We weren't in a position to let things play out and see where they led. We only had a few fleeting moments, and I wanted to take advantage of every single one.

"I'd like that too, and hopefully we'll become better acquainted with each other than we did in the past."

Her tone was light, but her eyes showed a bit of hurt.

"We will." I grabbed her hand and wrapped my fingers

tightly around hers. "One of my biggest regrets is not paying better attention to you in the past."

That seemed to appease her. And I was quickly learning that making Kinley Roberts happy was my number one goal.

When I walked her to the door, we both hesitated once we got to the landing. I tried to think of an excuse to keep the conversation going because I wasn't ready to leave yet.

Reaching up, I brushed her hair off her shoulder. She wore it down today, and the long blond locks felt soft under my fingertips. "When can I see you again?"

She planted her hands along my shoulders and leaned up on her tiptoes. "I could probably fit you in tomorrow sometime between my naptime and dinnertime."

"And she has jokes." I laughed and hauled her into my chest so I could capture my mouth with hers. Every doubt and worry I had about coming on too strong melted away. The kiss was gentle and slow, yet it had the power to make me lose my mind. Everything about that night came rushing back to me: her taste, her scent, the little sounds she made that drove me insane.

I bent my head to deepen the kiss; my hands found her hair, and every part of my body craved her. And when she let out a faint whimper, I felt like a bomb ready to detonate. I dug my fingers into her scalp. Never in my life could I recall ever wanting to worship a mouth like this. I moved her back against the railing, not caring one bit that anyone driving by could see us.

A throat clearing caused me to tear my mouth away from hers too quickly. Kinley lost her balance, but I caught her before she fell.

"Well, well. What do we have here?"

I grabbed on to Kinley's shoulders, making sure she was steady on her feet. We both turned to the voice that belonged to a little old lady leaning against the door wearing a floral muumuu. Her hands were in the pockets, and the corners of her mouth were uplifted into an amused smile.

I dropped my hand and rubbed the back of my neck, feeling like I'd been caught doing something I shouldn't have.

"Grandma." Kinley closed her eyes and drew in a deep breath. "I thought you were going out to eat with your friends from the Red Hat Society."

She folded her arms across her chest. "I did, but some dumb cow accused me of jumping in front of her at the buffet line at the Golden Corral. If her face wasn't buried in her phone, she would have noticed that the line was moving."

I raised a brow, with a million questions running through my head, but her stare was so intimidating that I was afraid to talk.

Kinley groaned next to me. "What did you do?"

"I smacked her with my pocketbook, that's what I did and I'd do it again. She started screaming and called for security." She shook her head in disbelief. "Your generation is so sensitive today."

It took everything in me to hold in my laugh because the woman sounded like a handful.

Kinley cleared her throat and waved her hand in my direction. "This is my friend, Maverick." She introduced me a little too quickly, like she was trying to shut this conversation down. "Maverick, this is my grandma, Deanne."

I don't know why she made me so nervous, but I wanted her to like me. Something told me that staying on her good side was the smart thing to do.

I extended my hand and gave her my game-winning smile. "Maverick Cross, a pleasure to meet you, Deanne."

She placed her hands on her hips and looked me over. "So, you're the one who knocked up my sweet little granddaughter, huh?"

I shifted uncomfortably on my feet as her eyes inspected me from top to bottom. Probably trying to figure out if I was good enough. Judging by how her eyes narrowed, my guess would be that I failed the test.

"Grandma, be nice." Kinley's voice was louder than usual.

"You don't need to shout." She tugged on her ear. "I got my hearing aids adjusted earlier. I can hear everything now."

"Great." Kinley smiled and dragged me into the house. Her grandmother ambled in front of us. The scent of her strong perfume floated in the air. It had a distinct smell; if you asked my opinion, it should have been discontinued decades ago.

"Mom," Kinley called out as we headed into the living room. The walls were lined with photos, and a cozy fireplace was in the back with bookshelves on either side. "I have someone I want you to meet."

An older version of Kinley muted an episode of *Family Feud* playing on the television and stood from the beige couch to greet us. "Oh." Kinley's mom was beautiful in a classic way. She had the same blue eyes and high cheekbones. "You must be Maverick. Thanks for bringing her home. I'm Michelle."

"My pleasure. It's nice to meet you, ma'am." I extended my hand, but she brushed it away and pulled me into a hug. "Unlike my mother, I'm a hugger, and please call me Michelle." Her embrace was warm and friendly, and I briefly wondered if she had been adopted. The two women I just met couldn't be more opposite.

Deanne made herself comfortable in the recliner and picked up a bowl of ice cream on the table next to her.

"How are you feeling?" Michelle smiled at Kinley and then at me. "Are you guys hungry? I have some leftover pasta I can heat up."

"We already ate, but I appreciate the offer." I wasn't sure why I was so nervous. Maybe because I felt unprepared to meet the family, and it wasn't something I could remember doing—ever.

Michelle picked up the remote and turned off the television. "Please sit down." She gestured to the loveseat against the wall.

"All Shook Up" by Elvis Presley started playing from Deanne's wrist. She pushed a button and reached for a pill container next to her. "That's my alarm," she explained, then dumped a pile of pills in her palm and threw them back like a cheap shot of bourbon. My eyes widened when she picked up a can of Pabst Blue Ribbon to chase them down. She swallowed and patted her chest. "It's rude to stare, quarterback."

"Quarterback?" I asked, making sure she was talking to me.

She picked up a napkin and wiped the side of her mouth. "Isn't that what you are?"

"Yeah." I swallowed, completely unsure how I should take this woman. She was nothing like my meemaw. This woman was a handful and then some.

"Anyone ever tell you, you've a handsome face?" She squinted her beady little eyes at me. If I didn't know any better, I would think she was enjoying watching me sweat.

"Not in those exact words."

"Well, you do, so maybe you should consider shaving that beard off so everyone can see it?"

Kinley fired her mom with a look, pleading with her silently to shut this conversation down. Even if she tried, I was pretty sure nothing could deter the woman.

"Grandma," Kinley scolded. "Why don't you finish your ice cream before it melts."

Her grandmother ignored her. "I need to ask the quarterback a few questions first."

I wanted to say hell no, but let's be honest, I had to earn her grandmother's approval somehow. It's been a long time since I had to prove myself to anyone, so hopefully, I wouldn't be too rusty.

"Ask away." I gave her a reassuring smile, like I had

nothing to hide, which was partly true. I stayed out of the headlines—mostly. I showed up for practice on time, got along with my teammates, and donated a good chunk of my money to charity. No famous sex tapes were floating around on the internet, and the only woman I've ever knocked up was her granddaughter. At least, that's the only one that I knew of.

"Are you a republican or a democrat?" was what she led with.

I scratched the back of my head, trying to think of a way to deflect or change the direction of this conversation. She couldn't possibly expect me to answer that, could she? It would be rude to ignore her, and I was reasonably confident she wouldn't allow me to, even if I tried. Deanne could give those reporters a run for their money. Very rarely did I get tripped up on the first question.

"Uh…" I ran a hand over my mouth and then my chin, stalling for time. I wasn't sure if I should laugh at the craziness or be scared shitless. What I did know was I needed a damn drink.

"You don't need to answer that," Kinley cut in, trying to end this interrogation. Thank God for small miracles. She shot her grandmother a glare, but the old lady just winked.

Deanne pushed her bowl of ice cream aside and unwrapped a piece of butterscotch candy. "I'm not going to judge. I really don't care which way you vote." I highly doubted that. "I just want to know what kind of household you'll be raising my great-grandbaby in."

Finally, Kinley's mom interjected. "Mom, stop trying to scare the young man." She looked at me with a mixture of embarrassment and worry. "She doesn't mean to be so rude."

I was certain Deanne didn't give a crap about how she came across or what came out of her mouth.

"If he can take a tackle from a three-hundred-pound linebacker, he better be able to handle a few questions from an eighty-year-old grandma."

"Wait." My head snapped to the side. "Do you watch football?"

She sat up straighter in the chair. "Every Sunday, Monday, and Thursday night." Well, shit. I ran a hand through my hair. She must have seen the excited look on my face, because she leaned forward and patted my knee. "I'm a Tampa Bay fan. Think you can get me some one-on-one time with Brady?"

"You want to meet Brady?" I asked for clarification. Brady was a rival and a damn good friend. We hung out a few times during the off-season. I'd call his ass up right now if it got me in this woman's good graces.

She stared at me as if I was slow to catch on. "Just because I'm old don't mean I'm blind. He looks mighty fine in that uniform they make you boys wear."

I threw my head back in laughter and glanced at Kinley, who looked like she was ready to crawl into the floor and hide. "I guess the whole tight pants thing runs in the family," I teased with a wink.

"All right." Kinley stood. "Maverick has to get going." She moved toward the front door like she was trying to do whatever she could to get me out of this conversation. "I'm going to walk him out to his truck."

"I bet you are." Her grandmother smirked and leaned back in her chair.

After saying a quick goodbye, and a promise to introduce Deanne to a few football players, I followed Kinley outside.

As soon as I closed the door, my chest shook with laughter. "Your grandmother is very…interesting."

"I love her to death, but she drives me crazy," she muttered.

"Hey." I pulled her in by the waist. "Don't be embarrassed. She's got a great sense of humor and seems young at heart." Wisps of her hair blew in the breeze, so I tucked a strand behind her ear. "I hope we're all like her when we get older."

She grabbed on to my wrist and stared into my eyes. "Thank you for being such a good sport."

I eyed her carefully, wishing I could mold my lips against hers and finish where we had left off. But something told me to slow down and not get carried away. Rushing into this wasn't going to get me what I wanted. But what I wanted and needed were two different things, and I needed her to know that I planned on exploring these feelings. We could take our time and get to know each other in all the ways that mattered.

I pressed a gentle kiss to her temple. "I'll call you later. Get some rest."

And with that, I walked back to my truck and forced myself to drive away. The hardest moments in life were sometimes waiting for the right moment, like knowing the exact second to release a pass so the receiver was in their spot to catch it. I waited during those moments, knowing that a herd of men twice my size were rushing toward me. I'd trained my mind to focus and knew when I needed to be quick or slow down. Those traits have served me well and would come in handy as Kinley and I navigate this unexpected path.

And I knew I could wait as long as it took to make her mine.

CHAPTER 13
KINLEY

"You're nervous?" Maverick squeezed my hand as we walked up the steps to his childhood home.

"I don't feel prepared. I'm not ready," I whispered, even though we were the only ones within hearing distance. "I feel like I'm going to throw up."

"My family loves you. Besides, it's not like you've never met them before."

"I'm still worried about how they'll react."

His parents were pretty laid-back, but no matter how hard he tried to convince me I had nothing to worry about, I still felt anxious.

"Things might get a little weird when they find out about the baby, but nothing we can't handle."

I wish I shared his confidence.

The front door flew open, and a little boy rushed out. Maverick barely had time to prepare before he crashed into his leg. "Uncle Mav, Dad said I had to wait for you to get here before we played Madden."

This must have been Declan's son.

Maverick laughed and ruffled his hair. "I'm surprised

your dad is even brave enough to play me seeing that I kicked his as…I mean butt last time."

He pointed and started laughing hysterically. "You almost said ass."

"Shh…" He placed a finger over his nephew's lips for him to keep quiet. "You look like you've grown ten inches since I saw you last. What are your parents feeding you?" he asked, holding him at arm's length.

The little boy pushed a fistful of bangs out of his eyes. "Depends on who is feeding me. Mom makes me eat a lot of fruits and vegetables, but Dad lets me eat pizza and McDonald's when she's not around."

I giggled at how cute he was.

He tilted his head and locked eyes with mine. "Who is this?"

Maverick paused for a moment as if he wasn't sure what he should introduce me as. "This is Kinley," he settled on.

He thought bringing me would be easier because I already knew his family. However, if you asked me, it only seemed to add another layer of complexity to an already fragile situation.

"Maverick, you're just in time." I turned my head, my eyes catching on his mom standing in the doorway. Her snowman apron was tied along her waist and a potato peeler dangled from one hand. Her gaze lit up when she saw her son and slid over to me in confusion. "Did you guys come together?"

Maverick flinched at how tightly I gripped his hand. She gazed at us across the lawn like she was working on a puzzle and trying to get the pieces to fit together. Now that we were here, I wished we had done this privately, as opposed to the front yard, where any nosy neighbor could hear us.

"Easton," a woman I'd never met before yelled from the porch. Her red hair was pushed back, and a reindeer headband sat on top of her head. "I told you to wait inside."

I recognized her now from the pictures that Rylee had posted online. She was Chelsea, Maverick's sister-in-law. The last I knew, Declan had moved to Chicago a few years ago. I didn't know him that well because he was five years older than Rylee, but I knew he was an engineer for some big energy company in the city. Speak of the devil. Declan came to an abrupt stop and drew his eyebrows together, making a huge dent in between his eyes.

"Kinley Roberts, is that you?" Interesting. Even Declan recognized me. In Maverick's defense, it's only been five years since I last saw Declan, as opposed to twelve.

"Hey Declan, it's great to see you."

"Kinley?" Rylee stepped around her brother.

Every muscle in my body tightened as she leaned against the door. She crossed her arms and narrowed her eyes into slits. I knew that look; I'd seen it countless times on her face. This was my first time on the receiving end of it, though.

"Is that what you wanted to talk to me about?" she asked, directing the question at me.

My eyes pinched shut, and my stomach turned over. There was no way to avoid this confrontation. She was making it obvious that she wasn't happy, and I couldn't blame her. I should have listened to my gut and met with her privately before ambushing her in front of the entire family. Instead of handling it as I should have, I chickened out.

"Yes." I ran my hand through my hair, feeling guilt eating away at me. "I didn't want to show up like this. I'm sorry."

When I called her last night, it went to her voicemail. I left a brief message, letting her know I was in town and wanted to talk to her. Instead of trying to reach her one more time, like I planned, I allowed Maverick to convince me that it would be a good idea to tell his family together.

And now I regretted it.

Beth shot Rylee a sidelong glance. "Why don't we go

inside." She nudged her daughter with her elbow. "I need to finish cutting up the fruit for the salad."

We all filed into the house, and I immediately smelled the turkey baking in the oven and spied three different pies on the cooling racks. Maverick walked to the fridge, helped himself to a beer, and handed me a bottle of water. The room was tense and quiet; if we didn't get this conversation over with, I was going to lose my mind. I took a slow sip of my drink and tried to ignore the strange looks coming at me from every direction.

"All right," Maverick braced his arms along the granite countertop, "I guess I'm going to go first."

His dad wrapped an arm around his mom's shoulders. His concerned gaze stayed on his sons. "Go ahead, Mav, say whatever it is you have to say."

I wasn't sure what the hell we were thinking showing up like this. In fact, based on the reaction from everyone in this room, it was a terrible idea.

Maverick swiped a hand over the top of his lip and let out a slow breath. "I'm sorry we've taken you guys by surprise here, but we wanted to have this conversation face-to-face."

"*We?*" One of Rylee's eyebrows lifted slowly. "Can you repeat that, please?" Beth elbowed her in the side and shushed her. I wrung my nervous hands in front of me and willed the contents in my stomach to stay where they belonged and not unleash the bagel and cream cheese I had for breakfast all over Beth's beautiful tiled floor.

Vinny cleared his throat. He was probably itching for a cigarette, and for the first time in my life, I was starting to see the appeal of nicotine. "Son, whatever you have to say will be fine." He winked at me, but it did nothing to calm the eruption in my stomach.

Please, Dear God, do not let me vomit.

Rylee slumped down on one of the stools at the counter,

her eyes darting back and forth between us. "Am I missing something here?"

Other than things being uncomfortable, I had no idea what to expect, but damn, this was worse than I imagined. Heat crept up the back of my neck at the thought of how blindsided they would be. Hopefully, once the shock wore off, they would consider it good news.

"We have something to tell you." His jaw worked back and forth, mulling over his words before he spoke. I wasn't sure how he would handle it if his family disapproved. Just thinking about it was enough to send me into a panic attack. "Kinley and I are having a baby together."

His mother's hand flew to her mouth in a gasp. His father's face turned white, and it felt like someone had turned up the thermostat to a hundred and fifty degrees.

"I'm going to assume this wasn't planned," Declan said, his eyes drifting between the two of us.

"No, it wasn't. We were both surprised by the news."

"Oh, my goodness." Beth stepped forward with tears brimming in her eyes.

"What the hell is happening right now?" Rylee's tone had my back going straight.

Maverick's hand landed on my shoulder in silent support. "I know this is a shock right now," he said, shooting his sister a death glare. "But Kinley and I would like to take some time to figure things out and we would appreciate y'alls support."

Vinny leaned forward; his hands landed on his hips. "Are the two of you a couple?"

A pang of unease hit me, and I did my best to push it aside. It reminded me how much shit we still had to hash out.

"We are just having a baby together," I said, finally finding my voice. Maverick's hand tensed on my shoulder.

Vinny nodded his head, looking disappointed. "So, what's the plan?" He kept his focus on me. "Are you moving back to Georgia?"

I wasn't expecting that question, although I probably should have. Beth and Vinny were old-fashioned. They weren't as strict as most southern parents, but they held their children to certain standards.

"Dad, we haven't gotten that far ahead yet."

Rylee stalked over to refill her wineglass. "I'd like a word with both of you."

I nodded my head because refusing her would only make matters worse. We followed her through the house and onto the back patio. Rylee's sleek, dark-brown hair swayed across her shoulders. The scent of familiar Marc Jacobs perfume floated in the air. It was the same one she wore in high school. It had only been a few months since we last spoke, but it seemed like forever. My stomach twisted in guilt, and that tightness in my chest kept growing with each passing second. Would she hate me? Would she feel betrayed?

Worry and doubt seemed to fill my head as I started to imagine every worst-case scenario.

"Let me get this straight." She sat down, and the wine in her glass swished as she set it on the table between the two chairs. "You guys are having a baby together?"

Maverick rubbed the back of his neck and unleashed a grin. "What are the chances, huh?"

She smacked his injured knee. "Are you kidding me right now? A joke?" Then she turned her hard, suspicious eyes on me. "And you, I can't believe you kept this from me. I know we don't talk often, but you're one of my oldest friends. We've been through a lot together. We've never kept secrets from each other."

I was transported back to when we would have sleepovers and stay up all night crying over broken hearts and hurt feelings. She never knew that I had a crush on her older brother. I hid it from her. But then again, it was one-sided, so I hid it from everyone.

"I'm sorry you're just finding out about this now."

She didn't seem mad, but I wouldn't say she was happy either.

"How long has this been going on?"

I twisted my hands in front of me. "He didn't even know who I was until just a few days ago."

Maverick's hand dropped from my shoulder, and he cursed under his breath.

She reared back, her eyebrows nearly reaching her hairline. "What do you mean, he didn't know who you were?"

Great. I had the pleasure of reliving one of the most embarrassing moments of my life.

"We ended up on the same flight out of New York right before Thanksgiving. Only a storm hit, so the plane never took off. Maverick didn't recognize me, and I never told him who I was."

"Wait a minute." Her frosty glare moved over to her brother. "You slept with her and didn't realize it was her? Do you still have a concussion? How the hell did you not recognize her? She practically spent as much time in this house as you did growing up here."

"She looks different." He looked at me for a little help, but he was on his own with this one. He let out a frustrated sigh and raked his hand through his hair. "It's been twelve years."

She shook her head. "You are such a bonehead. I blame it on all the hits you've taken to the head over the years playing football. They should study that brain of yours after you pass away."

My lips lifted into a smile at her reaction.

He placed his hands on his hips and glared at both of us. "I see how this is going to go. You two are going to gang up on me now, aren't you?"

We all shared a laugh, and it felt like a weight had been lifted.

"I can't believe you're having a baby together." She scrunched up her nose. "It's so weird to think about, but it all makes sense now."

"What makes sense?" I asked.

"Every time he would walk into a room, you would sit up straighter. It's like the clouds would part, and the sun would shine down on his arrogant ass." My cheeks heated. I didn't realize my attraction to her brother was like a flashing neon sign. "You would smile and laugh at all his jokes, and…" She pointed her finger as if she had just figured something out. "You always wanted to hang out at my house. I could never explain it, but I always got this weird vibe from you. You turned weird whenever he was around."

"Wow," I said, feeling completely mortified. "Some friend you are. You could have kept some of that to yourself."

Maverick threw his arm along my shoulders. "Doesn't feel good to be on the other side now, does it?"

"I want to make something perfectly clear." She pointed to me. "I know we've talked about our sex lives in the past. But I swear to God, if you ever go into detail about you and my brother, that will be the end of us."

She shivered, and I did my best to smother my laugh. Rylee always had a gift for lightening the mood.

"And you." She poked her finger in her brother's direction. "If you hurt her, it's going to cause a lot of problems between us." She leaned back. "Now, I'm going to do my best to stay out of y'alls business. I love you both, so I don't want to have to pick sides and be caught in the middle. As far as I'm concerned, what happens between you two stays between you two."

I had to admit, this conversation went much better than planned. I didn't sleep a wink last night due to the fact that I was too worked up about today. Rylee took the news better than I expected, and a small part of me was filled with guilt at all the years we wasted. We both could have done a better job of keeping in touch. There was no denying that we'd grown apart over the years. Hopefully, this baby will bring us closer together.

CHAPTER 14

MAVERICK

Kinley was rummaging through a plastic bin, singing "Feliz Navid" completely off-key and making sure she didn't miss a single lyric. The woman made me laugh more times today than I had in years. If it wasn't for the two hours we wasted looking for the perfect tree, the day would have been ideal.

There was nothing worse than spending an afternoon in the forest, searching for the perfect tree with a woman who couldn't make up her damn mind. A pregnant woman, nonetheless. Everything was too short and lumpy and had too many bare spots. Not sure what she expected to find a day before Christmas Eve.

I walked over, grabbed an ornament out of the box, and hung it on one of the branches. "At least it doesn't look like a Charlie Brown tree," I said, standing back and looking for any bare spots.

"Hush." She bumped her hip with mine. "I'll have you know that *A Charlie Brown Christmas* is my favorite holiday movie."

"Pretty sure it's considered a children's cartoon and not a movie."

"I'll tell you what it is," she said, placing a scented candle on the mantel. "It's a holiday classic."

"Sure, if you're five years old," I teased.

She took the lighted garland and started hanging it along the window. "And what's your favorite movie?" She turned and pointed. "And don't you dare say *Die Hard* because that is most definitely not a holiday movie."

"Not even close," I said, helping her drape the garland along the hooks. "My favorite is *It's a Wonderful Life*."

She snorted and stepped off the stepladder.

"What's so funny?"

"Besides the fact that it's aired in black-and-white and my grandmother's favorite, it's long and boring."

I smacked her ass. "It is not boring, and now that I know that fun fact, I'll make sure to invite Deanne over to watch it with me. Maybe I can use it to my advantage and we can bond over our admiration for Bedford Falls and George Bailey."

"Sounds like a perfect date." She winked and stood back to admire her hard work. "Do you think I went a little overboard with the decorations?"

I skimmed my eyes across the room, my entire condo had been transformed in a matter of hours, and it shocked me how much I liked it. The tree had gifts wrapped underneath the branches, stockings were hanging from the mantle, and a Christmas throw was hanging over the back of my couch.

"I think it's perfect."

Mariah Carey's "All I Want for Christmas Is You" started playing.

I held out my hand. "Dance with me."

"What?" She hesitated and looked around like she wasn't sure what to make of my request. "Why?"

"Because I want to." Our time together was limited, and I had this undescribed need to be close to her. The days were passing by too quickly, and I would have done anything to slow them down, or convince her to stay.

She took my hand, and I gathered her in my arms. "Fair warning, I'm not a very good dancer."

"I guess I'll just have to hold you extra close then."

My arms slid along her back, and I gathered her as tight as our bodies would allow. Over the past few days, we'd fallen into a comfortable routine. I didn't realize things would be this easy between us or how much I needed this time with her. It's been a nice change of pace. I couldn't remember the last time when my days and nights didn't revolve around football. If this is what having a real life felt like, then I wasn't in a hurry to get back to my old one.

She laid her head down on my shoulder and smiled up at me. "You realize holding me close will only make it easier to trip over your feet, right?"

I gave her a little twirl and brought her back to my chest. "Do your worst, but I won't let you fall. Plus," I kissed her temple, "it gives me a chance to hold you."

She folded her hands along my neck and gazed up at me. "I never knew you could be so sweet."

"That's because you only knew the teenage Maverick Cross. The young jock who thought he was God's gift to the universe."

"And what does the adult Maverick Cross think?"

"Besides the fact that it's weird that we're talking about him in third person." We both laughed. "He thinks becoming a father will end up being his greatest accomplishment."

Her feet stopped moving; she lifted her head and blinked up at me. "I think you are going to be a great dad, Maverick."

I traced the edge of her nose and spread my palm along her cheek. "Thank you."

I wasn't sure if it was the thought of her returning to New York that had me panicking or all my doubts and fears about raising a child together. But never in my life had I been so unsure about one thing and a hundred percent sure about another.

"And thank you for not making fun of my dancing skills." She laughed, trying to lighten the mood.

"You're welcome, but you just need to relax. You're too stiff."

She smacked my chest. "I'm not used to this."

"Used to what, dancing?" I wrapped my arms around her waist and led us through the living room.

"Affection and spontaneity."

"I plan on spoiling you, so get used to it." I winked. "And don't worry, I'll teach our kid how to dance."

"Good, because you're much better at it than I am. I'm pretty sure you're good at everything."

"Not everything. I couldn't have done all this decorating by myself." My fingers played with the ends of her hair. "I can only imagine how festive your apartment looks."

"Actually," she looked away sheepishly, "my apartment doesn't look anything like this. I have a little fake tree on top of a table and a few decorations scattered around. That's about it."

"What?" I reared back. "Are you serious or just pulling my leg?"

She brushed her hand along my shoulder and nibbled on her bottom lip. "My place is too tiny to do this much decorating. I don't have as much space as you do to display all this."

"I don't think I've ever been inside a New York City apartment before."

"You're not missing much."

A lump formed in my throat when she circled her arms along the back of my neck. We swayed to the music, our bodies in sync like we'd danced together our entire lives. "I know it's a little early, but I want to start looking into some real estate next time I'm there. I know nothing about the neighborhoods, but I want something close to you. I figured it would make it easier for when the baby is born."

Her eyes widened. "You would do that?"

"Why was it so hard to believe? I thought I made it obvious that I wanted to be involved."

She tried to pull away, but I wasn't having it. "Maverick, you have no idea how expensive Manhattan is. I'm already stressing out about finding something bigger."

"Kinley, I have more money than I could ever spend in one lifetime. I've worked my ass off and sacrificed enough. If I don't spend some of it making sure my child is safe and provided for, then what's the point? What else am I going to spend it on?"

She squinted her eyes, and a slight frown took over her face. "You're talking about buying a place for you for when you come to visit, right? Because there isn't a chance in hell you're buying me an apartment."

I brushed my lips against her forehead. "Let's table this for another time, okay?"

The woman was stubborn, that was for damn sure. I had no idea how I was going to convince her to let me help out with expenses. Her independence was one of the things I admired most about her, but that didn't mean we couldn't compromise. She was going to have to meet me in the middle somewhere. If I had my way, she'd never leave the state of Georgia again. Unfortunately, that wasn't my reality, and I would be lying if I said I wasn't worried about how we would make this work.

She was quiet, so I knew her head was spinning as fast as mine.

I grabbed her chin and forced her to look at me. "I know you're nervous and we have a lot to figure out, but I promise I won't make any decisions that you're not one hundred percent on board with."

That seemed to appease her. She closed her eyes and rested her head against my chest. Our movements were slow and unhurried as we glided back and forth across my living room. She ran her hands over my shoulders and down my back like she needed to be as close to me as I did her.

When the music stopped, those blue eyes looked up at me. They were smiling; she looked happy, and I wanted to soak up the moment. I held her face in my hands and brought my mouth to hers. The kiss was soft and gentle, but with every breath between us, I felt my body coming alive. Normally, kissing a woman led to sex, but with Kinley, I'd be perfectly content right where I was. If this was all we could ever be, I didn't care.

"Maverick." She swallowed, seeming unsure of her words. "Do you really think we can do this?"

"Do what?" I ran the back of my knuckles along her cheek. "What exactly is it that you want?"

She shook her head. "There is no way I'm answering that before you."

I pulled her tighter against me. "Why are you so afraid to tell me how you feel?"

"Are you kidding me? You're famous, and I'm a nobody. You date models and celebrities." Her cheeks turned pink as she kept going. "You ride in the back of limos and fly in private jets. You get invited to award shows…"

I cut her off with a laugh. "Are you forgetting how this all started? It started in a public airport as we fought over who was getting the next seat on a commercial flight. As for the models and celebrities, I never dated them. I took them as dates, that's different. I don't bring them home to my parents' house. I don't go picking out Christmas trees with them." I looked into her eyes so she could understand how serious I was. "I don't plan out my future with them in mind."

"I know this is different for both of us." She sighed. "I'm

just worried about what people will think. I'm not your usual type."

I tilted her chin up, not liking that comment one bit. She was overanalyzing everything and twisting things around in her head. "What's my usual type?"

She looked down at the floor, unable to meet my eyes. "I know what your typical date looks like, and it's not me."

"Kinley, most of the dates were arranged by my PR team," I explained, wishing I could erase the doubts she's been having our relationship. "I couldn't even tell you who half of them were. There was nothing memorable about any of them."

For such a strong, independent woman, she seemed to carry around a lot of insecurities. But given the life I lived, I guess I could see where some it was coming from.

"I know I sound ridiculous, but your life is constantly in the spotlight. The fans, the media circus, it all weighs heavily on me." She rubbed her hand slowly along my back. "But you're right, what they think isn't important. The only thing that matters is how we feel, and in case you haven't noticed, I'm crazy about you."

My heart did a little flutter, and I felt a bit of frustration melt away. "Good, because I'm crazy about you too." I dropped my forehead to hers. "You don't see the guy wearing the jersey, you see the man without it. This connection we have is the only real thing I have in my life right now that feels right. I don't even question it, and I probably should."

"Maverick, I've had eyes for you before you even owned a jersey, so you're right. None of that matters to me, it never did and it never will."

I grinned. "You've been smitten the whole time, huh?"

"Totally."

"How is it that I never realized how perfect you were for me when I was younger?"

She leaned back and cocked her head to the side. "Because you were the big man on campus and…"

"A cocky pain in the ass," I added.

She grinned. "I'm not going to dispute that fact."

If I could go back to the past and do things differently, I would have definitely paid more attention to her.

I blew out a breath, glad we got that conversation out of the way. "Are you ready to open your gifts now?"

"I asked you not to get me anything," she said as I walked over to the tree and handed her the small box. Kinley snatched it out of my hand so fast, I almost lost my balance. Those big, blue eyes lit up with excitement as her fingers started ripping through the wrapping paper.

I crossed my arms and laughed at how enthusiastic she was. Watching her rip the package open like it would disappear in five seconds if she didn't have it completely unwrapped was entertaining. "You don't seem too upset that I didn't listen to you."

"I'm just curious," she said, as she flew through the tissue paper. I bit the inside of my cheek at the frown on her face. "You bought me underwear?" She looked up at me, looking a little taken aback by what she found.

"Pull them out and take a look." I covered my mouth to hide my grin.

She held up the little red and white scrap of fabric between her fingers. "You've got to be kidding me. They actually make women's thongs with your name and number?"

I shrugged. "Trust me, I was just as surprised as you were. I thought, what better way to stake my claim than have you wear my name across your pussy."

I was tempted to tell her that I owed her a pair. She still had no idea that I found and kept hers from our night together. At some point, I planned on giving them back to her, but for some strange reason, I wasn't ready to do that yet.

"You did not just say that?" She threw it at my chest.

I chuckled and walked over to grab the other gift. This was a bigger box, and I noticed that her hands worked more slowly to open that one. She reached in and pulled out the basket. It was filled with La Perla bath lotions, body scrubs, a long silk robe, and a pajama set. In addition, there was a pair of UGG slippers, scented candles, and an assortment of teas and crackers.

"The basket is for nights when you need to relax, and I can't be there to take care of you."

Her blue eyes filled with moisture. "This is so thoughtful. Thank you."

"There's one more." I stood up and walked into the kitchen. I hid this one from her because I wanted it to be a surprise. I opened the drawer and pulled out the flat square wrapped box. The first gift was a gag; the second was just something I threw together to let her know I'd be thinking of her. This one, though, was more sentimental. If she got misty-eyed from the basket, I could only imagine what her reaction would be to this.

"Here." I held the box out, and she carefully took it from my hands.

"You didn't need to get me anything else." She stared down at the box like she was afraid to open it. Maybe she could sense my nervousness because she slowly undid the bow and pulled the top off. Her hands flew to her mouth when her eyes caught on the charm bracelet.

I pulled it out and held it up for her. "My mom has a charm bracelet that my dad bought when she was pregnant with my brother. Each year, she gets a new charm for Christmas." My fingers toyed with the two platinum charms I added.

"Oh, my, God. It's an airplane." She looked up and smirked at me. "And look at this one." She held up the silhouette of the New York City skyline with an apple nestled inside. "Maverick Cross, you are an old softy." She started half crying and half laughing. "This is perfect."

My shoulders sagged in relief at how much she seemed to like it. I wanted to give her something that would always remind her of when we reconnected.

Kinley wiped her eyes and shook her head. Then she surprised me when she leaped into my arms and kissed me. I wasn't sure if this was a thank you or if she was simply doing it because she wanted to. Either way, I was happy to have her mouth on mine again.

I grabbed the bracelet and clasped it around her wrist.

She walked to the door to grab the big gift bag with red and green tissue paper. I've stared at it a few times, trying to figure out what it could be. She placed it in my lap, and I immediately reached in and pulled out a big wicker basket. Inside was a popcorn bucket, a few snacks you'd find at a movie theatre, and a hand-printed ticket that said, "movie night for two," and my eyes bugged out when I saw the DVD at the bottom. *"Back to the Future?"*

She nibbled on her bottom lip. "I remember you were obsessed with that movie in high school."

"It's a classic." I flipped it over and studied the back. It's been years since I've seen the movie. It dawned on me that she didn't just buy me a random gift or a pair of cufflinks she saw in a jewelry store. She gave me something even better, a gift of her time. This gift was meant for the two of us to spend together, and I couldn't think of a better gift than that.

CHAPTER 15

KINLEY

"Thanks again for going along with this." Maverick handed me a sweatshirt. "I promise, it's nothing too crazy."

"Relax," I tried to reassure him. "I'm a big girl. I can handle being around a few hunky football players."

"On second thought." He was about to restart the engine. "Maybe we should stick with our original plan and stay in."

I laughed and pulled his hand away from the start button on his truck. "These are your friends, so I want to meet them."

He leaned over the console and kissed my cheek. "I appreciate you being so cool about this."

When he mentioned his friend was having a bonfire and asked if I wanted to go, I wasn't sure If I was ready for this next step. But these people were important to him, and I couldn't bring myself to tell him no.

He reached for my hand as we walked around the cars parked along the circular driveway. The smell of burning wood was in the air as we followed the sound of loud voices and music in the backyard.

As we got closer, I recognized a few faces of the guys gathered near a fire pit drinking beer. Another group played beer pong in the garage, while a circle of girls danced to country music off to the side.

"JP," Maverick called out to his friend, sitting at the patio table with a tiny brunette on his lap.

"Mav." He grinned and leaned forward for a fist bump. "It's about time you showed up. Drinks are in the cooler and there is food in the kitchen if you're hungry."

"Thanks, dude." He tilted his head to the side. "This is Kinley."

"So, this is the famous Kinley from New York?" He dragged a hand over his beard. "My buddy here was one phone call away from hiring a private investigator to track you down. Glad to see he finally found you."

"Okay, you can shut up now." Maverick laughed.

JP's eyes floated over to Maverick's; they were dancing with humor. "Why? Am I messing up your game?" He took a puff of his cigar. "Are you playing hard to get or something?"

Maverick squeezed my hand and glared at his friend. "You're a jackass, you know that?"

JP boomed with laughter. "Somebody has to keep the great Maverick Cross humble." And then those playful midnight blue eyes turned to me. They softened into something warm and friendly. "Nice to finally meet you, Kinley."

The woman on his lap paid me no attention, and it didn't go unnoticed that he didn't introduce her either.

"You too. Thanks for having me. You have a beautiful home."

When he shifted the woman to his other leg, I couldn't help but notice the size of his arms. If muscles could grow muscles, then JP was walking, living proof it was possible. Not only did he look like he could lift me in the air with one finger, but the man was covered in tattoos.

In my opinion though, the playful glint in his eye didn't match the tough guy exterior. "My pleasure, darlin', help yourself to whatever you want."

"I'm thinking that I might want to hang out with you for a bit and hear a few embarrassing stories about this big guy here." I poked Maverick in the chest. "It seems like you guys are all pretty tight."

JP boomed with laughter, and his eyes bounced to his friend. "Trust me, I've got a whole arsenal of stories, but my buddy looks like he's ready to piss his pants, so we might have to wait until we're alone if you want to hear the good ones."

"Knock it off." Maverick chuckled, his hand pressed deeper into my side. "Unless you want to find another icy hot rubbed in your jockstrap, I'd think twice about opening your mouth."

"Your threats don't scare me, pal, but it sounds like you're afraid I'll try to steal your girl," JP teased with a grin.

Maverick rolled his eyes. "I don't think I like you very much right now."

JP's hand went to his chest. "You wound me."

"You'll get over it." Maverick shook his head. "Come on, let's go get a drink." He placed his hand on the small of my back, leading me over to the coolers by the sliding glass door.

I looked up at the starry night sky and started feeling nostalgic. The campfire smell reminded me of happier times before I worried about work and paying bills. It brought me back to my teenage years, when life was simpler and less stressful. The only things I had to fret about were getting sick from cheap whiskey and doing something stupid I would regret the next day.

After living in the big city for so long, I forgot how relaxing it was to be outdoors.

"This place is massive," I said, taking the water bottle from Maverick's hand. There was a swimming pool, a hot tub, and a tall garage to the left with ATVs and dirt bikes. This was nothing like the parties I went to back in the day. "I take it your friend likes to have a good time."

"JP is a showoff." He laughed and led me to the group of people clustered by the fire. One of the guys got up and grabbed an extra chair for me to sit on.

"Thank you," I said to the man whose head was mostly shaved except for the bright red strip along the middle.

"What's up, Morris." Maverick jutted his chin out in greeting and made quick introductions. "That's Morris, Rhett, and Elliott." The one on the end waved. "Everyone, this is Kinley."

"It's nice to meet you guys." I smiled shyly. Seeing them on television was one thing, but meeting them in person was intimidating. All these men were huge.

Maverick pulled me into his side. "Whatever they say, don't believe any of it."

The one with the red mohawk grinned. "Afraid she'll come running in my direction, Mav?"

Maverick responded by flipping him the middle finger.

I noticed all the men were ripped and handsome. Some had baby faces, and a couple were a bit more rugged, but as I listened to them rib on each other, they seemed like regular guys just having a good time.

"So, Kinley." Rhett brushed a curly strand of hair off his forehead. I recognized him right away because he was always in the tabloids. "How did you meet this old man? Are you a football fan?"

"Watch it, rookie," Maverick warned his friend, who hooted in laughter.

"I hate to break the news to you guys, but I don't pay that much attention to football. The only sport I watch is baseball and that's only if the Yankees are playing."

Rhett sat up straighter in his chair and scratched his clean-shaven chin. He had a reputation for being a party boy, and I could tell just from our brief greeting that he loved the attention. "I bet I can get you to change your mind if you ever want to come and watch me play sometime. I still have a lot of stamina, unlike your old man over here."

He winked in my direction, and I felt a blush hit my cheeks. Maverick might not have been as muscular as some of his teammates—he was toned and lean—but I could say with one hundred percent certainty that his stamina was just fine.

Maverick flicked a bottle cap at his head. "Are you seriously going to flirt with her right in front of me?" He looked around at his friends, shaking his head. "Do I need to remind you animals to be on your best behavior?"

A dimple popped out on Rhett's cheek. "This is awesome. Never thought I'd see the day."

"What are you talking about?" The guys looked amused at Maverick's puzzled expression.

"I actually like this," Rhett said to Morris while Elliott nodded his head in agreement. "It will be fun getting him all riled up now that we know where his weak spot is."

They all high-fived each other, seeming pretty pleased with themselves. As much as they enjoyed ruffling each other's feathers, I could sense the strong bond they shared. They weren't just teammates; they were practically brothers.

"Y'all are a bunch of delinquents looking for trouble."

"Speaking of trouble." Rhett stood. "I'm going to find myself some now." He made a beeline for the girls dancing, and the guys whooped and hollered as he approached a blonde in a tight pair of jeans. He pulled on her long ponytail and started grinding against her. I just shook my head and smiled. He was certainly living up to his reputation.

There was a slight breeze making it cool, so I moved the chair closer to the fire and sat down. "Are you cold?" Maverick asked, squeezing into a seat next to mine.

"I'm good." It was in the mid-sixties, but the fire was throwing off enough heat to keep me comfortable.

I spent the next ten minutes getting to know Elliott and Morris, and it was impossible not to like them. They were easy to talk to and fun to laugh with. Morris and I bonded over the fact that he lived in New York when he played for the Giants. He was traded to Atlanta during his fifth year for a number one draft pick. He and Maverick had played together for the past seven years and were considered the veteran players, which in football years was considered ancient.

"Are you guys feeling ready for the game on Sunday?" Maverick asked Morris and Elliott. I didn't know much about football, but there had been a lot of excitement building as it got closer to the playoffs.

"We've got our work cut out for us, that's for sure," Morris said before tipping his beer back.

"What do you think, Mav?" Elliott asked. "Think you could handle a little pain and suit up for the game. You're our best shot at making the playoffs."

"Yeah," Rhett added as he walked back over to grab a beer from the cooler. "Maybe if you plead with the coach and offer to suck his dick, he'll let you on the field."

My eyes slid over in Maverick's direction, waiting to see how he would answer. We didn't talk much about his injury, but I knew that football was his life.

"Never say never." He shifted in his seat. "But you can bet your ugly asses I'll be pacing the sidelines, screaming into the headset, and cursing at all your shitty plays."

They all laughed. "You going to be our coach now?" Morris asked.

Maverick smirked and scratched his chin. "I wouldn't mind taking over as the offensive coach. God knows we'd have a better chance at winning if I did."

"Ooh…" Rhett settled back in his seat and smacked Maverick on his injured knee. "I'm tellin' on you."

Maverick winced and punched his friend in the shoulder. "You're such a fucker."

Rhett chuckled. "Well, I do like to fuck, so I guess it fits."

They all clinked their drinks and started talking about the upcoming game. I didn't miss the curious glances from a few of the guys or the scowls from a group of girls that showed up. Maverick kept his attention solely on me instead of engaging in the back-and-forth banter with his friends. He didn't once pick up his phone or leave my side. Everyone came to him, and he made a point to introduce me to everyone who approached.

"Hey, Maverick." I looked up at the woman with long auburn hair, a short mini-jean skirt, and a pair of heels more suited for a club than a bonfire.

"Della, I didn't know you were coming tonight." He shot up from his chair to greet her.

"I just got back today. My parents said hello." She went to kiss him on the mouth, but he turned his head to the side, so her lips landed on his cheek instead. When he pulled away, she made a point of brushing her boob against his arm. The woman was desperate to get a reaction out of him, and I wasn't going to complain one bit that he stepped back and put a little space between them.

Relief washed through me when he came to stand at my side. The new girl blinked slowly, and I watched her face transform into something sour. She looked disappointed, probably because she came here tonight to see him and wasn't expecting me.

"Who's your friend?" she asked, stepping closer and throwing me a saccharine smile. I was pretty good at reading people, and I would bet every last cent in my 401K that it was as fake as the eyelashes covering half of her face.

"Della, this is Kinley," he said as she dragged a chair over to join us. Great!

"Nice to meet you." I smiled and dug my sneakers into the grass. Why the hell did I dress for comfort? Oh, I knew why, because we were going to a bonfire. But as I looked at what little clothing some women wore, I felt seriously over-dressed.

She mumbled something that sounded close to "you too," but I couldn't be sure, and she gave a little finger wave to the group. "Hey, guys."

There were a couple of silent nods and casual greetings, but that was it. I noticed no one else jumped up to hug her. Only Maverick.

"How do you two know each other?" she asked, crossing her legs and leaning sideways.

"I grew up with his sister," I explained, trying to get my mind to relax. She was coming across as friendly, but I didn't trust her as far as I could throw her.

"Rylee?" Her eyes squinted in confusion, and she looked around. "Is Rylee here?"

"Nope." Maverick took a sip of his beer. "It's just me and Kinley."

She didn't look like she liked that answer at all. "I'm sorry. I'm having a hard time following." She glanced between the two of us. "Is she here with you as a family friend or as your date?"

"That would be your business, why?" He gave her a stern look.

A few chuckles rang out from the guys, and I tried to hide my smile behind my water bottle. Maybe I wasn't the only one who didn't care for this woman.

"Sorry, I didn't mean it like that." She attempted to sound sincere, but she sounded anything but sorry. She was clearly digging and failing at hiding her displeasure at what she was finding. She bumped Maverick's leg with hers. "Are we still on for Tuesday? I need to get my hands on those muscles and work my magic."

The water I had just swallowed came spraying through my nose. Rhett handed me a napkin and shot me a look of sympathy. I wiped at my burning nostril and coughed to cover up my embarrassment.

"I have the physical therapy session penciled in my calendar," Maverick replied, and edged his eyes over to mine in apology. He placed his hand on my knee in support, and I felt my shoulders relax slightly.

"Good. I need to loosen you up a bit. You seem like you are wound up tight tonight." She flipped her hair over her shoulder, doing everything she could to keep his attention. "I thought we could have lunch at Atlas when we're done. I know how much you love their black truffle fettuccini."

"Sorry, but I'm not available this week."

Our little group had gone quiet since her arrival. Morris was peeling the label off his beer, Rhett was pretending to scroll through his phone, and Elliott was poking the fire with a stick, even though it didn't need it. Meanwhile, the others just stayed silent during this little exchange.

"Oh." She took a sip from her red solo cup. "What about New Year's Eve? We always spend it together."

I tried to concentrate on the music behind me and focus on the couple dancing by the barn. The guy had his hands buried in the woman's shorts, and she had her tongue shoved down his throat. Basically, I was going out of my way to make it seem like I wasn't paying attention to what she was saying because it was obvious the woman was trying to get under my skin.

"I'm going to have to pass this year," he replied coolly. I guess he was catching on to her little game too. "Kinley is only in town for the week, so I'm spending New Year's Eve with her."

"You are?" I snapped my head to his in surprise. We hadn't made plans, and this was the first I'd heard of it.

"Uh…yeah, why? I assumed we'd spend it together. You didn't already make plans, did you?"

"No." I assumed he already had party invites or planned

on going clubbing. Isn't that what celebrities did on New Year's?

He settled back in his folding chair. "Well, now you do."

I peeked a glance over at his little friend. She didn't look happy.

"So, Kinley," she said tightly, "where are you from exactly?"

"I was born and raised in Georgia, but I live in Manhattan now."

"New York?" Unease settled in my gut with how bright her eyes lit up. "So, you're just here visiting then, gotcha ya."

Della seemed to perk up at the thought of me being so far away. My thoughts, however, seemed to dip into a sea of insecurity. I might not have liked her, but even I couldn't deny how stunning she was. There was no way I could compete with someone as beautiful as her. Even on my best day, I wouldn't be half as pretty, and my body would never be as toned and fit. In a few months, I'd probably have stretch marks and leaky boobs. My hips, my stomach, everything was going to get big. Why on earth would he want a fat, hormonal pregnant woman when he could have that? And the worst part was, I couldn't even blame him if he did. The more my mind started to wander, the more paranoid I got.

I stood up and looked everywhere but at him. "Does anyone know where the bathrooms are?" There was no way I could sit here and act as though I belonged here. I didn't fit in with women like her, and they were obviously close. How close was a question I was afraid to ask?

Rhett jumped out of his chair. "I'm headed that way. I can show you."

Maverick put his hand out. "I got it, stud."

"Really, Maverick," his catty friend called out. "I'm sure she can manage finding the bathroom on her own."

What started as a fun night seemed to go downhill fast, and I wasn't sure how to turn it around.

The woman brought out a violent streak in me. I was close to ripping her little diamond stud earring out from her nose and stabbing her in the forehead with it.

Like a woman on a mission, I kept a brisk pace ahead of him. "Is something wrong?" Maverick asked from behind me.

"No." I sighed at how unconvincing I sounded. I just wanted to sit somewhere and stew in private.

"Hey." His hand landed on my arm, pausing my steps. "Are you mad at me?"

"I'm not mad at you," I told him honestly. "I'm just not sure what to make of Della."

"I'm sorry about her. She's just a close friend and gets territorial sometimes."

I wasn't buying it. Call it intuition or whatever, but the vibe I got from her was not good. There was more to the story. I could feel it in my bones. And I was pretty sure when I scrolled through his Instagram she was one of the women I'd seen photographed with him.

"Maverick." I pressed my palms on his chest. "I know I don't have a right to ask, but are you sleeping with her?"

He grabbed my wrist and pulled me into him. "Of course, you have a right to ask. And the answer is no. The only one I want to sleep with is you."

My eyes moved across his face. His answer should have satisfied me, but for reasons I couldn't explain, it didn't. "There's really nothing going on with you two?"

"No." I raised my eyebrow, letting him know I didn't believe him. He sighed and looked away. "I dated Della briefly in college. It wasn't serious, trust me. We decided we were better off as friends."

I highly doubted she felt that way. I was a woman and knew competition when I saw it. She was still carrying a torch for her old flame; only he didn't see it.

I folded my arms across my chest. "But she's your physical therapist now?" I asked, trying to figure out the exact status of their relationship. It felt like I was playing a game that I was unfamiliar with and trying to learn the rules as we went along.

"She's the team's physical therapist." He brought me to his chest. "I promise you, there is nothing going on between us. That ship sailed a long time ago. I don't see Della as anything but a friend."

There was no way Della was happy being friends with Maverick. If I had to bet money, she was probably in love with him. Something told me she was going to stir up trouble. The million-dollar question was, how much?

CHAPTER 16
MAVERICK

My date was waiting for me in the lounge, wearing a red, snug-hugging top and another pair of black pants. The woman sure liked the color red, probably because it drew everyone's eyes to her perfect body like a siren. My eyes glanced around in irritation, hoping no one else noticed her sitting at the bar top by herself.

I raked a hand through my hair, wondering how I never saw her as anything other than my sister's best friend. I wasn't possessive. The only time I got territorial was when I was on the field. But looking over every inch of her was like looking through a totally different lens, and I really liked what was in front of me.

Her deep red lips were pursed in concentration as her fingers flew across her keyboard. She was completely unaware of me sneaking up on her.

I slanted my head to see what was so interesting on her phone. "I should have known you'd be checking your email."

"Jesus." She gasped and almost dropped the phone into her lap. That little sound was all wrong with what I was thinking because memories of our night together began to pile up in my head. And those thoughts couldn't have come at a more inconvenient time because there wasn't a damn thing I could do about them. "You scared the crap out of me."

When she finally looked up at me with those innocent blue eyes and tempting red lips, I silently told my dick to chill the hell out before things got awkward. I ran a quick hand through my hair and wondered how I was going to keep my hands off of her.

"What are you drinking?" I pointed to the glass on the coaster. It was a damn miracle I could articulate any words.

She held it up and rolled her eyes. "Tonic water with lime."

I rested my arm along the bar. "I'll have the same," I yelled to the female bartender as she passed by. I could tell Kinley wasn't all that thrilled with the no alcohol rule that pregnant women had to follow, and I couldn't blame her.

"No beer or whiskey?" She raised an eyebrow, and I noticed her makeup was more pronounced than usual. She looked like she had spent extra time preparing for tonight, which made me smile.

"Nah, I'm good for now. I might have something stronger with dinner."

"How did the meeting with your agent go?" she asked, poking her tiny straw around in her glass.

"About what I expected."

"Why would he schedule a meeting on New Year's Eve?"

I drummed my fingers on the back of her chair and looked across the bar for a few familiar faces. "Because he's Julian and doesn't know how to relax. His idea of a fun time is updating spreadsheets and drafting up contracts."

She laughed. "Sounds like a fun guy. I hope he's not married."

I nodded slowly. "They just celebrated their ten-year anniversary last month."

She grimaced. "Poor woman."

"She's just as bad."

"Okay then." She took a sip of her drink. "Thanks for sending a car to pick me up, but it was completely unnecessary."

"It's the least I could do. If there was a way to reschedule it, I would have."

As soon as my drink was placed on the bar, the maître d' came over to let me know our table was ready. I helped her off the stool and brushed my lips against her cheek.

As we moved through the restaurant, several people stopped to chitchat. Vesper Hills was an elite country club that cost a fortune to belong to. The membership was invitation-only, and the waiting list to get in was over a decade long. Our team's general manager was on the board, so a decent number of players from the Arrows organization belonged.

"Don't take this the wrong way, but I wasn't expecting to see so many young people here," Kinley whispered in my ear as we made our way to the back of the dining room.

"None taken," I whispered back. "It's one of the reasons why I joined. Plus, it's not as stuffy as some of the other country clubs around here."

The older members usually minded their business while their wives pretended not to be bored out of their minds. There was a mix of everything in this room, people of all ages, and the best part was everyone left you alone.

I caught a few curious glances as we rounded a few tables. It wasn't like I had never brought a date before. It just didn't happen all that often.

"Are you sure I'm dressed okay?" Kinley asked timidly.

"You look perfect." I pulled her chair out and stared at her red silk top that hung off her one shoulder. Her hair was down in soft waves; she was the hottest woman in the room, and she didn't even realize it.

"Thank you." She placed her napkin on her lap. "You seem pretty popular. Do you come often?"

I removed my sport coat and folded my frame into the seat across from her. "It's one of the few places I can enjoy a meal and hang out without being heckled by fans." I rolled the sleeves up on my dress shirt and placed my arms on the table. "I joined more for the golf course than I did for the country club membership, though."

"I don't remember you playing a lot of golf when you were younger. Are you any good?"

"I never had the time back then. I mostly play during the off-season. And to answer your question, I am a damn good golfer."

Her lips twitched. "I'll have to see for myself."

"You golf?"

She chuckled. "Nope, but I would be happy to follow you around in a golf cart with a glass of wine and watch you play." She took a sip of her tonic water. "After the baby is born, of course."

I leaned back in my chair and smiled at her cuteness. "How hard is it to go without alcohol?"

"Not as bad as going without caffeine. I think I'm allowed to have one cup, but I'm waiting to verify that with my doctor first."

I was just about to ask her when her doctor's appointment was when George Aarons, our head marketing manager, clasped me on the shoulder. "What's up, Mav."

"How's it going, G-Man?" I shook his hand and watched his gaze drift to my dinner companion.

"Who is this pretty little thing?" His grin was wide, and his breath reeked of Maker's Mark.

"This is Kinley. My date," I said and left it at that, but if he didn't take his eyes off her in the next second, we were going to have a problem.

"Nice to meet you." She took a sip of her drink, and I suddenly doubted bringing her here tonight.

"Pleasure's all mine, darlin'."

Her cheeks turned pink, and I pointed a glare in his direction.

"Did you need something, G-Man?" I asked, in case he forgot that I was sitting right fucking here.

"The boys and I are going to Deluce tonight. You are more than welcome to bring your lady friend."

There wasn't a chance in hell I would bring Kinley to that club. It was nothing more than an upscale drug den that drew in the wrong type of crowd. The guys seemed to favor it because the dance floor was always filled with beautiful women who would do whatever was necessary to get into the VIP section.

When I said anything, I meant anything. With tonight being the biggest party night of the year, it would be wilder and crazier than usual. It wasn't the type of establishment you brought a woman like Kinley to unless you were asking for trouble.

"We're good." I picked up the menu, hoping he would get the hint and move along. "Thanks for the invite."

He gave me a nod and shot Kinley a wink, which pissed me off. "It's New Year's Eve, we have the blue room secured, it'll be a good time."

"We've got plans tonight, so the answer is still no," I said through gritted teeth. I wanted to spend my time getting to know Kinley, not at some club, getting shit-faced and fielding off half-dressed women.

He chuckled. "All right, dude. Enjoy your night."

Kinley's eyebrows dipped down as he walked away. "You know I wouldn't mind if you went out with your friends later. He's right. It's New Year's Eve. You should be out having fun."

"I'm right where I want to be." I flipped the menu over to see the specials. "Do you know what you want to order?"

Our eyes met; if I wasn't mistaken, she looked relieved. "Everything sounds delicious. What do you recommend?"

"You can't go wrong with anything. I've never had a bad meal here."

Kinley was relaxed while we waited for our food to arrive, and I spent that time hanging on to her every word and silently trying to figure out what made her tick. We kept the conversation light, sticking to easy topics that didn't mean anything. All the while, questions and thoughts started to tangle up in my head. We seemed to be tiptoeing around this invisible line in the sand.

She was leaving in two days, and the realization that I didn't want her to go had me shifting in my seat.

"So, what are these mysterious plans you have for us later?" she asked, pulling me from my thoughts.

I kept my face straight as she eyed me from across the table. "I thought we'd go party it up at the big Peach Drop at the Underground. They're expecting a huge crowd tonight."

"Ha-ha, very funny." She picked at a tomato on her plate. "If that's the case, I might have to go home and change my shoes. Not sure if I'll be able to run with a stampede of people in these heels."

The annual Peach Drop was a yearly event equivalent to New Year's Eve in Times Square. There were lots of people, drunk people, crazy people, who didn't mind getting crushed to death while watching the damn Peach descend from the tower into the Underground.

My lips quirked because she would be doing a bit of running tonight, but nothing she wouldn't be able to do in her bare feet.

"You really don't like surprises, do you?"

She had been texting me all day, trying to get me to spill the beans. She tried to bribe me, blackmail me, and even threatened to cancel dinner if I didn't give her a hint. I called her bluff, and she didn't like that very much.

"Not even a little. Do you remember what happened when Rylee tried to surprise me for my fifteenth birthday?"

"How could I forget."

My sister was six months older than Kinley. So, for Kinley's birthday, Rylee thought it would be fun to let her friend practice driving in the high school parking lot. The only problem was that Kinley drove alongside a lamppost and scratched the entire side of my mom's Dodge Caravan. My parents were livid. Not at Kinley, but at Rylee. I cringed at the memory. My dad didn't raise his voice often, so when he did, you remembered it.

"Yeah." She took a sip of her water. "I still have PTSD every time I get behind the wheel of a car. Thank God for public transportation in Manhattan because I don't think I'd be able to handle driving every day." She sighed and gave me a pointed look. "Which, by the way, is your fault."

"My fault?" I said in between bites of my food. "That's news to me. I wasn't even in the car with you."

Her face turned the same color red as her top. "You're right, you weren't in the car. You were on the football field, running around without a shirt on. I was too busy looking at you and not at the street."

I leaned forward and decided to play with her a little bit. "There must have been some pretty dirty thoughts going through your fifteen-year-old head to distract you like that."

She snorted. "Like I would ever tell you."

"You know"—my thumb swiped along my bottom lip—"if you want to take a little ride out to Henninger High, I can make all your teenage fantasies come true."

"Sorry to break the news to you, buddy, but you missed your chance."

"Nonsense."

She looked across the restaurant and lowered her voice. "Considering it's too late for you to take my virginity in the back seat of your Honda or let me give you a blow job underneath the bleachers, I'd say you're out of luck."

I adjusted myself and leaned in closer. Her smell was

intoxicating, and we were playing a very dangerous game. "I'm pretty sure I can find us a Honda by the time we're finished with dinner. And for your information, I happen to know the perfect spot underneath the high school bleachers."

Her head fell back in laughter. "I'm sure you do." She stopped laughing, and her eyes filled with mirth. "But I have to say, I already found the perfect spot underneath the bleachers after my junior prom."

I crossed my arms, no longer finding this game fun. "With who?"

"Wouldn't you like to know?" She winked, and I narrowed my eyes.

"You're fucking with me right now, aren't you?"

She lifted a shoulder. "Maybe."

I picked up my fork and pointed it at her. "That. Wasn't. Funny."

She laughed, and we fell into a comfortable silence. I noticed she'd barely touched her risotto but had been eyeing my steak and twice-baked potato with hungry eyes throughout the meal.

"Would you like a bite?" I asked, holding a piece out for her to grab.

"I'm fine." She dropped her fork and averted her eyes.

"Kinley, why aren't you eating your meal?"

"Maybe I'm not hungry," she said, but it lacked conviction. There was no way that flimsy salad filled her up.

"I'm not buying it." I moved the candle to the side to see her face better. "From what I can remember, which I know isn't much, you love a good filet."

"People change, Maverick. I'm not a young teenager anymore that can eat whatever she wants. Especially, since I'm already planning on being as big as a house in a few months."

My fork fell from my hand and clattered onto my plate. "Kinley, you don't need to preach to me about healthy eating.

If I want to play football and make money, I need to stay fit, but there is nothing wrong with eating a juicy steak or enjoying a bowl of pesto risotto every once in a while. And last time I checked, you had an office job that doesn't require you to follow a strict diet."

She puffed out a breath. "Like I've told you, I've seen your social media pictures."

I leaned back in my seat and narrowed my eyes into slits. "I don't think I like where this conversation is going?"

"The women you're seen with look like they eat celery for breakfast, lunch, and dinner. It won't be long before someone finds out about me. You must read the comments online and know how vicious people can be when they are behind a keyboard."

"First off, there is nothing wrong with the way you look. Not now, not ever. Second, you're carrying my kid. I don't care how big your stomach gets. By the way, I am a big guy so there is a good chance the kid will be big. The bigger, the better."

She kicked my leg under the table. Unfortunately, it wasn't the kind of foot foreplay I was hoping for. "Will you stop saying the word big."

"Babe, listen to me." Her eyes widened at the endearment. It slipped out, but I wasn't in a hurry to take it back. "I can't promise that there won't be media ready to attack. That's a downfall to the business. It sucks. I can, however, guarantee that if anyone targets you in any way, I will handle it, and it won't be pretty." I reached across the table, grabbed her plate, and swapped it with mine. "Now, quit worrying about shit that doesn't matter and eat the damn steak. It's your last meal of the year."

She glared at me, but it was a playful glare—I think.

She picked up a piece of tenderloin and started chewing away. "Now, this will be worth the apple I'll have for breakfast tomorrow." She moaned, and I turned my head to make sure no one else heard it because that sound belonged to me.

————

"I can't believe you did all this," Kinley said, her eyes landing on the table I had my housekeeper set up while we were on our date. "You really are trying to get me fat, aren't you?"

"You burned a few calories tonight. You earned that blueberry cheesecake."

"I still can't believe you scheduled a private tour at the College Football Hall of Fame." She licked her lips while studying all the desserts taking up space on the table. She looked like she was debating which one to try first. There was tiramisu, red velvet cake, a fruit tart, and blueberry cheesecake.

I swiped my finger through the heaping of whipped cream. "You have the VIP All-Access pass to prove it," I said, pointing to the lanyard around her neck.

She slipped off her shoes and did a little dance. "And don't forget, I completed the forty-yard dash."

I laughed. "My coach would be impressed. Maybe you should consider trying out for the team."

Kinley and I spent two hours exploring all the interactive games. She timed me on how fast I could run, and I challenged her on how high she could jump. She pretended to interview me, and for the first time, I got to say whatever the hell I wanted without worrying about getting my ass chewed out. She got to kick a field goal, and I got to walk her through my favorite section, where I was the virtual quarterback, throwing passes to my receivers. She accused me of being a show-off, but I'd say she had a great time with how hard she laughed.

I walked up and snaked my hands around her. "Speaking of impressed, are you amazed by my talents yet?"

She smoothed her hand over mine that was resting along her stomach. "Maverick, you don't need to take me to a museum that has a display of your signed helmet and championship jersey. While I think it's great that they recognize your accomplishments," she let out a slow breath and turned around in my arms, "the things that impress me the most are how you lead your team, by setting good examples. You treat your friends with kindness and take care of your family. It's your actions off the field that impress me more than any trophy you could win."

Everything I always wanted but convinced myself I'd never find was standing right in front of me. This woman didn't care how much money I banked, and the fame that attracted most people didn't even faze her. Kinley was perfection in every way. From her spunky personality to her witty sense of humor. Sure, she was beautiful, but she was also kind and caring, and she brought out a side to me that not many people got to see. All those things that went unnoticed in my younger years could be felt with a force that scared me because Kinley Roberts slipped through the cracks and landed in a place where no one had ever been. And after spending the last two weeks with her, I felt everything, and I wasn't sure how I would let her get on that plane tomorrow.

"I want to kiss you after that little speech," I said, noticing her lip gloss was faded, yet I still had the sudden urge to pull her mouth to mine.

"Really?" Her mouth parted open with a sigh. "What kind of kiss?"

"More than just a peck."

I'd gotten a taste here and there, but if I didn't satisfy this need soon, I feared I'd lose my damn mind.

"You mean with tongue." She blinked those blue eyes at me, trying to act innocent, but there was nothing pure with how her face heated. And the thoughts spinning through my head were downright sinful.

"Lots of tongue," I explained. I was two seconds away from bending her over my dining room table and showing her all the things we could do with my talented tongue.

"Then what are you waiting for?" Her smile turned into a full-blown grin.

Thank God she was going to put me out of my misery.

In my next breath, my mouth was against hers. My tongue plunged inside because I was too damn restless to take it slow. Hunger, like I had never felt before, was spinning out of control. My body hummed with an intensity that was so strong I couldn't push it aside any longer.

I wanted everything. Her touch, her smile, her laugh; I wanted it all.

My lips branded hers in a bruising kiss; her taste sent a shot of pleasure through every cell in my body. Strong fingernails trailed down my back, sending my head spinning out of control. Unable to stop myself, I lifted her and folded her legs around my waist. I almost came out of my skin when she rocked her center against mine.

On wobbly legs, I carried her over to the wall of windows, where a burst of fireworks exploded in the sky. All the plans I had for tonight were turned to dust. The only thought in my head was how quickly I could burrow myself inside her. The dessert spread I had delivered would be there when we finished. I had something much better to feast on and a hell of a lot more satisfying.

I started to slow the kiss, but her hands went to my scalp and held me in place. "Don't you dare stop," she hissed against my mouth.

"Not a fucking chance." I breathed against her lips.

The entire world could have burned down around us, but I was too busy devouring her lips to care.

All over, one little speech that turned me inside out.

My fingers were clumsy as I reached up her shirt to unhook her bra. Her hands fumbled with the button on my pants. My memory of how good she felt that night came roaring back. My length was throbbing against her center, and I needed to get our damn clothes off.

"Maverick," she rasped out.

"Tell me what you want."

"I want you inside me. Now."

CHAPTER 17

KINLEY

I leaned on my elbows, watching him pull the hem of his shirt over his head. I could never get sick of staring at the view in front of me. The man was gifted beyond reason. The urge to slide my palms along those taut muscles seemed to grow with each breath.

I quickly stripped off my clothes and threw them on the floor. Once I was completely bare, I expected to feel self-conscious, but with how he gazed at me, I'd never felt more beautiful in my life.

Instead of crawling over the top of me like I wanted him to, he just stood there and gazed at me for a minute.

"Why are you all the way over there?" I asked when he wasn't closing the gap between us. It was a miracle I could even form a coherent sentence.

His chest rose and fell in heavy breaths. He looked tortured. He looked beautiful. He looked like he was on the verge of losing control.

"I'm giving myself a minute because I know once I touch you, I won't be able to stop."

"Sounds like a solid plan to me." I darted my tongue out to lick my lips. "Maybe we should get started."

I wasn't sure where this confidence came from, but he seemed to like it.

His eyes darted down to where I lay completely naked on his couch. His expression looked pained while my body hummed with anticipation. He displayed a level of discipline that I'm not sure many men could. "Tell me exactly what you need so I can give it to you."

"I need you to touch me." I was afraid if he didn't, I would do something to embarrass myself. I was barely hanging on by a thread, and he hadn't laid a hand on me yet.

He clenched his fists at his side. "I need you to tell me if something is too much. I don't want to hurt you." He swallowed. "Or the baby."

"The baby and I will be fine. Now please get over here and make love to me."

In two quick strides, he ate up the distance between us. I leaned forward on the couch and met him halfway. His knees landed on the cushion, and I wrapped my hands along his strong shoulders, needing him to come closer. He kissed me deeply, with a hunger like I'd never felt before. Unlike the last time we were together, this felt different.

There was desperation in his touch as his hands caressed my skin. I could sense his control snapping at how my body responded to him. He took a nipple into his mouth and ran his tongue along the tip. I moaned and dropped my head back, allowing the sensation to take over. It felt like my skin was on fire. Every lick was hot and searing. He took his time, scraping his bearded chin across my chest. He was way too good at this, and I was pretty sure I could come from his mouth alone.

I slid my hands down his thighs, feeling those strong muscles ripple under my touch. Tingles took flight as the heat of his body wrapped around mine. When I ran my fingertips along the crown, he hissed out a breath. My eager hands wrapped around his shaft and squeezed.

"Christ, Kinley." His Adam's apple bobbed. "Spread your legs."

I did as I was told, and he shoved a finger in deep. My back arched off the cushions when he dropped his face to my clit. He sucked and licked, withdrawing every ounce of pleasure my body had. My cries filled the room every time he reached that bundle of nerves that set me off.

My hands gripped his hair and pushed his face tighter against my sex. Every touch made my body hum louder with pleasure. A part of me wanted to feel the relief of the orgasm, and the other wanted to draw this out for as long as possible. Everything in me tightened when he found that spot that brought me to the edge. He dragged his tongue roughly along my center as wave after wave started to wash through me. His name was on my lips as I crashed over the edge.

My body went limp as he took his time, kissing along my hips and briefly resting his head against my stomach. My fingers threaded through his hair, and I found myself memorizing the way his face relaxed right before his eyes grew intense. Every emotion, every touch, was heightened.

He settled his weight over the top of me and brushed the hair out of my eyes. "Did you enjoy the warmup?"

"I did." My smile was lazy as I wrapped my legs along his back. "Now I'm ready for the grand finale."

He positioned himself at my entrance and thrust forward without warning. "Good." I cried out as he filled me completely. "Because that's the best part." My fingers clung to his shoulders as he slid out and drove in again. His hands, mouth, and movements were in all the right places. "Fuck, Kinley. No one has ever felt as good as you."

Maverick moved relentlessly, and I knew it wouldn't be long before I shattered again. He rocked his hips into me, driving deeper and faster. Just from our one night together, he remembered what I liked, and lucky for me, he fucked like he played on the field. Fast and hard. Every thrust sent me higher and higher. He never slowed. He never went easy. He kept the punishing pace, determined to make me see stars. I swirled my hips, trying to bring him to the same place he had brought me minutes ago.

He squeezed his eyes shut and dug his fingers into my skin. "Kinley, unless you want this to end in about thirty seconds, you need to stop that." I tried to move, seeing how far I could push him, but he held me still. "I swear to God, if you do that one more time, I'm going to haul you into my bedroom and tie you to my damn bed."

That sounded like a pretty damned good idea to me.

"I need it harder." I panted or moaned; I wasn't sure. All I knew was I needed more.

"I'll give you harder, but everything you're doing right now will end this before we both want it to."

I stopped squirming, and his muscles relaxed. "My God, woman, you're trying to kill me."

That was the last thing I wanted to do because I was pretty sure I was falling in love with him.

He continued sliding in and out while pressing kisses to my jaw and chin and moving down to my mouth in a soul-searing kiss.

"Maverick." His name was a plea.

"I know what you need, sweetheart." He withdrew and pushed in deeper.

I'm glad he knew because I had no idea how to express the emotion I was feeling. Happiness didn't feel like a big enough word.

Seeing our bodies connect, the way he circled his hips and held me in place like there was a chance in hell I was getting up from this couch. The way his arms flexed, the way his jaw tightened was all I could focus on.

His tongue delved between my lips in a frenzy. I lifted my hips, trying to find the friction my body craved. He withdrew slowly and drove back in again. I was afraid no matter how deeply he filled me, that ache would never be sated.

Our eyes met, and I saw the emotion play across his features. The softness flickering in his eyes was unexpected. He was a man who was used to being in control, and I would be lying if I said that didn't make me fall just a little bit more in love with him.

His movements began to quicken, and his pace was more powerful. Intimacy was never this intense. With Maverick, it was beautiful. It was perfection. It felt like a tumbling freefall. And I was utterly addicted.

One more thrust and my entire body shuddered around him. There was no other way to describe it. Maverick's eyes pinched shut, and his legs tensed. He threw his head back as a rough groan vibrated from his throat.

His body collapsed beside me, and we lay there in silence in a post-orgasmic haze. His head dropped to mine, and he wrapped his arms around me. And just like last time, there was no awkward space filling us. There was no regret. There was just contentment.

My eyes fluttered open. "I think that was better than the first time."

A soft smile played on his lips. "I guess we'll just have to keep going at it then until it's perfect."

My hand ran lazily up and down his spine. "I think we're pretty close."

"That's because I'm learning all your signs?"

"My signs?"

"Yep, I'm paying attention to every sound, every expression. It's a force of habit with my profession." He shifted me on the couch so I was on top of him. "I learn to execute every skill and position. I'm good at reading people and memorizing."

I rested my chin on his chest. "You're also pretty good with your hands, too."

"You're good for my ego." He kissed the top of my nose. "I thought about you after that night," he said into the quiet of the room. "I wanted to find you, but I had no idea who you were."

I lifted up, supporting my weight on one arm. "I'm sorry I lied to you about who I was."

He reached up, placing his palm along the back of my head. He pulled my face to his. "I understand why you did."

"Can I ask you a question?" I chewed on my bottom lip.

He turned us sideways so we were facing each other. "You can ask me anything."

I started playing with the hair on his chest. "Would you have slept with me if you knew who I was?"

It was the one question I'd asked myself a thousand times but was always too chicken to bring it up.

"Kinley, I was attracted to you since the moment I laid eyes on you in that airport terminal. When I stumbled into the bar later that night, I knew it was fate. It wouldn't have mattered to me. I wanted you. It was as simple as that. If anything, we could have been doing this sooner because I would have known how to find you." He played with my hair. "Is that what you've been worried about?"

"Yes," I answered honestly. There was no point in lying or playing games at this point.

He smiled softly. "You don't have to wonder about anything anymore. This changes everything." My heart skipped a beat at his words. "I don't know exactly what yet, but I know I don't want to be with anyone else. I want to see where this leads."

I just stared across the room, feeling caught off guard. We needed to have a serious conversation. We couldn't keep putting it off. If we were smart, we would get it done and out of the way instead of worrying about applying labels and complications.

We were both quiet, and I thought he had fallen asleep until he said, "I'm scared too, you know."

My body went still. "About what?"

His palm slid along my side. "Of getting hurt."

"You think I would hurt you?" I searched his face to see if he was serious.

He brought me closer to his chest. "Not intentionally, but I'm developing feelings for you. I might not be an expert on relationships, but I know that they take work. My biggest fear is that I'll do something to piss you off and you'll realize I'm not worth it."

I reached for the blanket off the back of the couch and wrapped it around us. "I can assure you that there will never come a day where you won't be worth it. Don't forget, I'm the girl who crushed on you at fourteen. You are the man I compared every relationship with. You're the reason they all came up short. I know it sounds silly because I was so young at the time, but you were always special to me."

He sighed heavily. "That's just it. I'm afraid you've built me up in your head and put me on this pedestal. And I'm scared to death that I will disappoint you and it will be a long fall to the bottom."

I've never seen this side of him. In fact, I was sure not many people have. This was the real Maverick. Not the playful jock he pretended to be.

A spark of protectiveness bloomed in my chest. It made me want to wrap him up and shield him from the outside world. There wasn't a doubt in my mind that I wouldn't do anything for him. And as I looked into his eyes for a long moment, I knew he would do the same for me.

I guess this was what love felt like.

CHAPTER 18

MAVERICK

Waking up alone for the past seven days has been depressing. That's how long it's been since I've seen her. I have yet to have a minute to spare between team meetings, reviewing film, physical therapy, and a few PR obligations.

So, as I stood outside Kinley's door, my palms were sweating, and my heart beat like a drum in my chest. I've gone out of my mind missing her and panicking that I wouldn't be able to make her doctor's appointment tomorrow.

Realizing I couldn't stand here like a pussy forever, I knocked on her door. I heard the click of the lock, and the door swung open. Jesus, she took my breath away. One look at her and my insides turned soft.

"Maverick?" She blinked, and before I could catch my breath, she lunged forward, and I caught her with ease. The force of her jump had her blond hair falling into her face. I pushed it back slowly as her arms went around my neck. "I thought you were flying in tomorrow morning?"

"My meeting got canceled today, so I hopped on an earlier flight," I managed to answer between breaths. I lifted her up and curled my hands under her ass.

"Lucky me." She wrapped her legs around my waist and her ankles locked around my back.

"Now, kiss me, woman. It's been too long."

Kinley didn't need to be told twice. She pulled my mouth to hers for a hard kiss. The taste of her and the feeling of her in my arms brought me a sense of peace that I never knew I needed. I didn't know what I ever did on this earth to deserve her, but I would do everything in my power not to screw this up.

"Are you still staying until Sunday?"

I grimaced. "Actually, I have to be back Saturday night."

To say Coach wasn't happy that I took a couple of days off during playoff season was an understatement. If I weren't on injured reserve status, I wouldn't have a chance in hell of pulling this trip off. I had to meet with him privately and the team owners to explain my situation. I had less than forty-eight hours before I had to be back.

"That's only like a day and a half." She buried her face in my neck. At that moment, I was tempted to say fuck the twenty-five-million-dollar contract. She would be worth every last cent I had to forfeit.

"I'm sorry. I had to pull a lot of strings to get the time off," I explained, hoping she would understand how important it was for me to be here.

"I get it. Really, I do." She pulled back and ran her fingers along my scruffy jaw. "I just wish we had more time."

"Me too, sweetheart," I said, giving her one last kiss on the lips. I liked being able to kiss her whenever I wanted to. It's only been a week, but in my opinion, it was a week too long.

"You've got to be freezing." She pulled on my arm and dragged me into her apartment. "It's cold outside."

If you asked me, it was colder than death out there. Why people chose to live here, I would never understand. I dropped my bag to the floor and glanced around. This was my first time here, and nothing like I expected. It was a living room/kitchen combined with a bedroom off to the side and a bathroom next to it. A door in the middle of the room looked like it opened to a tiny patio. There was a small gray couch facing a wall holding a small flat-screen TV and a matching recliner with a gray and white blanket folded along the back.

The floors were painted dark wood, and the white walls were covered with all that Peace, Love, and Faith shit that women seemed to go crazy over. Scented candles were scattered around, and a writing desk was nestled in the corner.

Kinley took my hand and led me to her bedroom. "I know it's small, but you can put your bag on the bench and hang your coat up in the closet." She motioned to where a small wooden bench sat underneath a windowsill. "I was about to make dinner. Are you hungry?"

"Starving." And not just for food but for her kisses, her touch, and her smile. I'd missed her and our conversations, and I'd gone too long without sleeping next to her.

She took my hand in hers and led me into the kitchen. My eyes darted around as she whipped something up for dinner. The apartment was definitely small, but she made it a home, which was important.

She placed a vegetable panini on the table and sat down.

I took a bite and moaned out loud. "This is delicious," I commented in between bites.

"Thanks. I hate eating out all the time, so I try to keep my weeknight meals healthy and simple. I get the ciabatta bread from a local bakery and it's just pesto, mozzarella, sun-dried tomatoes, basil, and spinach."

"It's heaven is what it is." I smiled in satisfaction.

"If you like the sandwich, you're going to love the soup I'm making tomorrow. I stopped at the grocery store after work so we would have food to eat this weekend."

"Oh, yeah?" I lifted my eyebrow.

"Yes, I wanted to prove to you that I could cook." She

smiled, and I refrained from telling her that I didn't care if we ate peanut butter and jelly sandwiches as long as we got to spend the next day and a half together. That's all I needed. "So tomorrow, I am making a pot of homemade Italian Wedding Soup."

"You're never gonna get me to leave."

She laughed from across the table, and all I thought about was she was too far away. She must have read my mind because she reached for my hand. "In case you couldn't tell by my enthusiastic greeting at the door, I'm not in a hurry to have you leave any time soon."

The bracelet on her wrist caught my attention. "You're wearing it?" I said, staring at the bracelet I gave her for Christmas.

"Of course I am." She looked down at the charm bracelet. I couldn't tell if she wore it because she loved it or simply because I gave it to her. "The only time I take it off is when I shower."

Maybe it was a little bit of both.

After finishing our dinner, Kinley went to take a shower and change.

I was standing at the sink, rinsing off a dish when a knock sounded at the door. The building she lived in didn't have security, and it made me uncomfortable knowing she was always here alone.

Whoever it was, was getting impatient because they knocked harder.

I walked over and swung open the door. A dude who looked like he could pass for a Ken doll stood on the other side. "Can I help you?"

He sized me up, which was humorous because I had fifty pounds of muscle on him and, if my guess was accurate, a foot in height.

"Where's Kinley?" he asked with a hard edge to his voice that I didn't like.

I frowned. Whoever this guy was, he wasn't making a great first impression.

Kinley came strolling out of her bedroom. "Who is at the door?" My eyes caught on the thin top she wore with her nipples poking out. "Oh, hi Chad." She adjusted the towel on her head and smiled.

So, this was the friend? He looked exactly as I pictured him too—blond hair, blue eyes, thin, and dressed like he just walked out of Brooks Brothers.

He stuffed his hand in the front pockets of his pleated Dockers. "What's going on, Kin? Who is this guy?"

Kin? What a dumb nickname.

"I'm sorry." She moved to stand between us. "This is Maverick, my…"

"Boyfriend." I held one hand out and hooked the other around her waist.

Kinley's eyes shot to mine as I moved her in closer. We hadn't talked about what we were, but it was past time we had a label.

Her little buddy pressed his lips together as if he were trying to hold back on asking a million questions. He rocked back on his heels, trying to hide his disappointment. "I didn't know you were seeing anyone?"

The hurt in his voice didn't go unnoticed. Friend, my ass. The way he looked at her had me on edge. It seemed that this visit came at the perfect time. I knew she wasn't ready to announce our relationship to the world, but he was her friend, right? And when I went back to Georgia, I wanted this guy to know she belonged to me.

Kinley seemed to snap out of whatever trance she was in. "Yeah, it's new." She shot me a dirty look. Guess she didn't like being pissed on. "I was going to tell you. I've just been so busy with work, trying to make up for the time I took off, I haven't had a minute to spare."

The guy glared down at my hand resting on her hip. He

looked like he wanted to break every one of my fingers. "I guess this explains why we haven't talked since I took you to my company's Christmas party."

My body went stiff, and I focused on holding on to my restraint. "Yeah, that's my fault," I said. "She flew to Atlanta and spent the week with me during the holidays. Now I'm here to return the favor," I explained, leaving out our doctor's appointment tomorrow.

I wasn't sure if she had told him about the baby yet, but I was smart enough not to bring it up.

The guy furrowed his brows and snapped his fingers. "Wait a minute. You're Maverick Cross. I didn't put two and two together until you just said that."

"Are you a fan?"

Kinley snorted. "No, the only sport he watches is golf." They both shared a little laugh, like it was an inside joke. I didn't like that. She stepped back and walked toward the door like she was about to close it. "Maverick and I were just about to watch a movie. Would you like to join us?"

Oh, hell no.

"Kinley." I stepped in her direction. "I'm sure he has other things to do." My eyes met hers from across the room. "Your friend doesn't want to sit here and be a third wheel. Let him go out and have some fun, am I right, man?"

He rubbed the back of his neck in frustration. "Yeah, text me when you're free. We can either grab dinner one night during the week or do something next weekend."

I was seriously considering calling Julian and telling him to find a way to trade me to New York.

"That would be great." She kept her eyes on me.

Shit! I raked a hand through my hair. She looked pissed.

When he walked up and planted a kiss on her cheek, I had reached my limit and was ready to rip his face off. But I had already overstepped enough, and I had a feeling I was going to get a good talking to when we were alone.

"Was that necessary?" She slammed the door and marched over to me.

It looked like I was right.

"I needed to set him straight." I hated knowing that he was right across the hall from her. He was close. Too close. And I didn't care what she thought. The guy was in love with her. She just didn't see it.

She parked her hands on her hips. "He's my friend!"

"I was just trying to set some boundaries," I tried to explain. "I don't want to be eight hundred miles away and worry about him trying to get in your pants."

Her lip curled. "Yes, let's talk about boundaries." She clapped her hands a little too loudly, and I flinched. "Number one." She held up her finger. "You have no control over who I'm friends with or how I choose to spend my time with them." She started pacing and held up another finger. "And two, you don't get to be jealous when you've got your own *friend* to worry about." She raised her eyebrow in defiance. We both knew she was referring to Della. "And last," she held her third finger up in my face, "you need to trust me, and I need to trust you, or this won't work."

I blew out a heavy breath and hung my head. "You're right. I'm sorry. I'm not trying to make your life more complicated; I just don't like the idea of some other guy spending time with you when I'm not around."

"There is no reason to be jealous of Chad."

"I know." I rubbed a hand over my face. "This is all new to me, and I admit I could have handled it better."

The relief in her eyes made me feel guilty for acting like such a moron.

"You realize," she took slow, deliberate steps toward me, "we just had our first fight."

I grinned as she got closer. "I guess we did."

Her eyes were sparkling. "I also just found out I have a boyfriend."

I hauled her up against my chest. "I probably should have asked you first, huh?"

She shrugged her shoulders. "Probably."

I pushed her wet hair off her shoulder and held her face in my hands. "Kinley Roberts, will you be my girlfriend?"

Her eyes went soft. "I've been waiting fifteen years for you to ask me that question."

I brushed my thumb over her lips. "I'm sorry for being so slow to catch on. I promise to make up for all the time we lost."

She slipped her hands along my neck and stared up at me. "I'm going to hold you to that."

I had no doubt that she would.

My mouth hovered over hers. "Now that we got that out of the way. Can we have make-up sex now?"

She ran her fingers across my stubbled chin. "What about the movie?"

"Fuck the movie." I threw her over my shoulder and headed toward her bedroom. "I'd rather fuck my girlfriend instead."

CHAPTER 19

KINLEY

WHEN MAVERICK CALLED AHEAD AND ASKED IF MY DOCTOR'S office had a separate waiting room that would grant us some privacy, I thought it was overkill. But then, once he explained how it would look if someone recognized him and how quickly a story could leak, I was glad he did.

The receptionist met us at a private entrance and led me straight to an exam room. She handed me a clipboard filled with paperwork to fill out and told us the doctor would be in shortly. Maverick sat in the corner, reading through a magazine on the table, when a nurse in pink scrubs poked her head into the room.

"Hi, I'm Becky." The bubbly blonde smiled as she walked over to the scale. "I need to get your weight and ask you a few questions."

"Turn around," I told Maverick, because he didn't need to know my weight. Hell, I wasn't sure if I even wanted to see the number on the scale.

"You are unbelievable," he grumbled and rolled his eyes.

I waited until he was facing the wall before stepping on the scale. The nurse made small talk while she checked my vitals and reviewed the paperwork. Every time Maverick would crack a smile and tell a silly joke, she would blush and giggle like a teenage schoolgirl. I wouldn't say she was flirting, but I would bet if he asked for her number, she would have gladly handed it over.

"Okay." She stood from the rolling stool. "I will need you to put this gown on, keep it open in the front and ensure the sheet is covering the lower half of your body. Dr. Granger will be in shortly."

While I was undressing, Maverick walked over to the stirrups and studied them. "This is my first time seeing these up close."

He started flipping them around, and I swatted his hand away. "They aren't toys."

He smirked when I laid down on the exam table. "You sure? Because I bet we could have some fun with these."

He lifted the sheet and poked his head underneath. "I can see everything from here."

I pulled on the sheet and wrapped myself up like a burrito. "I swear to God, if you ask to play doctor, I'm kicking you out."

He laughed. "I think I'm in the wrong profession."

"I think I regret bringing you here."

Thankfully, the doctor knocked on the door. I knew he was trying to take the edge off, but no matter how hard he tried, I was still ready to come out of my skin. We would hear the baby's heartbeat for the first time, which made this pregnancy feel real.

"How are you feeling, Kinley?" Dr. Granger asked as he was reviewing my chart. He was an older man with a white mustache that matched his hair, thick black glasses, and a kind smile. This was my first time meeting him. The doctor I saw on my yearly checkups had switched to another practice.

"I'm doing well."

"No cramping or bleeding?"

I shook my head no.

"That's great." He walked over to the sink, washed his hands, and pulled the rolling stool up to the exam table. "Are you the father?" he asked Maverick.

"Yeah." He swallowed deeply. All humor from earlier was gone. He seemed nervous, so I reached for his hand. His palm was warm and clammy, confirming my suspicions.

"I'm going to start with a pelvic exam and then we will check for a heartbeat. It says on the chart that you are only around six weeks."

"Yes. Will we be able to hear the heartbeat today?"

"We usually wait until closer to ten weeks, but we should be able to detect something today." He smiled and slid a pair of latex gloves over his hands. "Now I need you to relax and lean back while I do a quick exam."

He pressed down on my stomach, and my eyes fluttered closed. Every time I would wince in discomfort, Maverick would squeeze my hand. I inhaled and exhaled whenever I felt a little bit of slight pressure. I opened my eyes and focused on the man at my side. It should have felt strange having him here; instead, it was calming. I was glad he flew into town for this appointment because I needed him more than I realized.

Once Dr. Granger finished, he removed his gloves and washed his hands again. "You're doing great, kid." He winked as he pulled the monitor closer to his stool and started clicking away at buttons. Maverick seemed to study his every move as he explained that this would be a transvaginal ultrasound and applied what looked like a condom and gel to the wand and inserted it inside me. Every few seconds, he would pause and click a few buttons on the monitor. "I'm just taking a few measurements," he said, seeming completely at ease. Then a whooshing sound filled the room.

Knowing I was pregnant was one thing, but this feeling was on a whole other level. It was as if reality had finally come knocking on my door. I glanced at Maverick; his eyes were glued to the screen as if it were the most fascinating thing he'd ever seen.

"That's a good, strong heartbeat," the doctor said, withdrawing the wand. "Based on the measurements, I'm estimating your due date to be at the end of August."

Maverick's head snapped up in a panic. "August?" he asked for clarification. It didn't take a rocket scientist to know why he was so nervous. Training camp started in July, and the season wouldn't be over until February. I would be completely on my own, which was fine. I reminded myself.

"Yes, in the meantime, the nurse will give you some follow-up paperwork and make sure you schedule your next appointment," he said, looking at me.

"Do either of you have any questions?"

We both shook our heads, still mulling over my projected due date.

As soon as he left, Maverick pulled me up into a sitting position.

He rubbed my back in a few comforting strokes. "I'm glad I didn't miss that."

He seemed lost in his own head. This was a lot to take in for both of us. As much as I wanted to offer him comforting words and ease his worry, I was struggling with my own emotions.

"It's going to be okay." I put on a brave face and tried to reassure him. "We'll find a way to make it work."

His lips flattened into a thin line, and he leaned in. "I can tell you're freaking out," he whispered, so only I could hear him. "So, stop trying to make me feel better. I'm a big boy. I'm more worried about you."

"I still feel bad because this will be a huge change, and you…"

"Do not finish that sentence. I was there. I participated, and I have no regrets." He entwined our fingers, brought my hand to his mouth, and kissed my knuckles. "You've given me a priceless gift, so thank you."

My heart melted into a puddle at the softness in his eyes.

As much as I kept trying to stop myself from falling in love with him, it was becoming quite the undertaking. My head was trying to stay on track, but my heart was proceeding at full speed. The crash was inevitable, so the only thing I could do was prepare for the landing.

"Would you like a picture?" the nurse asked, looking between us. I forgot she was even in the room.

"Yes," Maverick rushed out. She smiled and printed out two images. Maverick stared at his for a long minute before clearing his throat and stuffing it in his wallet.

The nurse handed me a card. "I'll give you two a minute alone. Here is your next follow-up. I sent a prescription to your pharmacy for some anti-nausea medicine in case you need it. It would be best if you also started taking prenatal vitamins ASAP. The receptionist will have a packet for you to take home and read over."

She gave us a polite smile and walked out of the room.

"Are you sure you're okay?" I asked as he handed me my clothes to get dressed.

He ran a hand over the top of his head. "Yeah, this all just seems real now."

"It does," I said softly and rubbed a hand over my stomach. "It was a beautiful sound. How are you feeling about all this?"

He stepped between my legs and rested his chin on my head. "Nervous. Excited." He swallowed as I gave him a minute to process his feelings. "I always thought there was no greater feeling than carrying a football down the field, but nothing beats watching you carry my child."

I reached up, placed both hands on his arms, and stared into his eyes. "I feel just as emotional as you do. The morning sickness and fatigue, is all worth it. I could listen to that heartbeat all day long."

He was quiet for a moment. "How can I love someone I've never even met yet?"

"I think it's normal to feel that way. I feel connected to this baby, too." I spread my hands along the space where our baby was growing.

He leaned down and kissed my stomach. "Thank you." His head lifted, and I knew I'd never forget the look of love and gratitude in his eyes at that moment.

He stood and drew my body into his. His strong hands framed my face, and he leaned in and kissed me. Everything else faded away, except us and the life growing between us.

CHAPTER 20

KINLEY

"Other than Times Square, did you have fun today?" I asked, taking a sip of my hot chocolate as we walked down Forty-Second Street. We spent most of the day wandering in the souvenir shops and stopped to watch the ice skaters in Rockefeller Plaza.

Maverick claimed he had been to New York many times, but all those times were spent in meetings and hotels. So, we spent the day touring different parts of the city; all the while, I tried to ignore the twinge of sadness in my belly about him leaving later today.

"I don't hate Times Square," he said as we reached a cross-walk. "I'm just not a fan of crowds."

"What about the crowds that fill up the stadiums you play in?"

"That's different." We stepped off the curb and headed toward the entrance of Central Park. "I'm running on a wide-open turf. They're up in the stands."

"That makes no sense, but whatever."

"Look around you. There are people taking up every inch of sidewalk."

If I was honest, I wasn't a fan of the continuous buzzing

energy either. It was great initially, but the excitement wore off after a while. That's why I usually avoided the tourist traps. There were parts of the city I still loved, just nct the places that people came to visit.

As we got closer to Central Park, I threw my empty cup in the trash and entwined my gloved hands with his. "At least I let you skip the museums," I teased, remembering they weren't his thing.

"You won't hear any complaints from me, but you did have me nervous when you pulled me into that art gallery that you worked at in college." He smirked.

Maverick didn't believe I worked at an art gallery until the owner, Davis, ran through the lobby squealing the second he spotted me stepping off the elevator. My former boss got even more excited when he saw the handsome man next to me. And not because he was a football fan, but because my boyfriend was exactly the type of man he was attracted to.

"I think you made a good impression on Davis," I said, trying to hold in my laugh.

"Really?" he said sarcastically. "I couldn't tell."

I giggled. "Thanks for being a good sport."

He pressed his lips together. "He was harmless, only patted my ass five times."

"I must have been distracted; I only saw him do it twice."

He scowled, and it was hilarious. "Thanks for the save, by the way."

We stepped aside so a young mother with a double stroller could pass us by. There was a toddler in the front bundled up in a pink snowsuit and a little boy in the back dressed in blue. They both seemed fascinated with all the dogs getting their daily exercise.

"So," Maverick said, glancing over his shoulder one last time, "I downloaded one of the books the doctor recommended. Did you know our baby is the size of a kidney bean right now and in two more weeks, it will be the size of an apricot?"

I tried hard not to swoon over the fact that he was already reading up on the growth of the baby. "I did not know that." My hands went to my stomach. "Wonder what he will look like in twelve weeks?"

"He'll be the size of a plum or an apple. I can't remember all the different fruits. Wait a minute..." He stopped walking and raised an eyebrow. "He? Do you know something I don't?"

I shook my head. "Just intuition."

He stared at me longer than necessary, trying to figure out if I was telling the truth. Once satisfied, he resumed walking. "The doctor said we could find out at twenty weeks. Do you want to know or be surprised?"

"What do you want to do?" I asked, curious to hear which one he'd pick.

"While it would make it easier to know if it was a boy or girl, I kind of like the idea of being surprised. I feel like it would make the moment more exciting."

I never thought about it like that. There was so much about the labor and delivery part that scared me. Maybe not knowing would give me something to focus on and look forward to.

I squeezed his hand. "Then we'll wait."

He looked surprised. "Really? Just like that?"

"Absolutely." I adjusted the hat on my head. "I think it will be fun having everyone guess and make bets on what the gender will be."

He looked at me like he was seeing me differently. "You are just full of surprises. This trip has been a real eye-opener."

"Predictable is boring, right?" I teased, bumping my shoulder with his.

"Yes, I'm still trying to get over the fact that you worked at an art gallery, considering you know nothing about art."

I laughed. "It helped pay the bills. Living in this city isn't cheap, but at least I got to meet a few celebrities."

"Oh, yeah? Anyone I know?"

I smiled at a memory that popped into my head.

"Usher was a frequent customer. We bonded over the fact that we were both from Georgia. He tried for months to get me to go on a date with him."

His glove-covered hand gripped mine a little harder than necessary. "I knew I never liked that fucker. I'm going to make sure he gets shitty seats next time he comes to the stadium."

I laughed. "That's too bad because he's a huge fan of yours."

"So, you and Usher talked about me, huh?" He draped his arm along my shoulders and pulled me closer.

I leaned into him. "I might have mentioned that I knew you."

"Excuse me." A young boy approached; his eyes were filled with wonder. "Are you Maverick Cross?"

Maverick pulled his hat down on his head and adjusted the sunglasses on his nose that didn't do much to disguise him. I tried to convince him to leave the glasses behind, that they would only draw more attention, but of course he didn't listen to me.

"Are you a fan?" he asked, lifting his chin to the other three boys standing off the side.

We'd been spotted a few times, and every time he dodged questions and quickened his pace to avoid taking a selfie. This was the first time today he stopped to talk to one of his fans. Then again, this was a young kid, so he couldn't ignore him without coming across as a jerk.

"My dad was." There was no mistaking the sadness in his voice. He couldn't be older than fourteen.

"Was?" Maverick let go of my hand to give him his undivided attention.

The kid swallowed and looked away. "He died last year. He was a firefighter. He ran into a burning building and the roof collapsed. Him and my uncle Tony both died that day." He looked up at Maverick. "He was a fireman too."

My hand went to my heart. I wanted to wrap this kid up in a hug and take away all his pain. I lost my father when I was in fourth grade, so I knew firsthand how heavy that grief was.

"I'm sorry to hear that." Maverick's voice was so composed, I had no idea how he could be so unaffected. "What's your name?"

"Joey Bove."

"It's nice to meet you, Joey. Do you have a phone?" Joey nodded his head and pulled it out of his coat pocket. "I want to program your number in my phone. I'll send your number to my agent. Next time we play in New York, I'll make sure you and your friends get tickets to the game."

"For real?" he asked, whipping his head over at his friends, who looked like they weren't sure what to do with themselves.

Maverick nodded his head. "It would be an honor to have you there." He waved the group of boys over, who looked a little starstruck. "You guys want a picture with me and my buddy Joey?"

Their mouths opened and closed a few times like they were afraid to speak. Finally, one of the boys pushed the others forward. I laughed and took their phones. After snapping a few photos, Maverick made them promise to wait to post them on social media. He explained that he would have to leave if people knew where he was.

I stood off to the side and watched him in his element as he answered their questions and gave them tips on things they could do to improve their game. He also asked what school they played for so he could send some equipment and memorabilia.

"That was really sweet of you," I said as the group walked away.

He shrugged like it was no big deal. "Happens all the time."

"Don't be so modest." I looped my arm through his. "You made their day. It's obvious you love what you do."

"You know," he said as we continued our stroll through the park, "I always wondered what I would have done if I didn't play ball."

I wasn't expecting that. Football had been his entire focus, even when he was a teenager. He still partied and had fun, but he was always disciplined and worked harder than anyone else on the team. It's become such a huge part of his identity I couldn't imagine him doing anything else.

"It's normal to think that way." I squeezed his arm. "To wonder what if? But you've spent your life doing something you love."

"It started out that way, but after the first few years, the shine wore off for me. I became obsessed with money and the fact that I'd never have to worry about paying a bill." He paused as if he were reliving a memory. "When I signed my first contract, I offered to buy my parents a house, but they refused to move, so I paid off their mortgage."

"That was awfully nice of you." I sat down on a wooden bench, needing a minute to rest my feet. Not to mention, I was out of breath. I was used to walking, but the pregnancy fatigue was catching up to me.

"My dad gave me shit. He's got a lot of pride." He slid in next to me and looked across the park. "They sacrificed so much for me. The camps, the equipment, the tournaments and the travel, that stuff wasn't cheap. They took out a second mortgage on the house to pay for it all."

"I'm not surprised. I always admired how close your family was growing up."

Vinny was a postal worker, and Beth was a school secretary. They were your typical blue-collar family who raised their kids to be respectful and insisted they volunteered their free time. Maverick got stuck doing landscaping around the neighborhood, and Rylee would have to babysit or watch a neighborhood pet for free once a month. I remember Vinny saying, *you take care of your friends and neighbors because that's the right thing to do. You don't ask for money if they need help. It's called being a part of a community.*

This conversation allowed me to remember that Maverick wasn't always the legendary star quarterback that he was today. But I still always assumed he loved playing the field, both figural and literally, which brought me to my next question.

"I'm curious about something," I said, playing with my glove-covered fingers. "You grew up in a house filled with love and lots of good memories. How come you've never wanted that life for yourself? How come you've never settled down with anyone?"

"That's a complicated answer." He blew out a breath and adjusted the beanie on his head. "In the beginning, I was young and immature. I was all about having fun. As I got older, my name started to mean something. People kissed my ass. Guys that I thought were my friends would invite me to all the important parties, but never wanted to hang out one-on-one. The women I thought were interested in me just wanted to sleep with me and take pictures so they could sell them the next day."

"Jesus." I reached out and squeezed his hand. "It sounds like they forgot you're a real person."

"As long as it got them the attention they were seeking, they didn't care."

There was so much more to Maverick than people under-stood. He'd sacrificed and given up more than I ever under-stood. The fans, the lack of privacy, and the media attention all went with the lifestyle. Sure, there were perks to being a celebrity and having money, but it came at a cost that most people could never understand.

He looked down at my hand resting on his and stared at it before bringing his eyes to mine. "Tell me about the guys you've dated."

I rolled my eyes. "There are so many, it would take all night to talk about them all."

He squeezed the tip of my nose. "Cute." He lifted his eyebrow. "Now spill."

"I've only had a couple serious boyfriends. My last relationship ended last year."

"What happened?" His gaze was curious. It felt weird talking about this, but then again, I asked about his past, so it was only fair.

"Carson got a job offer in San Francisco. When he asked me to go, I knew I wasn't ready, so I broke up with him."

"What the fuck kind of name is Carson?"

"Be nice." I bumped his shoulder with mine. His question was kind of funny because he sounded a little jealous. "Carson was a nice guy; he just wasn't the one for me."

"You never regretted your decision after he moved away?" His eyes filled with curiosity, like he wanted me to tell him more, but I didn't want to spend what little time we had left talking about my ex-boyfriend.

"Nope." I patted my stomach. "Everything worked out the way it was supposed to."

A smile tugged at the corner of his lips. He seemed pleased with that answer. We walked in comfortable silence for a few minutes before I asked, "So, what's next on your bucket list?"

He looked at his watch. "Do we have time to make a snowman?"

A slow smile touched my lips. Of all the things we could possibly do in Manhattan, he wanted to do something as simple as playing in the snow.

"Your flight doesn't leave until later tonight. We have plenty of time."

The thought of him leaving dimmed my smile, and I suddenly wished we could forget the world around us. This lighthearted and fun side of him had me craving more time alone with him.

We gathered snow and rolled it into two big balls. Our attempts at making a snowman were hysterical because it was the most ridiculous thing I'd ever seen. In my defense, we weren't dressed for this type of outing. We wore jeans instead of snow pants and fleece gloves instead of mittens. Our hands were freezing, and our pants were wet, but I had never laughed so hard in my life.

"What a joke." He shook his head in laughter. "You've lived here for twelve years now and you never learned how to make a snowman?"

I stood up and wiped the snow off my pants. "Maybe if I was ten, I'd have more time to play in the snow. There is this thing called 'work' that takes up most of my time."

"Excuses, excuses," he teased.

I picked up a handful of snow when he wasn't looking, packed it into a ball, and aimed it at his face. Of course, it missed. In seconds, he was tickling me so hard that we lost balance and fell into the snow. I tried my best to wrestle my way out of his hold, but my struggle was no match for his strength. We laughed and rolled around on the snow-covered grass until I was on top of him.

His hands went to my sides, that hurt from laughing so hard. My laughter slowed down when I saw the tenderness in his eyes. The moment shifted from something fun to something much more. Maverick looked up at me. His face never looked more relaxed or at peace.

He brushed some of the snow out of my hair. "Are you okay?" His eyes trailed down to my stomach. "We didn't hurt the baby, did we?"

"The baby and I are fine." There was a flutter in my stomach that had nothing to do with the little kidney bean growing in my belly. I could tell myself whatever I wanted, but I was in love with him. Not the teenager I had a crush on, not the quarterback that everyone liked to watch on television, but the man who made me laugh and smile.

The only man to ever have my heart.

He gripped the back of my neck and gently pulled my mouth down to his. His lips were warm against my cold skin. The words I love you were on the tip of my tongue. I wanted to tell him so badly but was afraid to say it first. I wouldn't be able to handle the embarrassment if he didn't feel the same way.

The city bustled around us as we lay side by side on the snow-covered grass. He rolled over and linked our fingers together. We were cold and wet, but neither of us was in a hurry to leave. We stared at the blue sky until it was time for him to head to the airport.

The shift in our mood could be felt when we returned to my place to grab his overnight bag. He didn't even try to fight me when I insisted on riding with him to the airport. We sat in the back seat of the town car, both of us hating that we were dragging this goodbye out, but neither of us had the strength to stop it.

I was fighting back tears and trying to be strong, but the moment we reached security, I had to turn away. This was harder than I thought it would be.

We stepped back from the line, and I took a calming breath. He reached for my hand and kissed the top of my head. "We are right back at the scene of the crime."

"Yeah, but this time there's no storm to strand you here." I wrapped my arms along his waist and squeezed him tight. Between our schedules, I had no idea when we would see each other again. So, I clung to him like my life depended on it.

"Sweetheart, I'm just going back to my condo in Atlanta, I'm not going off to war."

God, I was a hormonal love-sick mess.

"I know." I squeezed my eyes shut to keep them from leaking. "I just wish you didn't have to go."

He buried his nose in my neck and inhaled. "Fuck, this is hard."

I looked up at him, feeling tears spill down my cheeks. "I'm embarrassing myself, aren't I?"

He ran his fingers through my hair. "No, but these tears aren't helping."

"I'm sorry." I was overcome with emotion and was doing a horrible job of hiding it. "You better go before you miss your flight."

His thumb traced over my brow. "I hate this."

My fingers clenched his shirt in a tight grip. "So do I, but we need to get used to this, right?"

His face morphed into something hard and determined. Realizing that this was only the beginning, my throat grew sticky with dread. I was half a second away from giving up my job, my home, and everything I worked my ass off for just so that I could be with him.

I glanced over at the TSA line and was tempted to hop on that plane with him and say the hell with all my responsibilities. Instead, I closed my eyes and concentrated on taking a couple deep breaths. The urge to scream and cry was still strong, but I held those feelings back.

Maverick brought his hand up to my stomach. "Be good for your momma, little one." He leaned his forehead against mine and kissed my lips one last time. "I'll see you soon."

He picked up his carry-on, and I felt my bottom lip tremble as I watched him walk through the pre-check line at security. By the time he disappeared, I was a sobbing mess.

CHAPTER 21

KINLEY

I'd felt guilty about keeping my relationship with Chad at arm's length. He'd been one of my closest friends for years, but things were changing in my life, and I wasn't sure where he fit anymore. Knowing that he could potentially have feelings for me made me question if we could truly stay friends.

As I stood in front of him with my nervous fingers twitching against the door, I wanted to kick myself for not anticipating this visit.

"Hey," I greeted him, glancing at the wrapped gift in his hands.

His mouth brushed along my cheek as he passed me by. It was innocent, but all I could think about was how awkward this was going to be.

"If I didn't know any better, I would have thought you were avoiding me." His eyes narrowed slightly at the Atlanta Arrows hoodie I stole from Maverick's duffel bag before he left. It was thick, comfortable, and it smelled like him. But Chad stared at my outfit with an odd look on his face.

"You look nice. Are you going somewhere?" I asked, giving him a strained smile.

He looked down at his outfit and frowned. "No, just stopping by to see you."

He was dressed in a hunter-green sweater with a pair of dark khaki pants. His hair looked gelled, his chin was freshly shaved, and his shoes looked polished. He was wearing a good amount of cologne; all these things would have gone unnoticed until now. Maybe it was my imagination, but he seemed nervous.

"I didn't know you were stopping by, or I would have ordered you some food," I hurried to say just as he spotted the takeout container on my coffee table.

He lifted an eyebrow. "Is that a corned beef on rye from Katz's Deli I spy?"

"You know it." I motioned for him to take a seat on the couch. "And the matzah ball soup."

"Damn, I can't believe you didn't call me. You really know how to hurt a guy's feelings." He eased onto the couch and set the big, red gift box on the coffee table.

I closed the door and held up my hand. "Hold on one second." I scurried into my room and grabbed his gift off the dresser.

His favorite band, The Foo Fighters, was coming to Madison Square Garden in July. I went online the day the tickets went on sale before they sold out. "I've been meaning to give this to you, but life has been crazy," I said, handing him the small gift bag holding the tickets.

He placed it in his lap and handed me mine. "Ladies first."

I sat down and grabbed the box that he was eager to have me open. Unlike when I tore through the gifts Maverick and I exchanged, I slowly unwrapped this one like it might explode in my lap. My charm bracelet jingled as I ripped off the last piece of tape.

"Is that new?" He pointed to my wrist.

"Yes, it's a gift from Maverick," I answered quietly.

"I thought you weren't a fan of jewelry."

He was right about that. Unlike most women, I wore minimal accessories. It wasn't that I disliked jewelry. I just had a bad habit of losing it. So, I kept it simple, with diamond stud earrings and an occasional necklace.

I shrugged. "I'm usually not, but I can make an exception, right?"

I smiled softly at the memory and focused on opening the box on my lap. It was wrapped in more tape than paper.

"I forgot how crazy you get with a roll of scotch tape," I teased and pulled out a big floppy sun hat and sunglasses. "Um...thanks." I looked up at my friend, feeling confused.

He laughed. "There's more."

My fingers pushed through the tissue paper and plucked out a manila envelope. I flipped open the tab and pulled out a pamphlet for an all-inclusive resort in Mexico. A lump worked its way up my throat.

"What is this?"

His smile was wide. "You and I are going to take a break from the snow and cold. I booked us a week in Cabo."

My eyes widened in surprise. "You did what?" Holy shit. Maverick was going to freak.

"I know you just took some time off, but I think a week away would do us both some good. Besides, you love the beach."

"Chad." I shook my head. "I can't go to Cabo with you."

He leaned forward, resting his elbows on his knees. "I knew you would say that, but I already paid for the trip and it's non-refundable."

He was sitting too close to me, so I reached for the water on the table to put a little distance between us. I took a sip and moved to the opposite end of the couch. I didn't want to have this conversation, but I didn't see another way out of this mess.

"Then take someone else," I said, holding on to my glass like my life depended on it.

His eyebrows drew together. "I don't want to take someone else. I barely see you anymore. Surely, you can get away for a few days. You can even bring your laptop."

"It's not that." I leaned back and stared at him. It was time to set the record straight because this conversation couldn't wait any longer.

Chad put the gift down and narrowed his eyes. "Is this about your new boyfriend? You haven't been dating him very long, and if I'm honest, he didn't make a great first impression on me. The guy acted like a douche."

"He's not a douche, he's a great guy, but I do have something to tell you." I set my glass down and folded my knees under my chest. For a moment, I held my breath, worried that if I didn't get this out now, I would lose my nerve.

I rubbed at my throat, trying to keep a straight face and not show how uneasy I felt. "I'm pregnant."

His face fell. "You're pregnant?"

"I am." My chest ached because Chad was someone important to me, and I knew this would be hard for him to accept.

He closed his eyes for a second. "It's his?"

"Yes." I didn't know how else to respond. I was afraid anything I said would upset him.

"And you think he's going to step up and be a dad? Do you honestly think he gives a shit about you?"

Shocked couldn't even come close to describing how I felt. Logically, my brain understood why he was lashing out, but my heart was having a hard time accepting it. He thought he was being a good friend and looking out for me. Instead, his remarks were testing my patience and made me angry.

"Wow!" I blinked rapidly, trying to stop myself from saying something I wouldn't be able to take back. "I didn't realize you knew him well enough to make that assumption."

His glare was hard. "I know enough about the kind of man he is."

Talk about doubling down on an already offensive comment. Chad and I had never fought like this in all the years we've been friends. I expected him to struggle with this news, but being rude and lashing out was something I wouldn't tolerate. If this was so upsetting, that was his problem, and he needed to find a way to deal with it.

"I don't understand where this hostility is coming from?"

His gaze flicked from my face to my stomach. "How can you be sure that he isn't fucking with you? I mean come on, Kinley, the guy is a pro athlete who has groupies that follow him from city to city. Guys like him sleep with anything that walks. Do you even know anything about him? What kind of life he lives? For all you know, you're not the only one he knocked up."

His sharp words sliced right through my heart, hitting their intended target. I looked for any resemblance of the kind, gentle man that I called my friend. All I saw was a man filled with hurt and anger.

"You obviously have your opinions about him. I can't change that. If you want to believe in stereotypes and gossip you read online, then maybe you should keep your thoughts to yourself. I've made a decision to raise this child with him. Maybe this relationship will work, or maybe it won't, but I'm going to try. Not because he's the father of my child, but because I want to be with him."

He looked like he wanted to argue but stopped himself when he spotted the lone tear slide down my cheek. "I'm sorry. I'm not trying to be a dick. I'm just looking out for you.
"

"I know you are," I said, deciding to cut him a little slack, even if he didn't deserve it. "That's why you're one of my best friends. I don't want this to come between us."

"You don't understand, Kinley. I always believed that in the end, it would be you and me."

"You and me?" I repeated back to him, trying to keep the panic out of my voice.

"You are the only person I've ever thought about settling down with." He paused and reached for my hand. "I've loved you as more than just a friend for years. I thought I had more time."

"More time for what?" My brain started sifting through all the years we spent together, but nothing stood out. I knew there was a chance he felt this way because Maverick and Taylor both warned me.

"For your feelings to catch up to mine."

Fuck! My eyes slid closed again. What the hell was I supposed to say to that?

When I opened my eyes, there was so much hope in his that it broke my heart. "Chad, I swear to you, I had no idea you felt this way."

He settled his elbows on his knees to face me fully. "Would it have made a difference if you knew? Does it change how you feel about me now that you do?"

There was no way to answer that without damaging our friendship.

"Chad, I don't want to hurt your feelings, but I've only seen you as a friend, and that's all you'll ever be to me." I hated hurting him, but I couldn't give him any false hope. God, I felt stupid for not seeing the signs. "I don't want the same thing that you want."

His face fell, and he buried his head in his hands. "You're telling me that you feel nothing for me?" He lifted his head and leaned forward.

When I looked at my friend, I saw comfort, security, and a lot of good memories. But I didn't see him as anything other than a friend I enjoyed spending time with. There was no spark or physical attraction on my end because those feelings were reserved for someone else.

"I'm telling you that you deserve someone who feels the same way you do, but I'm not that person, Chad. I'm sorry."

He nodded, his lips forming into a flat line. "I see."

I went to squeeze his hand again, but he flinched. "Are we okay?"

He tried to keep his face calm, but I sensed frustration raging inside. This baby was a huge inconvenience that he wasn't expecting, and my new relationship was something he never saw coming.

"No, we're not okay." He shot up from the couch and threw the gift he gave me across the room. If I didn't see the pinch of pain in his eyes, I would have picked up my glass of water and thrown it at his head for his behavior. "I'm too late, aren't I?"

"Chad, it doesn't matter if I'm with someone else or not. We were never going to be anything other than friends."

He clenched his jaw and dropped his gaze to the floor. "So, you're choosing him? He doesn't deserve you, Kinley. Not to mention, you don't belong in his world."

It hurt having my own fears repeated back to me. "That may be true, but you're wrong about one thing. I didn't choose him, my heart did."

"Your heart?" He braced his hands on his hips in irritation. "It's a little early to be using those words, don't you think?"

"No, we have a much deeper history that you don't understand but that doesn't matter."

His eyebrows lifted slowly. "What kind of history and why is this the first time I'm hearing about it?"

I shook my head slightly because I wasn't going to get into it with him. "It's a long story," I said with a slight warning and softened my voice. "What does matter is that I don't want to lose you as a friend."

He worked his jaw back and forth. "You'll never lose me, Kinley. I just feel like a major idiot and need some time to lick my wounds in peace."

"I understand." I wrung my hands in my lap. I guess that was as good as I was going to get, and that was okay because it sounded more like a pause instead of an ending. Losing him as a friend would be devastating. I already had too much change and uncertainty in my life. I didn't need to add to my already growing pile. Maybe a little distance would be good for us.

He walked toward the door and paused when his hand touched the knob. "I meant what I said. He doesn't deserve you. Hell, I'm not sure there's a man on the planet who is good enough for you. Just know that when he hurts you, I'll be waiting. My arms will always be open and waiting for you."

When the door clicked shut, I leaned against the wall and let out a slow breath. His parting words were echoing in my head.

Just know that when he hurts you, I'll be waiting.

As much as I wanted to brush off his words, there was a niggling in my gut that I couldn't ignore. I wanted to pretend that even though my relationship with Maverick was new, it was also strong and solid. But even the things that we believed were unbreakable could still destroy us in the end.

CHAPTER 22

MAVERICK

I GLANCED AT THE CALENDAR ON MY PHONE AND RUBBED MY eyes, feeling exhausted from the back-to-back meetings I had to sit through today. There was a fundraiser this Saturday that slipped my mind, and it was something I couldn't miss. Usually, I would bring a random date arranged by my publicist, but now that Kinley and I had made things official, she was the only woman I wanted on my arm.

This wasn't going to be an easy sell. Her biggest hang-up wouldn't be about the short notice but rather the media attention that would follow afterward.

I ran a hand over my stubbled jaw and decided to bite the bullet and call her.

"Hey." Her soft voice filled the line. "You've got great timing. I was just getting ready for bed and was going to call you."

I smiled. "You love hearing my voice before going to sleep, don't you?"

"I love the sound of it better when you're lying beside me," she admitted.

That was good to know because I felt the same way.

I thought about easing her into this conversation but was

afraid I'd turn into a total chickenshit if I put it off any longer. That thought made me laugh. On the field, I had no problem getting hit on my blindside and showed no fear when an opponent ran me down for a sack. I even kept my cool when players twice my size spit at me through their helmets or taunted me, saying they were going to screw my mother. Yet here I was, afraid to ask my girlfriend to accompany me to a freakin' dinner.

"Listen," I paused and stared out the window, working up the courage to ask her, "I hate to do this over the phone and I know it's last minute, but I have a charity event on Saturday. Any chance you can fly down and be my date?"

The line went silent, and I could almost hear her mind scrambling for an excuse. Was it unfair to throw this at her at the last minute? Probably, but I was sick of hiding her. I needed her more than I cared to admit. Being eight hundred miles away from her was driving me crazy.

"Maverick." She stopped and hesitated. I steeled myself for the let-down I knew was coming. "I'm sorry. I'm swamped with work. I'm still trying to play catch-up for the time I took off."

My shoulders sagged in disappointment. I knew the rejection was coming, but it still sucked to hear her say no. This was bullshit.

"Kinley, I can book you a ticket for Friday after work and have you back at your desk on Monday morning."

"Maverick, I can't. I'm sorry."

I gritted my teeth in agitation. She wasn't even trying. She could have at least taken a damn day to think it over. Pretended to be upset about telling me no. Met me halfway, somewhere in the middle. Offer a compromise. Something. Anything. Instead, all I got was a simple "I can't."

"Just be honest and admit that this has nothing to do with work."

"You're right." I could hear the anxiety in her voice, and it made me think twice about snapping at her. "I know this is completely unfair to you, I'm just not ready to go public."

My stomach twisted as the reality of our situation hit me. I kept telling myself that Kinley would eventually get there with me, but I was suddenly having doubts if she ever could.

"Kinley, I live a life that sometimes puts me in the spotlight. I can't change that. But I can do whatever I can to make sure you're protected."

"Fangirls aren't always polite."

No, they weren't. They were vultures, ready to attack at a second's notice. Some were bat-shit crazy. That's why I was so conflicted. Her fears were valid, yet I couldn't change who I was. And whether she liked it or not, the press would eventually find out. The only thing I could do was protect her to the best of my ability.

"I'll deal with it."

"What do you think will happen when they find out I'm pregnant?" Her words had my agitation building. She was being so damn stubborn. It was one of the things I admired and hated. "They'll think I trapped you. They'll paint me as a gold-digger who is looking for an NFL baby daddy."

"First off, we will spin this story in your favor. The world will fall in love with you by the time my PR team is done. And second, you're not even showing yet. No one will even know you're pregnant."

"Yet."

Jesus Christ! I needed a fucking drink. "I don't know what else I can do here. This is the world I live in." Thank God she couldn't see me because I was about to lose my shit.

"I know that, but once the relationship is out there, it's done. I just want a little more time to enjoy my private life and prepare before I take on the challenge."

"I understand you want to protect your privacy." Frustration licked my bones. The way she was hell-bent on living in the shadows had me wondering if this could ever work. She couldn't possibly think she could hide forever. "But I can't change who I am," I said, feeling my face contort with frustration and sadness. I desperately wanted things to work out between us. This was the first time where I doubted what we had would be enough.

Why couldn't she see that I wanted to announce to the world that I had found something special? Show her off so everyone could see how happy she made me.

"I know, and I'm sorry I can't be who you want me to be right now. Trust me, I would if I could."

What the hell did that even mean? Did I even want to know? No, I did not.

"I just want you to be you, Kinley," I said, keeping my voice calm. I hated every part of this conversation. And I especially hated doing this over the damn phone. I convinced myself that I could persuade her if we had this discussion face-to-face, or maybe that was just wishful thinking on my part.

"And I want to be with you too." Her voice filled with sadness, and I wish I were there to comfort her. "I'm just not ready to face the judgment of your fans or prepared to see how the media decides to review our relationship."

I held back on what I really wanted to say. I wasn't happy with her decision, but going back and forth wasn't going to solve anything either. And as much as I told myself it was just the fear talking, her rejection still stung. "I guess I have no other option than to accept your decision."

"You sound mad?"

I ran a hand through my hair and blew out a breath. "Honestly, I'm crabby because it feels like you will never warm up to this life." I didn't want to go there with her, but my agitation had reached its breaking point. "Unfortunately, I can't do a damn thing about it. I get it, okay. It's the downside of being in the public eye. Do you think I like having to smile every time someone recognizes me or wants to take my picture? You don't think I wish I could walk into a sports bar with a few buddies and watch a game and drink a cold beer without being heckled by fans or haters, depending on the week? Do you have any idea how badly I would love to take my girlfriend out on a normal date? Do something as simple as walk into a random restaurant or take a walk through the park without being recognized?" I drew in a sharp breath and shook my head. "And you know what really sucks? I can't complain because I'm doing something I love and have achieved success at a level most people only dream about."

Instead of lashing back at me as I expected, I was greeted with silence. I thought getting it all off my chest would make me feel better. Instead, I felt like a grade A asshole. "I'm sorry for lashing out at you." I hung my head. "I'm just frustrated."

"You don't need to apologize to me. Logically, I know you don't have a choice. There is a lot of change and uncertainty in your life at the moment. The last thing I want is to come between you and your career."

"You're not." I stood up and started pacing the room. "Kinley, do you still want to do this with me?"

"Yes," she said softly, and I felt the relief leave my shoulders. "I might not be ready to come out as your girlfriend, but I know without a shadow of a doubt that I want to be with you. I just need a little patience."

"Can I be honest with you?"

"Always," she said into the phone.

"I'm not going to pretend that your decision doesn't bother me." I pressed my lips together. "But I understand that you need to prepare for my lifestyle. It's not for everyone, I get it…" My words trailed off. "Just promise me that if you don't think this is going to work between us, you will tell me. Whatever you decide won't impact my role in raising this child with you."

"I promise." Her voice shook with emotion. "But I do want this with you. I don't expect you to keep me a secret forever. I just want to enjoy each other's company and get to know each other better."

"I understand."

I would find a way to get my emotions in check. Maybe a good workout would help with getting my frustration out. As a matter of fact, a punching bag sounded like a pretty damn good idea.

"I wish I was there so I could give you a hug right now," she said quietly into the phone.

"Me too, sweetheart." I walked to the liquor cabinet and pulled out a bottle of Jack Daniels. I needed a stiff drink to help settle these feelings that were wreaking havoc on my emotions. I grabbed a glass out of the cabinet and filled it up. "Why don't you get some rest, and we'll talk in the morning."

"Are you sure you're not upset?"

"I'm not," I lied. "I've been in meetings all day and need to read through some plays before the game on Sunday."

"Okay, I'll let you go."

I gripped the phone in my hands. "Get some rest. We'll talk tomorrow."

I hung up and threw my phone across my desk. I walked over to the window and looked into the darkness. The city was lit up on the other side of the glass. I loved this view, and I was grateful for it. I just wish she were here to enjoy it with me. I sat in the chair and propped my feet on the ottoman. I picked up my whiskey and thought back to our conversation. I couldn't help but wonder if I pushed her too far tonight.

I got it, really, I did, but I couldn't do a damn thing about it. I hoped she would come around with some time, but maybe I needed to face the fact that she might never will. She asked for patience, and that's what I would give her, no matter how much I hated it.

CHAPTER 23

MAVERICK

EVERYONE HAD MOMENTS OF REGRET WHERE YOU KNEW YOU made the wrong decision but had no other choice but to accept it. Tonight was one of those moments. That may be why the whiskey I sipped on the way to pick up Della did nothing to take the edge off.

When my publicist found out I wasn't planning on bringing a date to the fundraiser, she immediately suggested Della. It wouldn't be the first time I'd brought her as my plus one. In fact, she was more than thrilled to step up and help me out.

Everyone on the team got the invite, Della included. And there has been gossip recently about why I haven't been seen in public with anyone. I didn't want the media to dig too deep, so steering their attention elsewhere seemed like a good idea. Kinley wanted her privacy, and I was respecting her wishes.

However, the closer I got to Della's house, the more I questioned if I had agreed too quickly. My gut instinct screamed yes; it had never steered me wrong before.

Just pick her up and ride together. It doesn't have to be a big deal. Walk into the event together, smile for the camera, and go your separate ways for all I care. If you don't want the media to start digging, then you better throw them a bone to chew on.

I replayed that conversation with my publicist in my head and stared through the glass from the back of the town car as we drove across town. That twinge of guilt I felt wouldn't go away, no matter how hard I tried to shake it.

I leaned forward and set my drink in the holder when we pulled up in front of Della's townhouse. I stepped out of the car and wiped a bead of sweat off my brow as I approached the door.

"Don't you look handsome." Della stepped forward to adjust my black tie. She knew how much I hated wearing these monkey suits.

"Thanks. You look great too."

Della was stunning, as usual, in her floor-length black evening gown. Her hair and makeup looked a little overdone, but then again, she always went all out for these functions. She looked perfect for what I needed tonight, but I still wished I had Kinley on my arm to show off instead.

I took her coat and helped her into it. "Shall we?" I gestured to the waiting car idling at the curb. She pressed her lips to the corner of my mouth, making the situation tonight weigh more heavily on me.

We made small talk on the way to the event. Once we arrived, we stepped out of the limo and were greeted with camera flashes. I nodded politely and ignored the questions that were thrown my way. Unless I was forced to answer, I didn't give them a second of my time. I tried to quicken my pace, but Della seemed to enjoy the attention.

The woman was in her element, smiling and chatting away with all the players and staff as we entered the ballroom. She was taking the attention off of me, which was another reason I didn't mind having her tag along.

After retrieving our drinks from the bar, we checked out the auction items and made a few generous bids. I spotted JP immediately and headed in that direction, but my steps faltered as I got closer. I blinked twice when I noticed the woman on his arm. Carrie Nolan was the soon-to-be ex-wife of our teammate Beckett Nolan. What the hell were they doing here together?

A waiter came by with a tray of hors d'oeuvres. I plopped a shrimp in my mouth and made my way over to the group. We all bumped fists in greeting. I usually dreaded these types of events, but this party raised money for the Make-A-Wish Foundation. JP's younger brother died from leukemia when he was fourteen. This was a cause near and dear to his heart and one I didn't mind supporting. Neither did the NFL, who was a generous benefactor to the event tonight.

"Mav," JP boomed and slapped me on the back. Beckett glanced our way, and his eyes shifted from Carrie's to mine. He took a deep swallow of whatever he was drinking and turned away. Beckett and I weren't close, but I felt bad for the guy.

"How you doing, Carrie?" I gave her a casual hug and exchanged a glance with JP. As team captain, we would be having words later. He wasn't an asshole, so I wasn't sure what he was doing bringing her here.

"I'm good." She smiled, but her lips flattened when her gaze moved over to my date. There seemed to be a lot of negative energy between the two ladies. "Della." Carrie took a sip of her wine. "I didn't expect to see you here, especially with clothes on."

JP's drink sprayed out through his nose. My gaze flew to Della's in alarm. She shifted nervously on her feet and pulled down tightly on her dress. Tonight was going downhill, faster than a bike with missing brakes.

"Why, Carrie, I have no idea what you're talking about." Her smile was tight, and I noticed she didn't deny it.

Everybody on the team knew that Beckett and Carrie were having marital problems, but I had no idea that Della was sleeping with Beckett. She's been acting different and disappearing a lot over the last few months, but I'd been so preoccupied with my recovery and Kinley I haven't given it much thought.

"Please." Carrie rolled her eyes. "Save the innocent act, Della."

"Maybe you should lay off the alcohol," Della said, trying to keep her voice low.

"And maybe you should stop screwing other people's husbands." Carrie's nostrils flared. "My damn kids did not need to see a naked picture of you on their father's cell phone."

"What?" I snapped my head to Della's. All I could do was stare at her. "Tell me you didn't."

"Oh, she did all right." Carrie swayed on her feet a bit but kept the words flowing. "On my anniversary of all days. We were on our way to meet my in-laws for dinner. Becket let Xavier play a game on his phone while he drove to the restaurant. Xavier clicked on the message when it popped up. It was a video; I'll let you connect the dots on what kind of video it was." Her lips curled in disgust. "Let's just say it wasn't the Disney videos my seven-year-old son was used to watching." Carrie grabbed a glass of champagne off the tray from a passing waiter. She raised the glass in a toast. "To home-wrecking whores." She tipped the champagne back and drained it. "Now, if you'll excuse me, I need to get some fresh air. It's starting to stink in here."

I scrubbed a hand over my face, trying to wrap my head around what had just happened.

"I had no idea she would be here tonight," Della whispered against my shoulder.

JP gritted his teeth. "Maybe if you weren't fucking half the team, you wouldn't have to worry about being dressed down by their women."

Della blinked back tears. "I don't need this right now. I'm

going to the restroom." She hurried away, unwilling to give him the satisfaction of seeing her upset. Hopefully, she'd make it to the bathroom without finding any more trouble.

I shook my head and looked across the crowded room. "What the hell just happened, and why are you here with Carrie?" I asked, pulling JP aside.

"I could ask you the same thing about Della?" He raised an eyebrow. "What does your girl back in New York think about you bringing her as a date?"

My jaw clenched. "Everyone knows Della is just a friend," I said, not admitting that I was too chickenshit to tell Kinley. Things had been a little rocky since our phone call the other night. And she'd been dealing with some drama with her friend Chad, and I didn't want to add to her plate.

"For a smart guy, you sure act like a blockhead sometimes?"

"What's that supposed to mean?"

"How do you think she's going to feel when she sees your ugly mug splashed all over social media with another woman on your arm?"

I pulled on the collar of my dress shirt. I wanted to be pissed that he was calling me out, but he had a solid point. Bringing Della didn't look good, but my publicist suggested it, so I went with it, and now I fucking regretted it. "I didn't plan on bringing Della. Sylvia set it up. We just drove together."

He shook his head in disappointment. "You are dumber than I thought."

"C'mon, man. You know Della is just a friend."

"You mean a friend you used to fuck?"

Tonight was clearly turning out to be a mistake, but it was too late to turn the train around now.

"That was years ago, and speaking of fucking?" I whispered, feeling the urge to turn the tables on him. "Why didn't you tell me about Della and Beckett? Don't you think that's something the team captain ought to know?"

He sipped his beer. "Didn't think you would care."

"I would have talked her out of attending," I said, narrowing my eyes. JP snorted, and I inched closer and lowered my voice even though no one was listening. "And speaking of making bad decisions. Carrie? Why would you do that to Beckett? You know how drama like that fucks with the team."

He stiffened. "I'm doing our friend a favor."

I looked at him like he had lost his mind. He lifted his head and nudged it to the left. My eyes followed until they landed on Carrie and Beckett, who were in a heated discussion.

A sly grin split my face. "You dirty bastard." I laughed. "I always knew you were an asshole, but damn."

"Oh, come on." He took a sip of his beer. "Somebody needed to open Beckett's eyes. He's been moping in the locker room and playing like shit. Carrie has been showing up after every practice and somehow thinks my shoulder is the perfect one to lean on. I got sick of playing therapist between the two, so I gave him a nudge."

"Well, I'll be damned." I laughed while watching the two of them walk away. Beckett had his hand on her lower back. Carrie turned her head and mouthed *thank you* to JP.

He smacked his hands together. "It looks like my work is done." His phone dinged with a text, and he pulled it out of his pocket. "My parents are looking for me. I'll catch up with you in a bit." He started walking away but stopped and turned to fully face me. "A piece of advice, brother. Don't let that snake Della fuck up what you have going on with Kinley."

I watched his retreating back get lost in the crowd and mulled over his words, which did nothing to ease my guilty conscience.

Speak of the devil. Della slid up to my side, wrapping herself around my arm. "There you are." I saw the camera flash go off from the corner of my eye.

I brushed her off and cleared my throat. "What the hell were you thinking getting involved with Beckett?"

"It's complicated," she grumbled without making eye contact. I mentally replayed all their interactions, trying to figure out what I missed.

"Seems pretty straightforward to me. You knew he was married. Had a family at home. There is no excuse for that kind of shit."

She chewed on her bottom lip. "I was lonely and he was saying all the right things. He took advantage of me and I regret it."

I frowned at her. Della might have been a good friend to me, but she was no victim.

"Everyone knows he's still in love with his wife. What you guys did was wrong. It's as simple as that."

Hurt flashed in her eyes. "If he was still in love with his wife, he should have kept his dick in his pants."

"And you should have thought about the team that signs your paycheck and had a little more self-respect."

For a split second, I thought about reading her the riot act, but decided against it. She wasn't my problem, and it wasn't my job to keep her in line. But if she was going to fuck with my team, then I needed to at least address it.

"Are you siding with him?" I could see the tears building. Della didn't have many friends; sometimes, it felt like I was the only one. She was visibly upset, and now I felt like shit.

"I'm not laying the blame completely at your feet because it takes two to tango." I reached for her hand. "Just try to do better next time. Don't sell yourself short."

I pulled her into my arms and hugged her because it felt like she needed one.

Melissa Marks, a well-known sports reporter, approached.

The event was mostly closed off to the media, but Melissa was one of the few who made the cut. "Hi, Maverick." She smiled and looked at Della on my arm. "Got a second to answer a few questions? I promise to keep them short and move along."

I stepped away from Della and put some space between us. I didn't want Melissa to get the wrong idea. I usually avoided the press, but Melissa was one of the few I could tolerate.

"Of course." I winked and prepared to answer questions about my injury. It was a sore subject but one I couldn't avoid.

"We've missed seeing you out on the field lately." She smiled and moved to the side so her camera guy could get a good shot. "How's the recovery going?"

I forced a tight smile. "It's definitely gotten a lot better. Every day I feel more strength coming back." I shook my leg out for show, and she laughed.

"Does that mean we can expect to see you on the turf next season?"

I tilted my head to the side. "That's a question you'll have to ask my physical therapist here."

"Oh, that's right." She turned to Della. "You are one of the team trainers. I didn't recognize you at first, all dolled up. I thought you were Maverick's date."

"I'm both." Della sidled up next to me again and rested her palm on my chest. I narrowed my eyes at her hand. What was her angle?

"I didn't realize the two of you were an item?" Melissa looked intrigued as her eyes bounced between the two of us.

I was about to tell her we weren't when Della stepped forward. "A lot of people don't know this, but we were pretty serious in college. I actually followed him here after graduation. We've been in each other's lives the entire time."

What. The. Fuck!

I gritted my teeth. "What she's trying to say is..."

"Actually," Della cut in, "I can't remember a time in my life when we weren't together."

I took a deep breath, closed my eyes, and slowly counted to ten. But, unfortunately, it did nothing to calm me down.

"I had no idea." Melissa's eyes lit up as if she had just stumbled upon one hell of a story. "Do you mind if I ask..." she started to say, but I shot a hand out, putting a stop to this shit.

"Will you excuse us for a minute, Melissa?"

Yanking Della by the arm, I led her out of the room to a small corner at the end of the hallway. The woman had lost her damn mind. Either that or this was some sick joke.

"What the hell were you thinking?" I seethed, feeling my face harden into granite. My six-foot-two frame towered over her. I've sent men three times her size running in the opposite direction with this look, but she looked ready to go toe to toe with me without batting an eye. "You basically told her we were a couple."

"And that's a bad thing?" She scoffed at my reaction. Never in a million years would I ever have thought she could have been so conniving.

How did we get from me consoling her over having an affair with my married teammate to this bullshit?

"Della, I don't have those kinds of feelings for you. We tried years ago, and it didn't work."

"It did work. You just weren't ready for that type of commitment."

I stood a few feet away from her. My chest rose and fell with heavy breaths. I looked at the empty glass in her hands, wondering exactly how much she had to drink tonight.

"Whatever it was you think we had, it was a long time ago."

"Excuse me? *What I think we had*?" She jerked back as if my words had knocked the wind right out of her. "We had a relationship. We were committed to each other."

I sighed, feeling frustrated over this conversation. "We were young kids. Barely out of high school. The only thing I was committed to back then was playing ball and making the big leagues."

Della and I dated for less than a year. During that time, I spent most of it trying to please her and do things I thought she would enjoy. It was a period when I was still learning a lot about myself. What we had was more infatuation; it was never meant to last. Football was my focus, and she was an afterthought. I was a shitty boyfriend. After things ended, we realized we were better off as friends. Or at least she tricked me into thinking that's how she felt.

"What's so special about her?" She raised her voice, and I glanced around to ensure we were alone. "You've never been serious about anyone before."

I gripped the back of my neck in frustration. "I don't owe you an explanation. What Kinley and I have is between us. If you can't respect my relationship, then you and I can't be friends."

I watched as the look of hurt settled in. What little grip she had on her temper, was about to boil over. "Whatever you think it is you have with her isn't worth it. And when she's done spreading her legs, you'll realize that she is just one of many." She sneered, and I felt a chill rush through my bones. "If you're stupid enough to give up what we have, then I guess you deserve the little slut."

My body stiffened. She had officially crossed a line. Suddenly, I didn't give a fuck about her feelings anymore.

"You've got some pretty big balls on you, you know that? First, you lie to that reporter and insinuate that we are in a relationship. Which. We. Are. Not," I stressed, in case she was still confused. "Then you practically admit that you set me up tonight. Now, you're insulting my girlfriend, who has done nothing to you other than breathe the same air. That's three strikes, *my friend*. We're done."

She looked away, as if she were processing the gravity of the situation. Probably finally realizing how bad she fucked up tonight. "I didn't plan for that reporter to be here. She asked the questions, and I answered them for you."

I leaned forward, putting my face in hers. "You don't fucking speak for me."

"This is all over *her*!"

"She has a goddamned name and this little conversation has nothing to do with Kinley and everything to do with the stunt you just pulled."

Her face twisted, and she squared her shoulders as if she were ready to go to battle with me. "You can be pissed all you want. We both know this never would have happened tonight if she wasn't in the way. I hope she's worth it."

I shook my head at what a fucking epic mess she was. "We're done! From here on out, you are on your own. We are not friends. We are nothing. I will request a new physical therapist first thing on Monday morning. If you see me, walk the other way. Delete my number from your phone." My body was raging. "If you even think about fucking with me again, you can kiss your job goodbye. Get that through your thick head and leave me the fuck alone."

She blinked at me. "You're done with me? Just like that?" she hissed out. "If she's so special, then where is she tonight? Why am I here?"

"You're here for the same reason you always are, for appearances. Something you agreed to because it benefits you too. You like the attention and I need to be seen. It's been our arrangement for years."

"Arrangement?" She let out a hard laugh. "I've stood by and supported you throughout your entire career and this is how you repay me? You are right about one thing." She stepped forward and pointed her finger at my chest. "I do love the spotlight. So, watch me turn it on your precious little

Kinley. Let's see how long she lasts once I tell the whole world how you left me for her!"

I clenched my fists at my sides. It took every ounce of control I had to keep them there. I've never wanted to punch a female so badly in my life.

"If I were you, I'd think twice about that little plan. You have no idea what I'm capable of when someone I care about is threatened."

"You don't scare me." She darted an angry tear away. "I've been a part of your life for years. I know exactly what you're capable of."

"You know nothing!" I hissed. "And if you even think about going after Kinley, I will make you regret the day you were born."

With those parting words, I turned and stormed away from her.

Our friendship was officially over.

CHAPTER 24

KINLEY

I leaned my head back, thinking of how I'd spent the entire week missing him and trying to come up with ways to make this long-distance relationship work. I really thought he cared about me. Yet, as I stared at the screen in front of me, I felt like a fool.

Apparently, when I declined his invitation, he neglected to tell me he was extending it to someone else if I said no.

The images on my laptop were now burned in my brain like a bad nightmare, and the headlines only seemed to get worse as I scrolled through them.

Mav Cross Blindsided by Baby Drama.

Love Triangle Off the Field.

Sacked With a Baby.

The photos showed us outside my ob-gyn office, and another was taken the day we spent in the park. There was a side-by-side photo; one half showed a very flattering picture of Della on his arm at the fundraiser, while the one next to it was a grainy image of us saying goodbye at the airport. It was the most unattractive picture of me I'd ever seen. My mascara was running down my face, my hair was a matted mess from rolling around in the wet snow, and my puffy coat made me look fat. Just great.

My eyes stung with tears at how good Maverick and Della looked together. She was stunning and everything I wasn't, and I hated her for it. And with every second that ticked by, my imagination went further and further into a place I wasn't sure I'd be able to find my way out of.

I ignored my phone ringing on the coffee table. It had been ringing off the damn hook since the rumors had started spreading all over the internet.

"Maybe there's an explanation." I glanced up into Taylor's sympathy-filled eyes.

I wanted to believe there was, but the images of the two of them together over the last several years and her comments only proved there was more to their relationship than he led me to believe.

He glossed over it, convincing me they were just friends. No wonder why she was so frosty to me when we met. It made me wonder what else he was keeping from me. God, I was so stupid.

"Can I get you anything?" Chad asked, turning the TV off. He had unplugged the cable and set the TV to stream Netflix. It didn't matter what he put on to distract me. I couldn't focus on anything other than the chaos in my head. I even left work early because I couldn't concentrate on my damn job. I sent two emails to the wrong people, screwed up on a marketing proposal that was past due, and kicked the copy machine because it was too slow. After my fifth meltdown for the day, they sent me home.

"No." I stared across the room and adjusted the blanket across my lap. "This is exactly what I was afraid of. I should have seen this coming."

"There is no way you could have predicted this." Chad stared down at me. His words were meant to console me, but they had the opposite effect.

My eyes traveled over the words in front of me. I was being dragged across the coals. "I knew there would be a bit of backlash but calling me a liar and suggesting I abort my baby," I shook my head, "this is exactly why I wanted to stay out of the spotlight."

He grabbed my MacBook off my lap and slammed the lid closed. "Do not listen to that shit. You don't deserve to stay hidden like a dirty little secret. What you need is that motherfucker to defend you."

"Chad," Taylor admonished. "This is not helpful."

"What do you want me to say?" He threw his hands up. "Because from where I'm standing, the guy cares more about his image than he does about protecting her."

"That's not true." I shot him a glance. "I insisted on this, and he would never want anything like this to happen."

"Then why the fuck is he allowing them to do this to you? Where is his statement?" He cursed under his breath and stared at me like he couldn't believe I was coming to Maverick's defense.

There was a knock at my door, and all three of us exchanged a glance. I knew it was him before Chad even had a chance to swing the door open.

Once he came into view, my breath hitched at the sight of him. His eyes locked on mine, refusing to break away. The look of misery on his face gutted me. Taylor watched me closely, but Chad hadn't stopped glaring at Maverick since he opened the door.

He came like I knew he would, and I've spent the last day waiting and dreading it. I've been ignoring his text messages and sending his calls to voicemail like the coward I was. It was silly of me to think I could buy myself some time and gather enough strength to face him. I wasn't sure I'd ever be strong enough when it came to him.

He stuffed his hands in the front pockets of his jeans. There was a beat of awkward silence as his gaze stayed heavily on mine. Heartbreak and despair couldn't even begin to describe how I felt.

"I'd like to see Kinley," he said to my friend, who was still standing at the door, blocking his path.

A small part of me wanted to run into his arms for comfort, but I stayed still and shook off the urge. I would not make this easy on him.

He tried to brush past my friend, but Chad put his hand out. "Not going to happen."

Maverick's face turned red. "I don't remember you getting a vote. Now, move out of my damn way. This doesn't concern you."

Chad folded his arms over his chest. "She doesn't want to talk to you."

"You don't speak for her." Maverick's jaw was clenched, his eyes were narrowed, and as much as I wanted to send his ass back on a plane to Georgia, I knew I had to step in before things got ugly.

I stood from the couch and walked toward him. "Is any of what she said true?" My voice was low and on the verge of breaking. My salty tears hit my lips, but I was past caring how I looked. The world could have stopped spinning, and I wouldn't had felt a thing.

Maverick shook his head. "Can we talk in private, please?"

"Talk?" My chest heaved. "Now you want to talk. You have barely spared me a second of your time up until last night, yet you show up here and expect me to drop whatever I'm doing so you can what? Throw me a list of excuses."

He flinched at my words, and as much as I hated to admit it, I was at fault here, too, because I knew what I was getting myself into. "I'm sorry you saw those pictures. Those articles are all bullshit. I was hoping you wouldn't even fucking see them."

I bet he did.

"How else did you expect me to find out?" My hands were shaking, and my body was filled with so much fury I didn't know what to do with it all. "Maybe if you weren't too busy with taking your *friend* on dates, you'd have more time to talk to me."

His eyes looked pained, but I would not allow myself to feel sorry for him. I was mentally replaying the brief calls and messages we shared over the week, trying to remember if he mentioned or hinted to taking Della, but everything was coming up blank.

"It's not like that." He cursed under his breath. "You have been ignoring my calls and texts all night. I took the first flight out as soon as I could."

"And you thought you would show up here and accomplish what, exactly?"

He cleared his throat and lowered his voice. "You have every right to be mad at me. All I ask is that we not do this in front of an audience." He glanced between my friends, who were standing guard and ready to jump in if I needed them.

I sighed and looked between Chad and Taylor. "Thank you, both, for coming over and staying with me, but I think it's best if Maverick and I talk alone."

"Kinley," Chad protested as Taylor grabbed on to his elbow and started shoving him toward the door. "You don't have to listen to him."

I knew he meant well, but I did not have the mental energy to deal with him at the moment.

"Thank you for your concern, Chad. We'll talk later."

He pursed his lips and nodded his head in understanding. As soon as they left, I walked into the kitchen to pour a glass of water. I could feel Maverick's eyes on me, but I wasn't ready to hash things out with him yet. I needed a minute to pull myself together because I was on the verge of breaking down. Everything I feared was happening, and I was feeling overwhelmed.

I wrapped my arms along my stomach, wishing we could turn the clock back and do things differently. We were so happy, so I didn't understand why he did it? Why did he have to take her? How could he do this?

I gave my head a quick shake, and spun around. The only way I was going to get answers was if I allowed him to explain. But when I got a look at his face, the anguish was enough to bring me to my knees. I leaned against the counter and crossed my arms, praying for God to give me strength.

"Thank you for hearing me out," he said, his eyes searching mine. "I wasn't sure if you would even let me through the door." He smiled sheepishly, but I kept my face frozen. I wasn't sure what he wanted me to say. All I knew was the longer I looked at him, the angrier I became.

"It's not like I can just turn you away." My throat constricted. "You have too much explaining to do."

He stepped closer and paused in the middle of my kitchen. "I can't tell you how sorry I am. I was a stupid idiot."

He started with an apology. I could work with that. At least he wasn't denying anything.

"How much of what she said is true?"

"Can we start with the pictures first?" He began pacing the room but stopped at the threshold when he realized he wasn't getting very far. "The picture of us at the fundraiser." He paused. "The only reason why she even went with me in the first place was because you said no."

My mouth dropped open. "You can't be serious?"

He ran his hands through his hair in frustration. "I told you before that I take women to these events for business reasons," he tried to explain, but nothing he could say would make me okay with this. "Della is someone familiar who knows how these functions work. My publicist suggested we show up together. I wanted to tell you, but I didn't want to give you a reason to be pissed off or doubt me. I didn't think it was a big deal. Without sounding like an insensitive asshole, you've made it clear that you want no part of that life. I was honoring your wishes."

"Is it against the law to go by yourself? Is there a clause in your contract that says you can't attend functions by yourself?"

He looked down at the floor and then to my eyes. "It looks better for my image if I bring a friend."

"Let's talk about your friend." I threw my hands up, no longer willing to stay calm. "I asked you point-blank a few times if you'd ever been in a serious relationship and you told me no."

"About that." He scrubbed a hand over his face. "I told you. It was a long time ago. I had no idea she still had feelings for me."

"Really. You didn't know she had feelings for you, huh? I'm starting to think Della and I have more in common than I thought."

His mouth dropped open. "You can't possibly think that?"

"Honestly. I don't know what to think anymore. I don't know the difference between a truth and a lie. I'm questioning everything."

He tilted his head to the side. "Do you think I slept with her?"

I squared my shoulders. "I don't know. You tell me."

His jaw tightened and his nostrils flared. "I wouldn't do that to you. There is nothing going on between Della and me."

"Those pictures and that article say otherwise." A deep part of me knew he was telling the truth, but my anger had taken over. I felt foolish for believing we could make it work when all along I knew we were destined to fail.

"Let me get this straight. You saw a few pictures and read a few headlines and assumed the worst?"

"What did you expect me to think?" He knew damn well how bad this would look.

"I expected you to have a little faith in me. If you suspected something or if you had doubts, you should have confronted me and given me a chance to explain myself, instead of ignoring my calls and not responding to my texts."

My back went straight. He was the one who messed up. All I needed was a little time to cool down and get my thoughts in order before we had this conversation. But he was partially right, I should have given him the benefit of the doubt, although, if he were so concerned about my feelings, we wouldn't be in this position to begin with.

"So you're saying everything that was printed was a lie? The pictures of you and Della over the years are fake?"

"Yes, most of what she said is total bullshit." He took a step forward as if he were testing me. Wondering if I would push him away and allow him to comfort me. "You have to believe me." His eyes were pleading, but he didn't reach for me or take a step closer. He didn't say another word. He just waited me out, and I was at my breaking point. This was exactly what I feared would happen. I should have listened to my gut all along. It's never steered me wrong before.

"I can't do this." I wiped the tears out of my eyes. "I convinced myself I needed time to ease my way into your world. I wanted it to work, but after today I don't think I have it in me. I'm questioning everything right now."

"What are you saying?" he asked, finally closing the distance between us.

I moved back, bumping into the counter. I wouldn't be able to handle it if he touched me. "Maverick. It's not just about what Della is implying; I'm being vilified on the internet. I have thick skin, but it can only hold so much."

"It kills me to see the media attack you." He pulled on the

ends of his hair. "My PR team is doing damage control. I've already drafted up a statement disputing Della's claims. That's where I've been, in meetings, trying to figure out how to get the media off your back." He sighed heavily. "Kinley, I thought she was a friend. I had no idea she would pull that shit."

I shook my head, trying to get rid of the doubt that was taking up space. "Some friend."

"Former friend and I already requested another team physical therapist."

My shoulders sagged in relief, at least she was out of his life. Unfortunately, that still wasn't enough to fix our problem.

"It's not just Della." I sighed, wishing his words were enough to take my pain away. "Your fans won't stop until they get what they want. And guess what? They don't want me with you. They think I'm a whore and a liar."

"I will handle my fans. I will set the media straight."

The media was a part of his life, and if I stayed with him, I would have to be okay with photographers flashing pictures of me everywhere I went. I would have to be okay with them calling me names and threatening my safety. I would have to be okay with them speculating and making up stories. I would have to be okay with them digging into my personal life. And none of that was okay with me.

"Maverick, this isn't going to work," I croaked out. My voice was hoarse, and my entire body felt like it was shutting down. I wished I didn't love him so much because maybe then, it wouldn't hurt so fucking bad.

"Don't do this, Kinley. Let me fix this." The pain was written all over his face, but it wasn't enough to stop that wall from raising up around my broken heart.

I kept telling myself that loving someone shouldn't be this difficult.

"Some things can't be fixed." I wiped my eyes, trying to

get the tears to stop flowing. "It hurt seeing you with her. It destroyed me to read all those comments. I hate that my privacy has been shot to shit, and this all happened when you decided you needed some arm candy for a damn fundraiser."

His face filled with regret. "You have every right to be mad at me. I fucked up and made a bad decision."

"Every decision has consequences," I snapped, scrubbing a hand against my wet cheek.

"So, you're going to punish me?" His voice broke. "Is that what this is about?"

I shook my head and squeezed my eyes shut. "Did you even stop to think how I would feel once I saw those pictures of the two of you on a date? Because let's be honest, that's exactly what it was."

His gaze fell to the floor. "I don't know what I can say at this point, Kinley, other than I fucked up. I'm sorry. I don't know what else I can do other than apologize and ask for forgiveness. I didn't cheat on you, that much I can promise you. I'm committed to you. Only you." He lifted his eyes to meet mine. "You're the mother of my unborn child. I have too much respect for you."

Somehow, those words had the opposite effect of what he was hoping for. They struck a chord with me because they'd been in the back of my mind since the beginning.

"The mother of your unborn child, is that what I am to you?"

His one eyebrow rose slowly. "Is that a trick question?"

"Do you want to know what I think? I think this relationship was built around the baby. If I wasn't pregnant there would be nothing else holding us together."

"You're jumping to conclusions. You think I'm with you because it's convenient?"

When I didn't respond, his face fell.

We might have started out with the best of intentions, but somewhere along the way, things started to change. Maybe we convinced ourselves that time was all we needed. We both wanted the best for this child, but my doubts and insecurities reminded me that a relationship might not be possible.

"How long have you been telling yourself that, Kinley?" His eyes flickered in panic. "I made a dumb decision, okay. And you deserve to be pissed, but the reasons why I'm with you have nothing to do with the baby. This thing started the second I laid eyes on you in the crowded airport. I wanted you then. I want you now. I'm pretty sure I will always want you."

I wiped at the tears flowing down my face. I had to brush my hair back because it was sticking to my skin. "I don't want you to just want me. I want you to love me."

"Kinley. I…"

"No!" I shook my head. "Don't say it now. Don't say it because you feel backed into a corner. When and if you say it, I want to hear the words because you mean them, not because you feel pressured to say them."

"You realize I'm in a no-win situation right now, right?"

My heart pounded in my chest, at war with what I wanted and what I knew was right. There was so much doubt in my head, and it was too much for me to handle. It felt like my life was spinning out of control, and I was being hit at every angle.

"I don't want to spend this pregnancy stressing and worrying." We stared at each other; so much emotion passed between us. I needed to get the words out before my throat started closing up. "I think it's best if we break up."

He staggered back with a look of devastation on his face. The pain in his eyes was unbearable. I wanted to offer him comfort, but I wasn't in a position to give it to him. My heart was decimated and it hurt a thousand times worse than I thought it would.

"I thought if I explained to you what happened, that you would understand and we would be okay. But I can see by this conversation, no matter how hard I try to explain my actions, you're still going to fight me on whatever I say. I can't change who I am, Kinley. I shouldn't lose you over a simple mistake. I never cheated on you. I never lied to you."

"This isn't just about those articles. This was a test and we failed. I should have trusted you. You shouldn't have taken her in the first place. You knew there would be cameras and reporters there."

"That's just it. I was trying to keep them from finding out about you."

My eyes welled with tears; everything hurt. I needed him to go and take this pain with him. I wanted nothing more than to fall into his arms and forget the last twenty-four hours happened. Only I knew it wouldn't be enough.

"What this proved is that I'm not cut out for this lifestyle. You asked me to promise to tell you if I thought I couldn't handle it, and here I am. As much as I want to be with you, we will never work."

"Yeah, I get it, I really do. I just wish you had told me before I went and fell in love with you."

I hiccupped a sob as the pain sliced through me. I wanted to take it all back. Beg him to stay and erase the last thirty minutes and start over. I didn't want to lose him, but something told me our ending was inevitable.

He walked to the door, and when he turned around, the despair in his eyes sent me over the edge. "I'll see you at your next doctor's appointment."

I couldn't hold back my sobs anymore; it was pointless. The dam in my chest broke loose, so I let it all out. Never in my life had I ever felt so hopeless. So shattered and completely broken. I always thought he would be the one to break my heart. But, in reality, I was the one who severed both of ours.

CHAPTER 25

KINLEY

"Thanks for helping out tonight," Chad said, wiping off the counter in the commercial kitchen, where we had prepped food for tomorrow. Once a month, he volunteered to help his staff prepare a few hot meals to be delivered to homeless people living on the street.

"You don't need to thank me, it felt good to be able to help out. This is a great program. I just wish there was more we could do to help them."

"Me too. Unfortunately, a lot of these people are dealing with drug addiction, mental health, and physical disabilities. We can give them a hot meal, emergency supplies, and try to connect with them, but many are reluctant to accept assistance. All we can do is let them know we aren't giving up and we're here and ready to help."

Hearing the counselors tell stories about their day-to-day struggles put things into perspective. I felt guilty complaining about my life. I had hot food, a warm bed, and a roof over my head. Most of these people had nothing.

I also had a broken heart that wouldn't heal and no one to blame but myself.

I'd spent the last week living on donuts and pizza,

watching Netflix, and avoiding social media. The only time I left my apartment was for work. Hiding from the world and pretending that Maverick didn't exist couldn't go on forever, though.

I knew the season was winding down, which was a busy time for him. The last thing he needed to deal with was a hormonal pregnant lady who couldn't get a hold of her damn emotions. So, I made the decision that we would talk once the season was over. He just didn't know that yet.

Chad placed his hand on my shoulder. "Are you feeling okay?" His concerned gaze searched my face.

"I'm just overwhelmed and emotional." I dashed a tear from under my eye. "It's just pregnancy hormones."

"I'm sure the paparazzi hounding you everywhere you go isn't helping either."

A heavy sigh escaped before I could stop it. "It was inevitable."

Every time a camera would flash in my face and ask me for a comment, I would keep my head down and continue walking. Thanks to Della selling her bullshit story to the tabloids, I was the most hated woman in America. My biggest fear had become my reality. The media was making me out to be the other woman, and there was nothing I could say or do to redeem myself in their eyes. All I could do was pray they would get bored with me and move on to the next story.

"Have you talked to him?"

"Just through text."

He made a point of letting me know he was taking care of things. Every text was short and straight to the point. And every day I'd fall further into depression.

"Good," he said quietly. "I don't know everything that happened between you two, I only know that he hurt you."

"I'm not innocent in this. We hurt each other." I blinked the tears away, hoping they would disappear. "I hate that I doubted him and didn't trust my instincts. I hate that I allowed Della to come between us, but that's all irrelevant because this story was just the tip of the iceberg if I stayed with him."

"I know you cared about him, but he wasn't the right man for you." His hands went to my shoulders, and my stomach clenched when I saw the look of longing in his gaze. "I meant what I said, Kinley. I'll always be here for you. I would never hurt you."

My body went still. I tried to think of something I could say, but my brain was misfiring. Maybe I was reading too much into it, because I thought we had turned a corner. Chad has been wonderful through all this, stopping by to drop off food, holding my hand while I cried, never once leaving my side, all the while ensuring me that everything would be okay. Perhaps, I'd been so messed up in my own head that I thought he understood that I only needed him as a friend. "Chad, thank you for all you've done for me, and I appreciate having you in my life, but I don't want to give you any mixed signals."

He nibbled on his bottom lip like he was mulling something over. "I know you don't feel that way now, but do you think with him being out of the picture, that could change?"

I knew what he wanted me to say, but I've always been honest with him and wasn't going to start lying now. "Chad, it doesn't matter if I'm with Maverick or not. My feelings about you will not change. Not now. Not ever." His hands dropped. "I'm sorry."

He nodded his head, and I hated the awkwardness between us. I thought with a little effort, we could return to where we were before. Now, I wondered if our friendship would ever be the same again.

"It was worth a shot." He sighed. "I just want you to be happy. I want to see you smile again." I wanted that too. I just wasn't sure if it would be happening anytime soon.

"Thank you. I know talking about this isn't easy for you."

He let out a hard laugh. "No, it's not. I hate him. I hate that he hurt you. I hate that he broke your heart. I hate that he had something so precious and let it slip away."

I shook my head, letting him know that wasn't entirely true. "I knew what I was getting into. I can't lay all the blame at his feet." I placed my hand on my stomach. "I also don't regret him, not when he gave me this."

He cleared his throat, and shifted on his feet. "Speaking of the baby, you need to eat something. Why don't you sit down on one of those stools over by the stove while I make you a grilled cheese sandwich?"

I decided not to argue with him because I was hungry. Plus, my feet could use a rest. "Deal. Let me take the trash out and I'll sit and watch you slave over the hot stove. I also wouldn't mind a cup of tomato soup to dip my sandwich in."

He held the spatula out and pointed it in my direction. "Now you're just taking advantage of me."

"That's what friends are for." I winked and picked up the trash to carry out to the dumpster. We were the last ones left, so thankfully this was the last bag. The kitchen emptied out half an hour ago, but the other workers cleaned up before leaving.

"Kinley," he called out when he spotted me carrying the black trash bag. "Sit down. I'll throw that out when I'm done."

"It's fine." I waved him off. "It's not heavy."

He shook his head and went back to spreading the butter along the bread while I quickly walked to the service entrance behind the supply room. I pushed the heavy door open and was hit in the face with a blast of cold air. The alley was dark and narrow and barely shoveled. The last thing I needed was to trip on the ice, so I raised the bag over my shoulder and aimed it toward the green dumpster, only it landed on the cold ground instead. I sighed and carefully left the door slightly ajar, in case it locked behind me. As carefully as possible, I walked over, picked up the black bag, and threw it on top of the pile.

Just as I turned around, a man stepped in front of me. He was skinny, with long, unkempt wavy hair, a beard that needed a good trim, and a pair of thick black glasses that looked two decades old.

"Can I help you?" I asked, noticing he had a camera strapped along his neck.

"You're Kinley Roberts." His beady little eyes dragged up and down my body. "Mav Cross's side piece."

I froze.

"How far along are you?"

I looked to the door and counted how many steps it would take to get inside. "No comment."

"Oh, come on." He edged his way closer. Every hair on my body stood at attention. "I just want to ask you a few questions. Don't you want to tell your side of the story?"

"You need to leave," I said, trying to hide the panic in my voice. I looked over my shoulder, hoping like hell Chad would come looking for me. The guy was giving me the creeps.

He tilted his head to the side. "How about a picture." He lifted his camera, and the flash was bright and unexpected, forcing me to cover my eyes.

"Please stop," I pleaded as he continued clicking away. I tried to cover my face, but he didn't seem to care.

"I'll stop when you start answering my questions."

"That's not going to happen," I said, feeling my back hit the wall.

"Is the baby his? Are you even pregnant?"

Panic swept through me when the bastard tried to touch my stomach. "Get the hell away from me!" I screamed.

"Why are you so afraid?" He kept snapping my picture. He was right in my goddamned face. I pushed him in the shoulder, and he stumbled back slightly.

"Hey, that was unnecessary, bitch." He shoved me hard enough that I lost my balance on a patch of ice and fell on my back. All the wind rushed out of my lungs. "Maybe I should kick you in the stomach to see if you're really pregnant."

My heart started racing, and nausea crept up my throat, but I forced it down. At that moment, protecting the baby was all that mattered. I kicked him in the leg, but he didn't budge. "Get out of here or I'm calling the police."

"And tell them what? That you slipped and fell on a patch of ice? I got mouths at home to fucking feed, so I want my story. I ain't leaving until you start talking."

"I have nothing to say to you," I spat out through the clattering of my teeth. It was freezing, the ground was cold, and the alley was dark. I tried to slow my breath and think of how I would get this lunatic away from me.

He stepped forward; his boot-clad toe landed on my hair. I yelped in pain. "You're hurting me."

He kneeled over the top of me, bringing his face close to mine. "You're not even that pretty." His spittle landed on my cheek. "Makes me wonder what someone like him ever saw in you."

"Please stop." I closed my eyes. My entire body trembled in fear. Never in my life had I ever felt so helpless. I wanted to kick this guy in the balls, but I didn't want to anger him any more than I already had. I promised Maverick I would keep this baby safe. I would never forgive myself if anything happened.

He stepped off my hair and lifted my head. "Are you ready to start talking yet?"

"What do you want from me?" I squeezed my eyes shut, not wanting to give him the satisfaction of seeing me cry. "A confirmation?" I swallowed back a sob. "We're not even together anymore."

He kneeled over the top of me and brought his face close

to mine. "I can see why he'd dump you. I guess your little plan to trap him didn't work, huh? Or is he paying you off?"

"Hey!" The back door burst open. "Get away from her!" Chad's frantic voice filled my ears as he charged toward the man. The guy cursed, and shoved me to the ground, causing my head to slam against the ice. A searing pain ripped through my scalp.

The guy stumbled to the ground before running away. Chad rushed over and kneeled in front of me. "Kinley, are you okay?" He lifted my head off the ground, supporting it in his hands.

"My head hurts." I groaned. My limbs felt weak and my head felt fuzzy. "I feel dizzy. I need to make sure the baby is okay."

"Shit!" He reached for my hand and pulled me up to a standing position. It felt like I was going to pass out. "Do you need an ambulance?" he asked, inspecting me from head to toe.

"I'm fine." I flew into his arms, where I felt safe and protected. I was finally able to breathe again. "You got here just in time."

"What the hell happened?" One of the maintenance workers came running through the door. He assessed the alley and looked at me. "Are you okay? Were you mugged?"

"No, it was just some deranged member of the paparazzi." I shook my head and immediately rested my palm on the back of my neck. The dizziness I felt earlier was getting worse.

Chad's eyes widened, and I followed his gaze. Blood dripped down my pants, and as soon as I noticed it, a sharp pain seared through my stomach.

Chad pulled out his cell phone. I heard him on the phone with 911. He was rattling off the address as they instructed him what to do. He was frantic and reassured me that I was okay. My only thought was that I couldn't lose this baby. It was the only thing in the world I had left. The physical pain was nothing compared to the emotional agony of losing the last connection to Maverick I had left.

That was my last thought as my eyes drifted shut without warning, and everything went black.

CHAPTER 26

MAVERICK

I WAS SITTING IN OUR TEAM EXIT MEETING, LISTENING AS OUR head coach went on about how we weren't good enough to play football and explained all the reasons why we lost the playoff game, when my cell dinged with a text.

My brows pulled together as I read my sister's message.

Rylee: *Call me ASAP.*

Glancing up, I noticed no one was paying attention, so I typed back.

In a meeting. Can I call you when it's over?

Rylee: *No. Call me NOW!*

Well, shit. I ran a hand through my hair and stood up. "It's my sister. There is some type of family emergency. I need to step out into the hall and take this."

Coach signaled for me to go ahead, and I felt a few jealous gazes on my back as I bolted out of the room. This was basically like being excused from the principal's office. Most of the players had their cars running in the parking lot, ready to get the hell out of there when it was over.

Rylee picked up on the first ring. "What's going on?" I asked, not even giving her a chance to say hello. "Is it Mom or Dad?"

"Neither. It's Kinley. She was accosted by some fucking paparazzi perp. Things got physical and she ended up in the hospital. She hit her head and was being treated for cramping and bleeding. That's all I know."

I leaned against the wall for support. "What. The. Fuck?" I growled into the phone.

"Maverick, you need to book a flight and get your ass to New York."

"Did you talk to her? Is she okay?" I asked, taking in a huge gulp of air. It felt like someone was sitting on my damn lungs.

"No, I talked to her mom. She called me and asked me to contact you. Michelle is freaking out because she has the flu and can't fly."

"What about the baby?" I swallowed back the burning sensation in my throat. Someone was going to fucking pay for hurting the two most precious things in my life.

"I don't know. She was helping out at a soup kitchen and went to take the trash out. Her friend Chad chased the guy off. I don't know anything else other than she was brought to the hospital to get checked out."

"Send me her mom's number." I gritted my teeth, and willed my heavy beating heart to slow down. "I'm on my way."

I pinched the bridge of my nose and stormed back into the meeting.

"I have an emergency. I have to go." I was surprised at how calm my voice was.

Beau Landers, the owner of the team, popped his head up. "Everything okay? Do you need anything?"

"I have to fly to New York. My girlfriend was attacked by a shit member of the paparazzi. Any chance I can borrow your jet?"

"Done. I'll have it ready for you in thirty minutes."

I breathed out a sigh of relief. "Thank you."

He picked up his phone and started barking out orders, while every single person in the room asked what they could do to help. I didn't stick around long enough to answer them. Instead, I headed straight to the airport.

My phone call with Kinley's mom did nothing to soothe my fear and anger. I was relieved that she was okay, but I wasn't sure how I would handle seeing her or if she would even want me there. I tried to call her, desperate to hear her voice, but her phone went straight to voicemail. Either it was turned off, the battery was dead, or she didn't have it with her.

When we pulled off the highway and into the private airport, I was relieved to see the jet ready and waiting for me. The car came to a stop, and I wasted no time running up the stairs and onto the small plane. I buckled my seat belt and clenched the armrest as soon as we took off. I might not have been able to get through to her, but I sure as fuck was going to try to get some answers.

After being transferred and put on hold for half the flight, I finally got a hold of someone at the NYPD. It had only been a few hours, so there wasn't much information, just endless questions from me. After throwing every name I had at my disposal around, the only thing I got was a promise to call me with any updates. I bit the guy's head off and threatened to sue the department if they didn't find the fucker. The detective told me my money and threats didn't mean shit, and I needed to back off and let them do their job. So, I sat and stewed in my seat until the plane touched down at Teterboro. A private car was waiting at the stairs when the door of the jet opened.

As I was sliding into the back seat, Kinley sent me a text, letting me know that she had been released from the hospital and was home resting. Due to the heavy traffic and a shit ton of construction, the forty-minute car ride seemed to take forever. By the time I made it through the front door of her building, my heart was thumping painfully hard in my chest. I used the key she gave me when I stayed here last time, not even bothering to knock.

I sucked in a sharp breath at seeing her buried under a mountain of blankets. Chad and Taylor were hovering over her, saying what I had no idea. My shoulders slumped in relief when I saw that she was okay.

Chad pushed off the couch as soon as he saw me. I shoved him out of my way and crossed the room in three quick strides. No one and nothing was going to get between us again.

Kinley sat up and straightened against the pillows. "Maverick?" She hiccupped a sob. "How did you get here so fast?"

Chad glared at me, and Taylor smiled, seeming relieved.

"My boss let me borrow his jet." I knelt next to her. "Are you okay? Is the baby…" I choked out the words, unable to finish the sentence.

She ran her fingers over my stubbled cheek. "I'm fine, and so is the baby."

"Thank God." I sighed, leaning into her touch.

"I just have a few scrapes and bruises."

"And a concussion," Taylor added.

A bit of tension in my shoulders eased until my eyes landed on Chad. "Why was she by herself?" I barked out.

He leaned against the wall and folded his arms across his chest. "Maybe if her name and face weren't splashed all over the internet, she'd be able to do something as simple as taking the trash out without being hounded by a crazed celebrity chaser."

A muscle in my cheek ticked. I didn't think I just moved. "I'm getting really sick of your attitude."

"All right, you two." Taylor stood between us and held her hands out. "This is not helping."

"Maverick, come here," Kinley called out. I glared at the fucker one last time. I knew I had to calm down, but the shithead was pushing every single one of my goddamned buttons. That lid I had on my temper was ready to pop off.

Kinley grabbed my hand and entwined our fingers. I was still visibly shaking, but the brush of her fingers helped settle my nerves slightly. "This is not your fault." She glared at her friend.

"Yes, it is." I scrubbed a free hand over my face. "You could have been seriously hurt." I was pissed and terrified. As much as I hated to admit it, Chad was right. I should have done more to protect her. Instead, I spent the last week with my public relations people and sitting in team meetings trying to come up with a solution. I thought seeing her would calm me down, but it only fueled this raw panic swirling inside me.

"I'm just glad I got to her in time and chased him off," Chad said, trying to act like he was some kind of white knight. I grounded my teeth together in an effort to keep my mouth shut. That strategy lasted for two whole seconds.

"You never should have allowed her out in that alley alone," I barked out, needing to take my anger out on someone.

"You're right," he said. His voice was calm, but I could tell he wanted to tear me apart. I should have let him try. At least I would have been able to release some of my fury. "Just like you shouldn't have allowed those pictures to hit the internet, so I guess we're both to blame."

I sighed and hung my head, hoping I could somehow get it to settle down. "I'm so sorry, Kinley. Chad has a point, I'm partially to blame for all this."

Her eyes softened in understanding. "You have nothing to be sorry for, so please stop blaming yourself."

I shook my head. "I feel like I failed you, and I promise you, I will never make that mistake again."

She leaned forward, and I pulled her into my chest. Never in my life had I been so scared. I pressed my lips to her forehead, not trusting the words that threatened to come out of my mouth. I wanted to lock her away and never leave her side.

Taylor cleared her throat. "Why don't we give you guys some time alone." She looked at Chad. "Kinley needs her rest. We can check in with her tomorrow."

Chad didn't like that idea very much, but he was smart enough not to argue.

After they left, I palmed her face in my hands and studied her. "Let me run you a bath."

"Wait. Can we talk about what happened and the things that were said the last time you were here?"

I sighed. "I'd rather not. I don't want to hear you tell me you can't be with me. I can't handle that right now. I just want to hold you. But I also want to make something perfectly clear." I titled her chin up. "I'm hiring you a bodyguard. Between the media hounding you and what happened tonight, I'm not taking any more chances." I stared into her eyes. "Please don't fight me on this."

"I won't." She leaned into my chest.

"Thank you." I pulled her into me and breathed her in, thankful that she was allowing me to hold her and not pushing me away.

"I need you to understand something too," she said, leaning back, but keeping a firm grip on my shoulders. "I was coming for you when the season was over." That made me smile. "The second you left; I knew I made a mistake. I should have trusted you. I should have believed in us and I regret giving up so easily."

I brushed her hair off her shoulder. "Kinley, I'd like to forget that conversation ever took place." My hands trailed down along her neck, and I settled my palms against her warm skin. "I'd also like to set the record straight on one more thing and then we are done talking about this."

"Okay?" Her blue eyes captured mine in a way that almost made me lose focus.

My determined gaze held hers. "We are not broken up."

Her lips lifted into a smile. "So, I'm stuck with you?"

I laughed. "Damn straight." My lips brushed against her forehead. "Now, let's get you ready for bed. You've had an exciting day and need to rest."

She wavered a bit when I pulled her from the couch. "What did the doctor say, exactly?" I asked, keeping my hands firmly planted on her hips to steady her in place.

"He said my body is going through a lot of change and the stress and hormones probably triggered the bleeding. They did a thorough exam and confirmed everything was fine. He wants me to rest and take it easy over the next few days."

"Thank, God."

When I stepped inside her bathroom, I frowned. Her tub was tiny, not nearly as big as mine. I didn't have anything against her apartment, just that it wasn't mine. I wanted her back in Georgia. I wanted her safe and close by. Basically, I never wanted her out of my sight again.

I kicked off my shoes and hung my suit coat on the hook. I was rolling up my shirt sleeves when she came up behind me. "You're going to ruin your suit," she said, wrapping her arms around my middle.

I turned in her arms and placed my hands on her shoulders. "That's the least of my worries."

"I'm so sorry," she said, drawing small circles on my chest.

I lifted her chin so she was looking at me. "For what?"

"I know you're busy and you obviously went to a lot of trouble to get here so quickly."

My lips were on hers before she could finish. She chuckled against my mouth. "That's a good way to shut me up."

I kissed the tip of her nose. "There is nothing more important to me than you. Nothing," I repeated, hoping the words would finally sink into her stubborn head.

She gave me a tight squeeze before sliding away. She looked exhausted, both mentally and physically.

There was nothing sexual about the way I helped her strip out of her clothes. Once everything was off, she sagged against my chest. Her fingers skimmed up and down my back. Holding her calmed me in ways I couldn't fully comprehend.

Her body sank into the hot water while I sat on the cold tiled floor next to her. Kinley closed her eyes like she just wanted the stress to melt away and forget the past few days ever happened.

"This feels nice." She glanced at me with a soft smile. "I needed this."

I leaned in and kissed her softly. "Let me wash you."

"You've already done enough. I can handle it from here."

I shook my head. "I know you can, but I want to. Not because you're some obligation, or because you're pregnant with my child." I grabbed the body wash on the ledge and squirted a good amount into my palm. I started massaging her shoulders and ran my hands down her arms. "But because you're my entire world." She looked like she was ready to fall asleep, so I trailed my hands down to her stomach and paused for a moment. The events of the last few days were finally catching up with me. My entire body shook, feeling overcome with emotion. "I love you, Kinley." Her eyes flew open at my words. "Both of you."

"Maverick." She reached out and touched my arm.

I swallowed thickly at the softness in her eyes. "I don't just love you. I adore you. I treasure you. And I need you more than I've ever needed anything."

"I love you too." She pulled me closer. "I never fully understood the meaning of the word until you. I never knew it could feel this way."

She didn't have to explain because I knew exactly how she felt. This was a first for me too. I didn't know what other couples went through. I didn't know what they did or what they said. I had nothing to compare this to. All I knew was that I'd never felt this way before. Every time we're together, it never felt like enough. When we weren't together, I missed the hell out of her. All I wanted was to be with her and take care of her.

I kissed her one last time. "Come on, let's wash your hair." Gently, I scrubbed her scalp and offered her comforting words every time I'd touch a tender spot. I wanted to hunt the bastard down and kill him with my bare hands.

Once I was finished, I wrapped her up in a towel and guided her into the bedroom. I grabbed a pair of pajamas from her dresser and slipped the top over her head. "In case I forget to tell you. I'm glad you're here," she said softly.

"Me too." I brushed my thumb along her cheek.

She pulled on a pair of sleep pants and lay on the bed. I pulled the covers back and climbed in next to her. I dragged her body into mine, careful of her bruises.

She rested her head on my chest and tangled her legs with mine. "I like being in your arms. I feel safe."

I lay there quietly, thinking about what happened and how it could have been so much worse. We've been through so much these past few weeks. I didn't want to make her any promises because I still had a lot of shit to sort out, but we couldn't keep doing this.

I palmed the side of her face gently, and decided to just go for it. "Kinley, I hate to ask, especially after tonight. But would you consider moving back to Georgia? I know my timing sucks and I'm putting you in an uncomfortable position, but I have to know if there is a chance. If you would consider it."

She sighed softly. "I have considered it. Actually, I've thought about it a lot recently." She drew lazy patterns on my chest as I gave her a minute to mull over her thoughts. "I love my job and my friends. I've built a life here, but I know things are changing and I need to do what's best for us. It's not that I worry about being unhappy or resentful. I just wouldn't be able to handle it if things didn't work out between us. I'm not saying they will, but we both know anything can happen."

My heart had never been so torn because I understood where she was coming from. I respected the hell out of her for the life she's made here. This city is known to eat you up and chew you out, but she made it and should be proud of her accomplishments. But that didn't help my current situation.

"You have some valid points. I'm not trying to pressure you, just trying to come up with a plan that has us both living in the same zip code," I explained, leaving out that I didn't share the same fears as she did about us not working out. As far as I was concerned, that wasn't an option for me. "I love you, Kinley. I've never said those three words to anyone outside my family before." Tears filled her eyes, but I kept going. "I thought I loved the game, the fame, all the awards, but there is a difference. What I feel for you is different. I am a different person with you and I like the person I've become. I don't just love you for who you are. I love who I am when I'm with you. You ground me, humble me, and I'm a better man because of you."

She clung to me, and I could feel her shoulders shaking. "I guess it's true what they say; love is patient. I've been waiting half my life for you to declare your love to me."

I laughed while running my hand through her hair. "Was it worth the wait?"

"It was totally worth it." She shifted up on her elbow so we were face-to-face. "I love you and promise I will give it some serious thought."

I blew out a breath and squeezed my eyes shut. It wasn't a no. I could work with that.

CHAPTER 27

KINLEY

"Are you ready?" JP asked, his lips hooked up into a smile. He'd been teasing me since he picked me up from the airport.

I blew out a breath and pulled on the sleeves of my shirt. "Ready as I'll ever be."

His grin was wide. "Let's go make some noise."

He offered me his arm and led me through the doors to the training facility. Maverick had no idea that I booked my flight last night on a whim. Or that I sent JP a private message through Instagram and asked for his help.

As we stopped at a security desk, where I had to hand over my identification, I realized there was no way I would have been able to pull this off on my own. There was so much security, you would have thought it was Fort Knox.

We made our way deeper into the building, and I kept my head down, ignoring the curious stares and glances from people as they passed us by.

My fingers tightened on JP's elbow. "I thought you said this place was going to be deserted."

"Did I?" He scratched the side of his cheek.

I stopped walking, forcing him to pause his steps. "I will murder you in your sleep if you set me up."

He barked out a laugh. "Relax, most of the guys have already cleared out their lockers and left for the season."

I glanced in every direction and wondered if I should believe him or not. A few people were milling around the hallways. Some were carrying trash bags; others were carrying large black duffel bags. JP wasn't kidding when he said they cleaned house at the end of the season.

I smoothed a hand down my front and pressed it against my stomach. My heart pounded in my chest the second we stepped into the weight room.

It was nothing like I pictured. It looked more like a rec center than a weight room. The white walls spilled into the beige carpet. There were free weights, benches, every machine known to mankind, and a squat station with yoga mats. What really got my attention was the projector screen hanging in the middle of the room in place of flat screens.

Did they watch movies while working out or review film? My guess was the latter.

I spotted him immediately. He was hunched over, nodding to whatever the guy on the rowing machine was saying. JP cleared his throat loud enough to get his attention.

"Kinley?" Maverick's eyes lit up in surprise. The booming laughter and chatter that greeted us when we first walked in stopped. No one moved, but I could feel every single eye in the room on me. I licked my dry lips, trying to keep my expression even, despite being a nervous wreck inside.

"I didn't think there would be an audience here." I grimaced, and I looked at the small crowd in front of me. So much for doing this privately.

"Rhett?" JP whistled, and Rhett came jogging over. "The instructions were to bring him to the weight room, not the entire team."

Rhett cracked a smile. "He was getting suspicious, so the guys thought it would be better if we all kept him busy."

He looked proud of himself until JP smacked him upside the head. "You're an idiot."

A few of the guys snickered. I practiced my speech the entire plane ride here. Now, it felt like someone tangled my tongue up in a knot.

Maverick stood and walked toward me. "What are you doing here?"

His dark hair was thick and wild, needing a trim, and his smile was so big it lit up his entire face. He was dressed in a simple white T-shirt and black track pants. And when he came to stand in front of me and pulled me into his arms, I knew I had made the right decision by coming here.

"I told you when the season was over that I was coming for you," I said, running my hands up along his chest.

He lifted an eyebrow. "I'm confused. Didn't we already go over this?"

"Yes." I hesitated and reminded myself to breathe. I couldn't believe I was doing this in front of all these people. "I came here to surprise you." I pulled back but reached for his hand. "You asked me a question last time we were together, and I told you I would think about it. Do you remember what it was?"

"I do," he answered slowly. "Have you come to a decision?"

"I have." Maverick eyed me skeptically, while eagerly waiting for me to continue. "I regret not doing this sooner, but I allowed my fear and insecurities to get in the way." I smiled, even though my nerves were on edge. "I allowed outside influences to impact my decision-making, because I didn't believe in myself enough and didn't trust my gut." Maverick's eyes softened, and as much as I wanted to melt into his embrace, I forced my gaze away so I could get this off my chest. "You see," I said to his teammates. "I've been in love with this man since I was fourteen. But it wasn't until recently that he finally noticed me." A few boos rang out, and I laughed. "The truth is, we've been secretly dating since Christmas, and it was foolish of me to think that keeping our relationship private would help control the outcome. And if I learned anything over the past two weeks, it's that some things can't be controlled. So, just to set the record straight, Maverick and I are expecting a baby together, and I decided that it would be best if I moved back to Georgia so we can raise our family here together."

"Seriously?" Maverick gasped.

"Get it, Mad-Dog," someone shouted. It sounded like Rhett.

"Yes." I turned completely in his arms. "I spoke to my employer and they are allowing me to work remotely. There is no reason for me to stay in New York. My life is here with you."

He picked me up off the floor and kissed me hard. I wrapped my legs around his waist and folded my arms along his neck. Kissing him had never felt so good, and I'd be content to do this all night long, not caring that the entire football team was watching. The guys started chanting and whistling, causing Maverick to laugh against my mouth. Our little celebration came to a screeching halt when the door swung open behind us. I didn't even need to turn my head to know who it was. The silence in the room gave it away. Maverick slid me down slowly until my feet touched the ground. He kept a firm grip on my side and trained his gaze over my shoulder.

"My invitation to this little party must have gotten lost in the mail." That snarky voice I would know anywhere got closer, and my entire body tensed.

The temperature in the room dropped so quickly you would have thought snow was about to start falling from the ceiling.

"Do you need something, Della?" JP stepped in front of her, but she brushed past him. The guys all straightened their shoulders, preparing for whatever destruction she was about to cause. I finally understood the meaning of your team having your back.

"Guys," Maverick's voice was tense, "I appreciate the support and well-wishes, but would you mind giving us a minute. Kinley and I would like to speak to Della privately."

They all nodded, clapped him on the back, and shook his hand before they dispersed in a single file on their way out the door.

"What do you want, Maverick?" She crossed her arms in front of her chest, setting the tone for this discussion.

"What I want is for you to stop telling lies and causing trouble."

"Why would I do that?" She popped her hip out and stared me down. "The media believes me. Your fans feel sorry for me."

"Because they are all lies."

"Prove it." She smirked.

Nope. Nope. Nope. I wasn't putting up with this. It was time for me to put a stop to this little game of hers.

"Is this about revenge?" I asked, trying to hang on to my composure. "Because I have no idea what your motivation would be. He is your friend, so I don't understand why you would want to hurt him."

"Being his friend no longer works for me," she said flippantly. "But having a little extra cash does."

That made me angry on his behalf because this was someone he cared for and trusted. She took advantage of that, all because she was bitter and jealous.

"What doesn't make sense to me is that you supposedly care about Maverick. Yet, your actions are damaging his reputation. You're hurting his career, his teammates, and his family. All for what? For revenge? For money? All because he doesn't return your feelings?"

Her eyes turned into slits. "Look at you, getting all protective of him. Do you honestly believe you'll be in his life forever?"

My fists were clenched so tight my nails dug into my palms.

"Enough!" Maverick's jaw was hard. "You are not going to stand there and talk to Kinley like that."

She rolled her eyes. "Give me a break. The way you two are so quick to jump in and defend each other is nauseating."

He shook his head. "I had no idea you were so toxic, but, man, did you have me fooled."

She scoffed. "Maybe you should have paid better attention. If you didn't cut me out of your life and choose her over me, you wouldn't be in this mess."

He ran a hand through his hair and blew out an exasperated breath. "Della, you brought this shitstorm to my door all on your own, and I'll never forgive you for it. What you're doing is inexcusable. It's all lies and bullshit and it needs to stop...Now."

"Or what?" Her eyes narrowed. She didn't appear to be backing down anytime soon. "Just because you knocked her up doesn't mean I have to change my story. If anything, it makes you look like a bigger asshole."

My body tensed. She was a walking, talking nightmare and hell-bent on causing as much havoc as humanly possible. The woman was clearly on a power trip. All over a bruised ego and hurt feelings.

He scrubbed a hand over his face. "About your little story. You don't have a leg to stand on. You have fucked around with too many members of the team, leaving a long line of bitter wives and girlfriends who are looking to take you down a notch. You want to know how I know?" She held his stare without flinching. "Want to take a guess what we were talking about before you came in here? It seems you're not as popular in the clubhouse when you're not spreading your legs. The women are pissed, and the guys are desperate for you to go away. You want to talk about having a bad reputation." He whistled. "Yours is about as low as it goes. Every single person you fucked over is coming forward. Game over."

Her face was a mask of indifference, but her body language was another story. His words definitely got to her.

"Your threats don't scare me," she said, looking at her watch as if she were bored. This conversation was going nowhere. "I've got better things to do with my time. I'm out of here."

She started to storm away, but he blocked her path. "Another piece of 'friendly' advice, start looking for a new job. Your days here are numbered."

Her brows furrowed, and for a split second, I saw fear. I thought for a moment he'd gotten through to her until her eyes sliced over to mine. "Enjoy him while it lasts. I'm not the only one whose days are numbered."

She stalked off, leaving us alone in heavy silence.

"I don't think that's the last of her." I sighed, trying not to imagine what she would do next. In my attempt to defend him, I feared I might have made things worse.

"I don't give a flying fuck. The only thing I care about is getting you home." His hand curved along my bottom. He squeezed my butt cheek and pressed his body against mine. "The only concern I have right now is how fast I can get you naked and in my bed." He was edgy and wound up. The thought of him taking all that aggression out on me had my core muscles tightening in excitement.

I batted my eyelashes, playing innocent. "I thought maybe you'd want to help me look for an apartment?"

He cocked his head to the side and brought my hand down to his erection. He was already hard. "Does that feel like I'm in the mood to go house hunting?"

I swallowed. "It feels like you're in the mood to go hunting for something."

I gave his erection a slight squeeze, and his eyes slid shut. "Kinley, I don't think you want to play this game with me right now. Seeing you so riled up on my behalf has me so turned on, I can't think straight. So, unless you want me to strip you of these clothes and lay you down on a sweaty workout bench where anyone could walk in, I suggest we start moving toward the parking lot."

I fake gasped. "Are we going to have sex in your truck?"

He grabbed my wrist and pulled me out of the room. "You bet your ass we are." He swatted my behind as I started to run ahead of him. We were both laughing hysterically until we reached his parking spot and came to a stop at his truck. My only thought then was, thank God for tinted windows.

CHAPTER 28

MAVERICK

"You wanted to talk, son?"

My father's voice startled me. I'd been leaning against the desk in my office, lost in my head.

My gaze was fixed on the Heisman Trophy I won in college sitting on the top shelf. Next to that were my three Super Bowl rings resting in glass cases. Everywhere I turned, there were pieces of my career scattered, taking up space.

I stood with my back facing him, staring at my accomplishments. "I think I'm going to retire," I finally said, turning around.

His eyes grew big. "You think?" His gaze moved down to my leg. "Is it because of your injury?"

"Not really. It's actually getting better. It doesn't hurt like it used to, but I'm not sure I want to take the chance of further damaging it. I'm afraid I won't be able to play at the level I played at before. Look at Peyton Manning and Brett Favre."

"It sounds like you've been doing a lot of thinking." He crossed his arms. "You know, Peyton and Brett both thought retiring would be easy until the reality of it all set in. They ended up changing their minds once they realized they still had a love for the game."

"I don't want to let anyone down, Dad. I want to leave while I'm still on top. I'd rather do it this way than be forced out or traded."

He leaned his hip against the wall. "If you don't feel ready and if you're concerned that you might not get there, then take some more time to think it over. If you're worried about losing your spot on the team, then I suggest being upfront and addressing these issues with the team doctors and management."

"It's not just that." My nervous hands folded along the back of my desk chair. "I'm scared, Dad. It feels like no matter what I do, someone is going to feel let down. I'm scared of becoming a father. I'm scared about disappointing the people I care about. I'm scared of letting my fans down. I'm questioning everything. I'm losing sleep. I don't know what to do."

"You better get used to losing sleep." He chuckled, and I did too. Talking to my dad about this stuff was easier than talking to my mom. My mom was too emotionally invested in my well-being, while my dad tended to keep an open mind.

He sat down in the chair and rubbed his jaw. "Is the thought of being a father tying you up in knots, or never playing football again? And before you answer that, what's the one driving these feelings the most?"

My head dropped back. "Probably the responsibility of being someone's parent. What the hell do I know about raising a baby?"

"None of us do. Sometimes I still don't." We both shared another laugh. "All humor aside. How do you feel about Kinley? Do you see a future with her?"

I let his question hang in the air for a minute and looked behind me. For the longest time, football was the most important thing in my life, but that wasn't the case anymore.

"Kinley is different."

He smiled knowingly; if I wasn't mistaken, there was a hint of pride in his eyes. "Go on."

"She's easy to talk to. She's down-to-earth, and funny. I never have to question if she's genuine."

"Is that all?" He lifted an eyebrow, letting me know he wasn't letting me off that easily.

"I feel connected to her in a way that's hard to describe." I scratched at my beard. "I love her, Dad. More than I ever thought I could love someone. And she loves me and accepts me for who I am. Me!" I hit my chest. "Not the football player, not that guy who can buy her things. She doesn't care how much money I have in the bank, or how much my condo costs. Hell, I'm pretty sure she doesn't even like my condo. It's rare in my world to find someone that I can trust and depend on. I know without a shadow of a doubt that she'd be there for me, no matter what."

The look in his eyes told me he understood. "Those are all important qualities to find in a partner." He leaned forward and rested his elbows on his knees. "You still haven't answered my other question. Do you see a future with her? I'm not talking about as the mother of your child."

I knew what he meant, and the more that thought took root in my chest, the bigger it grew. "I do."

He linked his fingers together, looking smug. "She did give up her life in New York for you. Does she know about this plan?"

"Not yet. I wasn't saying anything until I was sure. I didn't want her to carry the burden of thinking she swayed my decision somehow. Although, I'm not sure keeping this from her is a good idea either. Shit." I rubbed the back of my neck. "I'm already screwing things up, aren't I?" I asked, laughing at my own joke.

"Son, I've been married to your mother for thirty-five years and I still screw up." He leaned back. "So, your mind is made up?"

"I think so." I looked up at the ceiling. "I don't want to just see my kid during the off-season. I don't want to break promises and beg for forgiveness when I can't follow through on things I said I would." I gritted my teeth, hating the very thought of it.

I didn't know much about being a parent, but I knew beyond anything that I wanted to be a part of my child's life. When I looked back at my own childhood and how supportive my parents were, that was what I wanted. They cheered me on from the stands, from Pop Warner football to the NFL. They didn't miss one school open house and were always around to help with homework and projects. I grew up eating home-cooked meals in my mother's kitchen and hanging out in my dad's workshop on Saturdays. They would host pool parties and movie nights in the backyard. That was the life I wanted. I didn't want to live out of a hotel room six months of the year. I didn't want to worry about missing a flight and not making a birthday party or anniversary dinner. I'd seen the toll it took on my teammates, and it sucked.

"Maverick," he said, twisting his lips in thought. "Relationships take work and you've never been afraid to put the time and effort into anything. Whether it's on the field or off, you've always managed to make things happen. Have a little faith in yourself and roll with the punches. It will all work out."

"But my life isn't just about football anymore, Dad."

His eyes softened in understanding. "No, it's life, son. It's messy, it's complicated, and it's hard. You're going to make mistakes. There is nothing about the walk of life that is straight and easy. It's cracked and filled with uncertainty. But if you stay on track and allow yourself to see through the cracks, you'll learn nothing is impossible."

Leaning forward, I scrubbed a hand over my face. "I want a normal life and I want my kid to have a normal life and we both know the paparazzi won't make that easy." I yanked on the ends of my hair, wishing I could punch something. "Have you been online lately? Have you seen the shit they're saying about Kinley?"

He steepled his hands under his chin. "Son, there will be another headline dominating the news by tomorrow. You know how the celebrity world operates. You can't protect her from everything. If she loves you, she will find a way to balance it all. But you need to prove to her that you are in it for the long haul."

"That's exactly why I think retiring now is the right thing to do. I want to be a dad, just like you were. I want my family to feel like a priority. I have to give up football eventually. I've already given the league all of me. I've got nothing left to prove and everything to lose. I don't want to lose time with my kid that I'll never get back. I don't want Kinley to feel like she's second best to my career. Family is forever. Football is not."

My old man's eyes were watery as they stared back at me. "I'm proud of you, son. And you are right; you've already proven all you need to prove. You don't owe football another thing. I'm proud of the man you are and always have been. But it takes a lot of courage to walk away from something you love for the unknown. You're going to make a great father and husband someday."

I wiped at my eyes. "Thanks, Dad."

"So," he cleared his throat, "it sounds like you've come to a decision."

"Yeah, I think I have."

"Good." He pulled a pack of cigarettes out of his back pocket. "Now, let's go out on your balcony and celebrate with a drink. I need a smoke after that chat."

I took a deep breath and stared at the message on my screen. "Good luck." I read my dad's text one last time before I powered down my phone. I walked into the large conference room. Coach Ludden, Julian, my agent, Jerry Fields, the GM, and the owner of the Arrows, Beau Landers, were congregated along the sleek glass table. Beau wore a black tailored suit, his white hair was combed to the side, and his signature mustache was neatly trimmed.

"It's good to see you." Coach Ludden extended his hand.

"Thanks for meeting me." I smiled as we all shook hands and made small talk. I asked Julian to put the meeting together after office hours. The press was usually gone by this time, and I didn't want this to get leaked.

Jerry cleared his throat, causing the chatter to stop. "Shall we get started?" He motioned for me to sit in one of the empty chairs.

"What is the reason behind this meeting?" Beau asked, flipping through a stack of papers on his desk.

"I wanted to talk to you about my contract next season." I looked over to Julian and met his eyes.

Beau leaned back in his chair. "While we appreciate your enthusiasm to return to the field, you have yet to be cleared to play, and we can't officially offer you a contract until the team doctor has his final assessment. Until then, nothing has been decided."

"Actually." I coughed into my hand nervously. "A decision has been made."

He snapped his head up, and all eyes shifted to me. "I'm not following?"

"I appreciate all you've done for me."

"Is this about money?" Jerry cut in.

"I wish it was," Julian mumbled, and I glared. To say he wasn't happy about my decision would be an understatement. We had a brief falling out when I informed him about my plans. My career was a huge reason why his even existed, so he didn't understand where I was coming from. He begged me to come back for one more season, but I stayed firm on my decision, and it pissed him off. He had other clients, but I was his biggest.

I cleared my throat and looked across the table. "Over a good chunk of my life, I've given football one hundred percent. I've loved the game and the fact that it's allowed me to live my dream and compete on a level that most players will never get the chance to, but I think there comes a point where you realize you've had your fill and it's time to move on."

It seemed every man in the room had a different reaction. Beau drew his eyebrows together and waited a minute to see if I was serious. Jerry looked like that was the last thing he expected me to say. Julian sat silently, letting me know how pissed off he was. And Coach looked like he had mixed feelings about my announcement.

"I wasn't prepared for this," Beau said, looking across the table. "Is there anything we can do to make you rethink your decision?"

"I'm afraid not. This wasn't an easy decision for me, but it's time for me to focus on the next chapter of my life." I kept my focus on Beau. "I want to thank the organization for taking a chance on me, for believing in me and giving me the opportunity to compete in a sport that I love." I moved my attention over to Coach Ludden. "It wouldn't be fair to my teammates who wake up every morning ready to put in the work that needs to be done. So, with that being said, I am officially retiring."

"So, this is it?" Coach Ludden asked; he didn't seem surprised. We've been together for the past ten years, and he paid attention to things most people didn't. That's probably why he didn't seem so shocked.

"Coach, I'll always be thankful for your leadership. Thank you for putting up with me. I know I was demanding at times, but you provided me with everything I needed to win. I've learned so much from you and will always be grateful for your leadership and friendship."

His smile was warm and genuine. "It's been one of the greatest pleasures of my coaching career."

Beau cleared his throat while rolling his expensive pen around his fingers. "Are you sure there isn't anything we can offer you? Maybe take some more time to think things over."

My eyes shifted to the different sets of eyes waiting for me to respond. "I appreciate that, but my decision is final."

"You know, you are the only shot we have to win the Super Bowl next year. We've invested a lot of money into this team." Beau pinched the bridge of his nose. "Wilson is too young, he still needs some fine-tuning. You are leaving us in a jam here. We will have to trade a draft pick or offer one helluva contract to replace you." He laughed lightly. "This is an unusual situation. You're the first athlete I've met who willingly retired so young. This isn't a situation where no one wants you or you're being pushed out. So, I'll ask you one last time. Are you sure this is what you want?"

"I'm sure. My reasons are strictly personal."

Beau leaned back in his chair, steepling his fingers under his chin. "Then we respect your decision. The only thing I ask is that you hold off on your announcement until the season is officially over. We might not be going to the Super Bowl next week, but the league doesn't need any distractions."

My shoulders slumped forward in relief. "You got it."

Everyone stood, congratulated me on my retirement, and wished me well. There were a few jokes tossed around about seeing me on SportsCenter or a State Farm commercial. The only person who wasn't laughing was Julian.

He pulled me to the side once everyone had left the room. "I'm not trying to be a hard-ass here, but I think I could negotiate a good contract for you in New York. Isn't that where your girl is?"

"Not anymore. Even still I couldn't imagine playing for another team."

The travel, the commitment, none of it would change. It would still be long days at training camp, hours spent watching film, and meetings with coaches and coordinators. The preseason alone required so much focus and time that I practically lived at the facility. And with the baby being due at the end of August, it wasn't going to work.

"You've lost your mind, you know that, right? You're giving up millions in potential income."

I patted his back. "Thanks for always looking out for me, Julian, but I'm all set."

"Wait. Did she make you do this?"

"No." My voice was firm and held no room for argument. He still didn't fully understand that this was my choice and that he needed to respect my decision. "She doesn't even know about this."

The last thing I wanted was to get her hopes up and promise her something I couldn't deliver.

I took one last walk through the tunnel and stared at the stadium. I was going to miss the fans cheering and the rush I would get every time I stepped onto the field. I would miss throwing that ball and watching it fly into the hands of a receiver. I would miss the hell out of my teammates and the pre-game rituals—the hazing, the camaraderie, even the victory dances that earned us hefty fines. I wouldn't miss getting hit, though. I wouldn't miss the shitty calls from the refs or the brutal press conferences after a loss. My team-mates, the coaching staff, and even the maintenance workers were people I'd become friends with. Those are the people I'll miss the most.

CHAPTER 29

MAVERICK

I was throwing my clothes in a duffel bag when there was a knock on my door. I grabbed the phone charger from the wall and shoved it in the bag before forgetting about it.

"Julian, what are you doing here?"

I was flying to New York to help Kinley pack up her apartment, so I was in a hurry to get to the airport.

"We have a problem." He breezed past me, walked over to my mini-bar, and poured himself a drink.

"What's going on?"

My nerves started to rattle. Did the owners of the team change their minds? Were they going to screw me over?

"Have you been on social media today?"

"No, I've been too busy packing."

He pulled his phone out and held it out for me to grab. "Everyone is commenting all over your Twitter and Instagram."

I took the phone and looked down at the screen. "Who the fuck leaked this?"

There was a picture of me standing on the field after I left the office yesterday on the front page of the Atlanta Chronicle. The headline read: *Maverick Cross has stunned the sports world by announcing his retirement yesterday, bringing his promising career to an abrupt ending.*

Julian knocked back his whiskey. "Keep reading."

My eyes scanned the article and paused on Della's name.

This is one of the hardest decisions of my life, and I wanted to set the record straight. Many of you know that Maverick Cross and I were in a long-term relationship until I recently discovered he got another woman pregnant. But I'm also the team's physical therapist and want to give his fans a heads-up about a press release coming out of the Arrows organization at the end of the season.

Their statement will be vague, and to clear up any confusion, Maverick won't be back next season, and the reason has nothing to do with his recovery. He is retiring to focus on his new relationship and their baby that is due this summer. The team owners are delaying this information from becoming public knowledge until after the Super Bowl. I know this is shocking, but his fans deserved to know the truth. It saddens me that the situation is being handled so poorly. His teammates, coaches, and owners all know about this. I feel bad for his fans because I know what it's like to be misled. So, it looks like Maverick Cross is willing to lie to his fans just as he has lied to me.

"I'm going to kill her," I roared.

How dare she act like she was the one hurt and betrayed? She was no fucking victim. I had plenty of regrets in my life, but Della was by far the biggest one.

"Now take a look at your Instagram."

I opened the app to thousands of comments, posts, and tags. They were making accusations based on Della's bullshit story. The male fans were pissed that I all but killed the Arrows chances at winning the Super Bowl next year and questioned my loyalty to the team. The female fans were even worse. There were a few crazies who were wishing harm to my unborn child. They were calling Kinley names and making Della out to be a hero.

"Get the PR team on this now!"

"Already done."

"I'm going to destroy her." I brought my hands to my temples to soothe my pounding headache. So many thoughts ran through my head as my brain desperately searched for a way to handle this.

"Not gonna lie, this doesn't look good for your reputation."

My reputation was the least of my worries. After what happened last time with the paparazzi, I was glad I put a guard on Kinley. Especially after a few admirers started messaging her vile comments, causing her to deactivate her social media accounts.

This fabrication was going to fuck up what little progress I made at restoring some degree of normalcy in our lives. Just as things started to calm down, that witch had to stir up more trouble.

I snatched my keys and wallet off the table and ran to the door. "What are you doing?" Julian called out.

I turned. "Something I should have done a long time ago."

I rushed to the elevator and banged on the button as if it would make it move faster. Once I finally made it out of the parking garage, I peeled out of there like a bat out of hell. My hands tightened along the steering wheel; my fingers strangled it in anger; it was a poor substitute for what I wanted to do to the lying, scheming bitch.

I've heeded a few warnings and dismissed some comments that made their way through the locker room. It was foolish of me to ignore the advice and brush off the stories because I thought and assumed it was just everyday drama. Until recently, the way she treated other people didn't impact me, so I never paid too much attention. She didn't start showing her true colors until Kinley entered the picture, and it's only gotten worse.

I didn't have the first clue about what was going on in her head, but I was done giving a fuck. When I pulled up to her townhouse, I made a decision that I was going to ruin her life. Drag her name through the mud like she did with mine. One way or another, she was finished.

I pounded my fist on the door, not bothering to ring the doorbell. Della swung the door open, looking all too smug. I shoved past her and stormed inside.

"Well, hello to you too." She slammed the door. "Did you come to tell me how sorry you were that I lost my job?"

Spinning around, I took her in. She was in a sports bra with a pair of tight yoga pants. Her long auburn hair was up in a high ponytail, and she had sweat dripping down her neck. There was a yoga mat on the floor and a set of weights sitting next to it.

"I didn't know you were let go, but I can't say that I'm sorry about that news."

That explained why she released that article.

"So, you're not here to offer me a job then?"

"Cut the shit." I snagged the towel off the couch and threw it to her.

"You're really pissed about the article, huh?"

I stepped toward her, trying like hell to keep my temper in check. "Did you think I'd be happy that you released my retirement to the press? That you threw me under the bus and brought my fucking unborn child into this?" I roared.

She wiped the towel across her forehead and then down along her chest. "Your fans deserved to know the truth."

"You don't give a shit about my fans, and you wouldn't know the truth if it sat on your face. The only reason why you leaked it was to stick it to me."

She shrugged. "Actually, that's not the only reason."

I raised my brow and waited for her to fill in the blanks.

"I got a nice little chunk of change to spill the tea. The extra cash will come in handy now that I'm unemployed." She picked up her water bottle and started chugging it.

My shoulders stiffened. "So, it's all about money and revenge for you?" Her silence only angered me. "Money can't buy happiness but it can lead to misery and I can't think of anyone more deserving than you."

She shrugged. "I'll deal."

"What the hell happened to you? When did you grow so cold?" I asked, searching for a glimmer of the woman I thought was my friend. How could I have trusted her for so long?

"When you chose her over me."

"There was never a choice. I'm sorry you thought there was." I tried to stay calm and keep my tone measured, even though all I wanted to do was strangle the woman. Something I would never do, but man, was I tempted.

"Once *she* came into the picture, I was forgotten."

"Maybe if you weren't so fucking petty, we still could had be friends."

"I never wanted to be your friend. That's the box you put me in. Look, I get it," she sighed, "you don't want me. You want a nice little family with the hometown girl you grew up with. But here's the thing, I want you, and I want money. So, if I can't have one, I might as well take the other."

"Money!" I looked up at the ceiling and back at her. "It always comes back to money. I would have given you the money to keep your mouth shut. You could have taken it all. I couldn't care less."

"It's easy to say you don't care about money when you have plenty of it."

"I would hand over every cent I own to keep Kinley and my baby safe. But thanks to your little revenge piece of crap that you sold to the highest bidder, the media won't let up.

She's pregnant and doesn't need the added stress. She's already been through enough. I won't risk her safety again."

"Please." She rolled her eyes. "She ended up with a bump on her head."

I angled my head to the side. "How do you know about that?"

Della and I haven't exactly been on speaking terms, so I knew for a fact that she didn't hear about what happened in New York from me.

Her eyes darted to the window, realizing her lies were catching up to her. "I thought that's what you were talking about."

"No." I shook my head as a missing puzzle piece clicked into place. "I'm talking about the comments online. But since you brought it up, did you have anything to do with that perp attacking her in the alley?"

She took two steps back and held her hands out in front of her. "Before you go assuming the worst, the guy was only supposed to scare her. He wasn't supposed to rough her up."

It took a second for the shock to fade. I came here intending on getting her to admit to leaking the story, this was not what I was expecting.

"Scare her?" I asked, making sure I heard her right.

"Yes." She swallowed. "I didn't think it would be a big deal. I gave him a few breadcrumbs and pointed him in the right direction. I told him if he could inject a little fear into her, I would send him a nice bonus on top of the money he collected from the sale of the article. She wasn't supposed to get hurt. You can't blame me for that."

"The fuck I can't." My voice was filled with ice. "She's pregnant."

"Are you not listening to me? I just sent him there. I didn't have anything to do with her getting hurt. You can't pin the blame on me."

"You and I have been friends for a long time. Long

enough to know that I won't tolerate being fucked with. She could have been seriously hurt and could have lost the baby."

I pounded my fist into the drywall, choosing the wall instead of her face. I paced back and forth; my body was vibrating with too much rage. I needed to get the hell out of there. I pulled my phone out and held it up so she could see that I'd been recording the whole conversation.

"Anything else you want to add?"

Her mouth fell open. "You recorded our conversation? Isn't that against the law?"

"Don't give a fuck if it is. As long as it exposes your lies, I couldn't care less."

Her eyes filled with fake tears. "I'm sorry. I didn't mean for her to get hurt. Please don't turn me in. I'll retract my story, I'll do whatever you want."

She wasn't sorry that Kinley was attacked. She was sorry her ass got caught.

"Save your fucking tears. There is a special place in hell for women like you."

I spun around and headed toward the door. She reached for my arm. "Where are you going? Let's talk about this."

I took her hand in a tight grip and shoved her off me. She stumbled back in a panic. "I hope you saved a little bit of that money you collected from the last article you sold, because you are going to need a good fucking lawyer. I will stop at nothing and spend every last cent I have to make sure you pay for all the trouble you caused. And you know the best part?" I smirked. "I'm not the only one. The wives, the players, the entire Arrows organization. Yeah, you pissed off a lot of people."

"You won't get away with this."

"You don't think so? Because I can handle this in one of two ways. I can contact the website who ran the article and tell them what happened and threaten to sue. Or I can throw my money around and find the perp my damn self. Either way, you're going down."

"Please," she sobbed. "Don't do this. I know you're angry, but you care about me. I know you do. You can't just erase all those years we've spent together."

I pulled on the door handle and looked over my shoulder. Her makeup was running down her cheeks; her body was visibly shaking. I felt absolutely nothing for her, but hatred. "You are dead to me!"

As I walked back out to my car, I called Julian. He answered on the first ring. "You need bail money?"

I huffed a laugh. "Not yet, but if you can track down the motherfucker who attacked my girlfriend, I might."

"Talk to me."

"Della sent him. I recorded the entire conversation on my phone."

"You want me to find this guy? I can threaten to sue whoever paid for the story."

I loved how he was straight to the point. He didn't waste time with pleasantries or fluff. "Yes, and yes," I said, hopping into my truck and starting the engine. I looked over at Della's house before backing away. "Spend as much of my money as you need to, and let me know the second you track the asshole down. But I want a go at him before your people approach him."

"Mav, you got a kid on the way. The last place you want to be is sitting in a jail cell while your girl is giving birth. I'll make sure the situation is handled. "

"I want him to fear for his life, just like she did."

"He will. I promise. I represent a couple heavyweights who get bored sparring with the same trainers every day. Trust me, they would be more than happy to use their fists on somebody new."

A smirk lifted my lips as I merged onto the interstate. "Thanks, Julian. I appreciate it."

"No thanks necessary. Now you better get going, don't you have a flight to catch?"

"Yeah, but I have to make a quick stop first."

"I'll let you know when the situation is handled. It shouldn't be hard to follow the money."

I blew out a sigh of relief. "That would be great."

"Now, go get your shit done so you can get your girl. And I want a copy of that conversation ASAP." He barked out and hung up the phone. I was going to miss the asshole.

But he was right. It was time to put this all behind me. I selected a podcast to listen to, hoping it would calm me down during my twenty-minute drive across town. My palms were sweating, and my heart was racing as I pulled into the familiar driveway.

Deanne was sitting on the porch, drinking a beer and doing a crossword puzzle. "I had a feeling you'd be showing up sooner or later."

"So, you know why I'm here?"

She arched a thin white eyebrow, looking at me like I was stupid. "Of course, I know why you're here. I'm no idiot, boy. The second that shrew announced your retirement, I knew it was only a matter of time."

I slid into the spot next to her. "Any chance you're going to go easy on me? Maybe offer me a beer?"

"What do you think?" she asked, lifting the can of Pabst Blue Ribbon to her lips and taking a long sip.

I cleared my throat and looked at my watch. "I'm running low on time, so what's it going to take?"

When the smirk stretched across her face, I knew it would be something big.

She patted my leg and looked over her shoulder. "Before my daughter gets wind of this and shows her face, why don't you and I have a private little chat? I have a case of beer out back."

CHAPTER 30

KINLEY

WHEN I WALKED OUT OF MY OFFICE BUILDING, THE SIDEWALK WAS swarming with paparazzi. They screamed and shouted questions as I moved toward the waiting car near the curb. The lack of privacy and interest in my personal life was something I'd never get used to, and I was pretty sure I would never warm up to it. But this was a part of Maverick's life, so I would have to learn to deal with it.

Ray, my bodyguard, rushed over and ushered me inside the waiting vehicle. I could see the flashes from their cameras going off as we pulled away.

Having a guard assigned to me full-time took some getting used to, but Ray was good at his job, and I felt safe knowing he was nearby if I needed him.

"Why are there so many of them? Did something happen?" I grabbed my phone and was about to click on the internet when Ray spoke up.

"Just ignore them. There is nothing new. I'll put some music on to help you relax. You don't need the stress."

I eyed him skeptically and debated clicking on the news when my phone buzzed in my hand.

Baby Daddy: *Are you on your way home?*
Me: *Yes, are you there waiting for me?*
Baby Daddy: *Just got in. I was delayed getting out of Atlanta.*
Me: *Damn. I was hoping you would have had my apartment packed up by now.*
Baby Daddy: *I told you, that's what I pay people for.*
Me: *Just because the season is over, that doesn't give you an excuse to start slacking off. You're not getting any younger. You can't let those hard muscles get soft.*

I smiled while waiting for his response.

Baby Daddy: *There is nothing soft about me, and I'll prove it to you in a few minutes.*
Me: *Promise? Because I'm wearing the underwear you gave me for Christmas. The ones with your name on them.*

I watched as the dots jumped across the screen, and they stopped and started again. He took a while to type his message, so I laughed when I saw what he wrote.

Baby Daddy: *You won't be wearing them much longer. Now put your phone down and relax. I need to do a few pull-ups before you get here.*

The streets of Manhattan passed by in a blur. I was so lost in thought that I wasn't even paying attention to where we were going. I assumed we were headed straight back to my apartment. Instead, we were headed uptown. I leaned forward, "Um...Ray, where are we going?"

"You'll find out in just a few minutes." I could see his smirk in the rearview mirror, which only confused me more. Ray was never playful. He was serious and professional. Never once had I seen him crack a smile.

The sky was turning dark, and snowflakes were falling gently along the windows. We pulled to a stop outside The Plaza Hotel.

Ray rolled down the window, and I looked around, confused, until I saw him. My breath caught in my chest as he strolled toward the town car.

"Maverick." My eyes ate him up. "What are you doing here? I thought you were meeting me back at the apartment?"

He pulled the door open and helped me step out of the car. "There has been a change of plans."

"You know how I feel about surprises," I said, trying to come across as annoyed, but I was pretty sure he could see the smile in my eyes.

One side of his mouth hitched up in a smile. "Are you not happy to see me?"

"Of course I am." I hit his chest playfully. "I wasn't expecting it to be here, that's all."

He drew me into him and ran his hands down my back. "I have some things I need to talk to you about."

"Okay."

My heart started racing at how serious he sounded. It was so out of character for him, and it caused my nerves to kick up a notch.

"Hey." He kissed my cheek. "Everything is all good. I swear." He grabbed my hand and dragged me down the shoveled pathway. "Let's go for a walk. "

We crossed the street and walked into the southeast corner of the park. We had some bad weather last night, so the trees and grounds were covered in snow. Kids were sledding, dogs were running around, and tourists and locals were taking in the sights. It didn't snow often, but when it did, the park turned into a winter wonderland.

"So," he pulled me to the side so a horse-drawn carriage could pass us, "there has been some news that has recently hit the internet."

My shoulders slumped forward. "What is Della saying now?" I was almost afraid to ask, but I had to know, so we knew what we were dealing with.

"Actually, it's the truth this time. She leaked something that wasn't supposed to get out yet."

I tilted my head up and studied him. "What are you talking about?"

"I retired."

"You did what?" His lips were on mine before I could say anything else. I tried to break away to ask what was going on, but he held me so tight I was afraid he'd never let go.

I clenched my hands along his shoulders as he deepened the kiss. Finally, he slowed the kiss, and we both backed away to catch our breath.

"Maverick, you love playing football."

"I do, but I love you more." His hands went to my face. "Kinley, I thought carrying a ball and scoring passes was all I wanted out of life, but that's not the case anymore." A lone tear slipped from my eye, but he quickly brushed it away. "I don't know who I am without football." He sighed. "But I know who I am with you. You make me believe that everything's going to be okay. You believe in me. You, the little lime growing in your stomach, this life we're building, is all that matters to me. I don't want to miss birthdays and holidays. I want to be there for every milestone, every celebration. So, if you still want me, I'm all yours."

"If I want you?" I blinked in amazement. A few snowflakes gathered on my lashes. "Is that even a question? Of course, I want you. But are you sure this is what *you* want?"

I wasn't trying to change his mind or make him rethink his decision. He was giving up so much, and I wanted to make sure it was for the right reasons.

He got down on one knee. "I've never been more sure about anything in my entire life."

Tears splashed onto my cheeks, and my throat clogged with emotion. I didn't trust myself to speak. I just stood there while my heart fluttered in anticipation.

"I never anticipated this ending, but you were the one play I never saw coming. I've spent my entire life focused on getting from one point to another. I was so busy chasing titles and trying to win championships that I never paid attention to the world around me. Now I feel focused in a way I never felt before. I feel like a different man and see with a new sense of clarity. My only regret is that I wish I had noticed you sooner. Some people think it's about finding the right person, but for me, it's choosing the right person. And I choose you. Will you choose me too? Will you marry me?"

My bottom lip started to tremble.

"Please don't cry," he said gently.

That only made me cry harder because I felt his love deep in my soul. I hiccupped a sob and clung to his shoulders. "Maverick, I wanted to marry you since the first day of my freshman year of high school, when you had to help me open my locker because I couldn't get the combination to work. I've loved you every day since then in some way, shape, or form. Nothing would make me happier than to finally call you my husband. My answer is yes."

He picked me up and spun me in a circle. I felt breathless and dizzy, but never in my life had I ever felt so right.

"What are you doing?" I giggled. "Do you know how much weight I gained?"

He slid me down his chest and held my face in his hands. "I bench press more than you." He reached into his pocket and pulled out a ring.

My heart raced at the feeling of the band sliding onto my left ring finger.

A smile played on his lips. "Aren't you even going to look at the ring?"

I brushed my lips against his. "I don't need to. If you're the one putting it on my finger, then I will love it."

His eyes bored into mine. "Look at the ring, Kinley."

I looked down, and OMG! I blinked up at him. "It's my grandmother's ring." I stared at him, dumbfounded.

He cleared his throat. "She gave it to me when I asked her and your mom for their permission to marry you."

"She did what? She said she was taking it to the grave with her."

"Yeah!" He looked away, embarrassed. "She traded it for a lunch date with Brady and box seats to the Super Bowl."

A laugh bubbled out of me at the strings he must have pulled. I remember going through her jewelry when I was younger and admiring her ring. It was an emerald-cut diamond with two small diamonds on either side. She swore up and down that the ring would never leave her possession. Maverick could have splurged on a big, expensive diamond. Instead, he gave me something much more meaningful. "You have no idea how much this means to me."

His fingers gazed down my cheek. "She told me you always wanted it."

"I got the ring I always wanted. The man of my dreams and a baby on the way. I'd say I just scored the perfect life."

EPILOGUE
KINLEY

We turned down a long gravel road, pulling up to a gate with a security panel. It felt like a secluded paradise, tucked away from the hustle and bustle of the city. If neighbors were nearby, I didn't see them, and the closest main road was a mile away.

The truck pulled up to a massive brick house with tall white pillars. Two rocking chairs were sitting on the wide-open porch, and I could totally picture spending my mornings there, sipping coffee while waiting for the sunrise.

"Whose house is this?"

Instead of answering me, Maverick unbuckled my seat belt and opened the driver's side door. Then he walked around the truck to unbuckle Zander from his car seat.

"Is there a reason why you're not answering me?" I asked, stepping out of the truck and grabbing Zander's diaper bag. My little boy was banging his tiny fists against his father's chest, begging to be let down. He was eighteen months old and always on the run.

"Not yet, little man." Maverick placed a soft kiss on his son's head, and I handed him the animal book he loved to carry with him everywhere he went.

"Maverick, don't make me ask again," I said, wobbling up behind him. I was nine months pregnant with our second child. I was moody, cranky, and ready to pop at any second. Mila Rose was expected to make an appearance any day now, and I couldn't wait to push the little thing out of my stomach.

He sighed. "Our condo is getting too small. I want our kids to have room to run around. I want barbeques and birthday parties in the backyard. I want movie nights on the couch and dinner out back overlooking the lake. And honestly, it would be nice to give this little guy his own play-room, so I don't have to worry about stepping on another plastic toy again." I laughed. "I want a home for us to make memories. When my realtor sent me this listing, I knew this was the perfect place to raise our family."

I brushed my lips against his. "It sounds perfect. Let's check it out."

"I want this house to be exactly what you want. If this isn't it, then we will keep looking." He linked his fingers with mine and started to move, but I stopped him.

"Are you and our kids going to live in this house with me?"

He raised his one eyebrow. "Well, I'm your husband and these are your babies, so yeah?"

"Then that's all I want. My home is wherever my family is."

"Fuc...fudge, I love you." He leaned in and kissed me deeply before Zander started pulling on my hair.

I laughed. "You are getting better with the potty mouth, but you still need to work on it a little bit more. Especially since this little guy started talking."

"Mama. I want down." Zander started kicking his legs out as we walked through each room.

Maverick lifted him on his shoulders, and Zander started slapping his head playfully. We both knew if he set him down, Maverick would spend the entire time chasing him around.

The house had five bedrooms, a finished basement, a theater room, a home office for each of us, a sauna, and a home gym. The house was empty and in move-in condition. But there was no way I'd be able to pull off designing a ten-thousand-square-foot mansion on my own. My daughter was due any day, so my free time would be limited, and I would need help.

We walked out back, and Zander spotted the kid's play-house immediately. He spent less than a minute exploring the little Fisher-Price house before running over to the sandbox and started digging away.

I halted in place and allowed my eyes to wander in every direction. There was a huge deck that ran the length of the first level of the house. I slowly made my way down the three steps in the middle that took me to a beautiful stone patio, I had to pause for a second. I couldn't believe this was going to be our home.

A giant in-ground pool and built-in hot tub took up most of the fenced-in yard. Off to the side sat a firepit and a grill with an outdoor kitchen resting under a gazebo. Spinning around, I took it all in. Holy shit! I knew Maverick had money, but this was ridiculous. There was a fully equipped kitchen outside with a seventy-inch-flat-screen TV built into a brick wall behind a man-made bar.

"Is that a kegerator?" I asked, pointing to the stainless-steel fridge with a tap.

Maverick laughed. "Turns out this place was owned by a teammate. He was recently traded to LA. I came here a few years ago for a barbeque and fell in love with the house. He had three young kids, so when I thought of a family home, this was what I envisioned."

"I'm not sure how the keg and built-in bar equates to 'family home,'" I teased.

"Think of all the entertaining we could do."

This was a huge plot of land that included trails to hike during the day and a boat dock leading out to a small lake. Everything I could ever want was right here, including the man of my dreams.

He couldn't have picked a more perfect home. Despite its grandeur, it didn't feel flashy or over the top. It felt like home. It was big enough that we could grow into it yet still fill it with love and memories.

"Pinch me." I held out my arm.

He laughed and twisted my skin a little too tight.

"Ow." I pulled my arm back and gave him *a what the fuck look?*

He laughed and rubbed the spot he had just bruised. "Sorry, I didn't mean to get you so hard."

"You could kiss it and make it better."

He grabbed me by the waist and pulled me into him. "I'd be happy to kiss it and make it better."

I could feel myself blush, and then I turned around to the massive house. "It looks like we have a lot of rooms to choose from. Maybe we should put Zander down for a nap and figure out which one we want to christen first."

"I knew there was a reason why I asked you to marry me."

"Probably the same reason why I said yes."

"Speaking of yes. What do you think?"

"I think it's perfect. Let's buy it."

He drew me in by the hips and stared into my eyes. "I think we're going to be very happy here."

I loved the quiet, the peace, and the feeling of contentment. "It's perfect."

When I left home at eighteen, I thought my life was all mapped out for me. I wanted to prove that I could make it on my own. But finding my own way in this world wasn't nearly as important as finding my way back home.

Zander came running up and started pointing at my leg. "Mama, pee-pee."

"Huh?" I looked down, and my eyes went big.

"Kinley, tell me that's not what I think it is?"

"Oh, my God. My water just broke." I started panicking. "My bag is at the condo. We'll have to bring Zander with us to the hospital. Call your parents and tell them to meet us there."

Maverick's face turned white. "But you're not cramping or anything."

"I'm telling you, it's my water. Pick him up. Let's go."

"Wait." He looked conflicted. "Shouldn't we wait until you have contractions? Maybe we should go back to the condo and monitor things."

I looked at my husband like he had lost his mind. "What is wrong with you?" He nervously chewed on his bottom lip and peeked at his Apple watch. Then it dawned on me "Are you for real?"

He looked at me and then back at his watch. "Kick-off is at six thirty. What do you think the chances are you'll be done by then?"

"Zero. Now get your butt moving toward that truck and get me to the hospital, because so help me God if you don't, your dead body will be on its way to the morgue before this baby is even born."

He flinched. "Right, but you won't mind if I put the game on in the hospital room, will you?"

"Maverick Cross, you can miss one Super Bowl. Besides, it's not like you're playing. Wasn't that the whole point of retiring?"

He picked Zander up and kissed my lips. "You're right, like always, wife. Besides, I can have JP tape it for me and watch it later."

I rolled my eyes as he helped Zander and me into his truck. And as it turned out, my husband didn't have to miss the big game after all. Exactly one hour and thirty-seven minutes later, Mila Rose entered the world at nine pounds and eighteen inches long. Daddy rocked his little girl to sleep while I rested comfortably in the hospital bed beside him.

And when the Atlanta Arrows won their fourth Super Bowl later that night, I asked my husband, "How does it feel?"

He brought Mila up to his chest and ran his palm along her pink cap. "Like this is exactly where I'm supposed to be."

———

Ready for JP and Rylee? Click here for Fumbled Beginning.

WOULD YOU LIKE MORE?

How about a peek into Maverick & Kinley's future? Click HERE to subscribe to my mailing list and you'll get instant access to an exclusive Fumbled Love bonus scene!

Already subscribed? Just click HERE to download it now.

———

CONNECT WITH ME

Want to stay up to date on all things S. Jones, get exclusive access to ARCs and giveaways, and be part of a fun, positive, and drama-free zone? Then, I highly suggest joining my Facebook reader group. It's a great place for me to get to know my readers on a more personal level. We play games, talk about books and life in general. Become a Sandy's Sassy Reader today. http://sjonesauthor.com/contact-s-jones

ACKNOWLEDGMENTS

Thank you so much for reading Fumbled Love. I am truly blessed to have such amazing readers.

To Marla and Virginia, you ladies are the best. I love working with both of you, thank you for polishing up my mess and making it shine.

To PA Carolina, even though you drive me crazy sometimes, you are a treasure and I appreciate all you do for me.

To Leanne, I would be lost without you. Words cannot express how grateful I am. You make my life a lot easier for handling things that would take me forever to learn.

To my Sassy Readers, you guys brighten my days and I am forever thankful for all the love and support you have given me. I love each and every of you.

To my team of bloggers, bookstagrammers and ARC readers, thank you for all your help with promoting this book. I'm so glad we connected and I look forward to working with you again in the future.

Thanks to my family and friends who support my writing wholeheartedly. And of course, to my book friends, thank you for all your guidance and support. I'm so lucky to be a part of this amazing community.

ABOUT THE AUTHOR

S. Jones is a contemporary romance author from Upstate New York. She has a strong passion for writing and reading stories that will rip your heart out before it's put back together again.

If she's not buried in her writing cave, she's usually reading or planning out her next vacation. She loves to travel to different places and spends all her free with her husband, and two college age children.

When the weather permits, you can find her outside walking her golden retriever or enjoying a nice cocktail by the pool. She loves cooking and entertaining for her family and friends.

When she's not holding a glass of wine in one hand and her kindle in the other, she loves to hear from her readers at:

Authorsjoneswrites@gmail.com

ALSO BY S. JONES

Fumbled Beginning

THE HARD SERIES

Hard to Love

Hard to Stay

Hard to Leave

THE PROTECTIVE SERIES

Whatever It Takes

Whatever You Need

Whatever You Want